'Davidson writes with precision and power that's hard to ignore . . . an excellent collection'
Independent on Sunday

'Craig Davidson is a young author who already displays the sure-footedness of a seasoned pro, and the best of these tightly balled, arrestingly visceral explorations of machismo's dark recesses uncoil with concussive power'
The Times

'Stark oppositions often pack the punch in these gritty tales about American tough guys on the ropes . . . This salty collection more than whets the appetite'
Guardian

'Now, here's a writer who know how to unsettle. This collection reaches in to the darkest places and is not afraid'
Herald

'Impressive . . . *Rust and Bone* might be described as "promising" were it not already such a finished piece of work'
Times Literary Supplement

'A pared-down style, an unflinching eye, a sympathy for the underclasses of America . . . a collection which is a heady brew of brutality and melancholy'
Big Issue

'What sets Davidson apart from his peers is the sheer energy and clarity of his prose, all eight of the stories blasting forth

Rust and Bone

CRAIG DAVIDSON was born in Toronto. He wrote
Rust and Bone in 2005 and his debut novel, *The Fighter*, in 2007.
His next novel is set in the Niagara Falls region and is titled
Cataract City. It will be published by Atlantic UK in early 2014.
Craig enjoys hearing from his readers, and encourages
them to contact him through his website,
www.craigdavidson.net.

Also by Craig Davidson

THE FIGHTER

Craig Davidson

RUST AND BONE

Stories

PICADOR

First published 2005 by Viking Canada, Toronto

First published in Great Britain in paperback 2006 by Picador

This edition published 2012 by Picador
an imprint of Pan Macmillan, a division of Macmillan Publishers Limited
Pan Macmillan, 20 New Wharf Road, London N1 9RR
Basingstoke and Oxford
Associated companies throughout the world
www.panmacmillan.com

ISBN 978-1-4472-2624-6

Copyright © Craig Davidson 2005

On page 101, lyrics from "Everytime You Go" by The Tragically Hip
written by: Baker, Downey, Fay, Langlois, Sinclair; used by permission of
Little Smoke Music / Southern Music Publishing Canada LTD

The right of Craig Davidson to be identified as the
author of this work has been asserted by him in accordance
with the Copyright, Designs and Patents Act 1988.

1 3 5 7 9 8 6 4 2

A CIP catalogue record for this book is available from the British Library.

Printed and bound by CPI Group (UK) Ltd, Croydon, CR0 4YY

Visit **www.picador.com** to read more about all our books
and to buy them. You will also find features, author interviews and
news of any author events, and you can sign up for e-newsletters
so that you're always first to hear about our new releases.

TO MOM AND DAD

Stories

RUST AND BONE

Twenty-seven bones make up the human hand. Lunate and capitate and navicular, scaphoid and triquetrum, the tiny horn-shaped pisiforms of the outer wrist. Though differing in shape and density each is smoothly aligned and flush-fitted, lashed by a meshwork of ligatures running under the skin. All vertebrates share a similar set of bones, and all bones grow out of the same tissue: a bird's wing, a whale's dorsal fin, a gecko's pad, your own hand. Some primates got more—gorilla's got thirty-two, five in each thumb. Humans, twenty-seven.

Bust an arm or leg and the knitting bone's sealed in a wrap of calcium so it's stronger than before. Bust a bone in your hand and it never heals right. Fracture a tarsus and the hairline's there to stay—looks like a crack in granite under the x-ray. Crush a metacarpal and that's that: bone splinters not driven into soft tissue are eaten by enzymes; powder sifts to the bloodstream. Look at a prizefighter's

1

hands: knucks busted flat against the heavy bag or some pug's face and skin split on crossing diagonals, a ridge of scarred X's.

You'll see men cry breaking their hand in a fight, leather-assed Mexies and Steeltown bruisers slumped on a corner stool with tears squirting out their eyes. It's not quite the pain, though the anticipation of pain is there—mitts swelling inside red fourteen-ouncers and the electric grind of bone on bone, maybe it's the eighth and you're jabbing a busted lead right through the tenth to eke a decision. It's the frustration makes them cry. Fighting's all about minimizing weakness. Shoddy endurance? Roadwork. Sloppy footwork? Skip rope. Weak gut? A thousand stomach crunches daily. But fighters with bad hands can't do a thing about it, aside from hiring a cornerman who knows a little about wrapping brittle bones. Same goes for fighters with sharp brows and weak skin who can't help splitting wide at the slightest pawing. They're crying because it's a weakness there's not a damn thing they can do for and it'll commit them to the second tier, one step below the MGM Grand and Foxwoods, the showgirls and Bentleys.

Room's the size of a gas chamber. Wooden chair, sink, small mirror hung on the pigmented concrete wall. Forty-watt bulb hangs on a dark cord, cold yellow light touching my clean-shaven skull and breaking in spears across the floor. Cobwebs suspended like silken parachutes in corners beyond the light. Old Pony duffel between my legs packed with wintergreen liniment and Vaseline, foul protector, mouthguard with cinnamon Dentyne embedded in the teeth prints. I've got my hand wraps laid out on my lap, winding grimy herringbone around the left thumb, wrist, the meat of my palm. Time was, I had strong hands—*nutcrackers,* Teddy Hutch called them. By now they've been broken so many times the bones are like crockery shards in a muslin bag. You get one hard shot before they shatter.

A man with a swollen face pokes his head through the door. He rolls a gnarled toscano cigarillo to the side of his mouth and says, "You ready? Best for you these yahoos don't get any drunker."

"Got a hot water bottle?" Roll my neck low, touch chin to chest. "Can't get loose."

"Where do you think you are, Caesars Palace? When you're set, it's down the hall and up a flight of stairs."

I was born Eddie Brown, Jr., on July 19, 1966, in San Benito, a hard-scrabble town ten miles north of the Tex-Mex border; "somewhere between nowhere and *adiós*," my mother said of her adopted home-town. My father, a Border Patrol agent, worked the international fenceline running from McAllen to Brownsville and up around the horn to the Padre Island chain off the coast. On a clear July day you'd see illegals sunning their lean bodies on the projecting headlands, soaking up heat like seals before embarking on a twilight crossing to the shores of Laguna Madre. He met his wife-to-be on a cool September evening when her raft—uneven lengths of peachwood lashed together with twine, a plastic milk jug skirt—butted the prow of his patrolling johnboat.

"It was cold, wind blowing off the Gulf," my mother once told me. "*Mío Dios.* The raft seem okay when I go, but then the twine is breaking and those jugs fill with water. Those waters swimming with tiger sharks plump as hens, so many *entrangeros borricos* to gobble up. I'm thinking I'm seeing these shapes," her index finger described the sickle of a shark's fin. "I'm thinking why I leave Cuidad Miguel— was that so terrible? But I wanted the land of opportunity." An ironic gesture: shoulders shrugged, eyes rolled heavenwards. "I almost made it, Ed, yeah?"

My father's eyes rose over a copy of the *Daily Sentinel.* "A few more hours and you'd've washed up somewhere, my dear."

The details of that boat ride were never revealed, so I'll never know whether love blossomed or a sober deal was struck. I can picture my mother wrapped in an emergency blanket, sitting beside my father as he worked the hand-throttle on an old Evinrude, the glow of a harvest moon touching the soft curve of her cheek. Maybe something stirred. But I can also picture a hushed negotiation as they lay anchored at the government dock, maiden's hair slapping the pilings and jaundiced light spilling between the bars of the holding cell beyond. She was a classic Latin beauty: raven hair and polished umber skin, a birthmark on her left cheek resembling a bird in distant flight. Many border guards took Mexican wives; the paperwork wasn't difficult to push through. My sister was born that year. Three years later, me.

I finish wrapping my hands and stand, bobbing on the tips of my toes. Tug the sweatshirt hood up, cinch the drawstring. Half-circle to the left, feint low and fire a right cross, arm cocked at a ninety-degree L to generate maximum force. Torque the hips, still bobbing slightly, three stiff jabs, turning the elbow out at the end. A lot of people don't like a jabby fighter, a pitty-patter, but a smart boxer knows everything flows off the jab: keeps your opponent at a distance and muffles his offense, plus you're always in a position to counterpunch. And hey, if the guy's glass-jawed or thin-skulled, a jab might just knock him onto queer street.

My father once took me on his evening rounds. August, so hot even the adders and geckos sought shade. We drove across the dry wash in his patrol Bronco, past clumps of sun-browned chickweed and pokeberry bushes so withered their fruit rattled like hollow plastic beads. He stopped to show me the vents cut through the border fence, chain-link pried back in silvery flaps.

"Tin snips stashed in a plastic bag tied to an ankle. Swim across the Rio Grande, creep up the bank and cut through." A defeated shrug. "Easy as pie."

The sky was darkening by the time we reached the dock. Walking down the berm to the shoreline, we passed a patch of agaves so sickly even the moonshiners couldn't be bothered. Our boots stirred up clouds of rust-hued dust. Stars hovered at the eastern horizon, casting slivers of metallic light on the water.

My father cycled the motor, pulling into the bay. Suspended between day and night, the sky was a tight-sheened purple, shiny as eggplant skin. The oily stink of exhaust mingled with the scent of creosote and Cherokee rose. To one side, the fawn-colored foothills of west Texas rolled in knuckled swells beneath a bank of violet-edged clouds. To the other, the Sierra Madres were a finned ridge, wedges of terra cotta light burning though the gaps. A brush fire burned distantly to the north, wavering funnels of flame holding the darkness at bay. Stars stood on their reflections at the Rio Grande's delta, a seam of perfectly smooth water where river met ocean.

My father fired a flare into the sky. As the comet of red light arced, he squinted at the water's surface lit by the spreading contrail.

"They don't understand how dangerous it is," he said. "The pulls and undertows. Fighting a stiff current all the way." He pulled a Black Cat cigar from his shirt pocket and lit it with a wooden match. "Shouldn't feel any responsibility, truly. Not like I make them take the plunge. Everyone thinks it's sunnier on the other side of the street."

I snap off a few more jabs as my heart falls into pre-fight rhythm. Sweat's coming now, clear odorless beads collecting on my brow and clinging to the short hairs of my wrists. Twist the sink's spigot and splash cold, sulfurous water on my face. A milky crack bisects the mirror, running up the left side of my neck to the jaw before turning sharply, cleaving my lips and continuing north through cheek and temple. Stare at my face split into unequal portions: forehead marbled with knots of sub-dermal scar tissue and nose broken in the center, the angle of cartilage obtuse. Weak fingers of light crawl around the base of my skull, shadowing the deep pits of my sockets.

Thirty-seven years old. Not so old. Too old for this.

On my fourteenth birthday my father drove me to Top Rank, a boxing gym owned by ex-welterweight contender Exum Speight. I'd been tussling at school and I guess he figured the sport might channel that aggression. We walked through a black door set in a flat tin-roofed building, inhaling air cooler but somehow denser than the air from the street. The gym was as spacious as a dance hall and dim, vapor lamps set in the ceiling. The ring erected in the center with a row of folding chairs in front. A punching bag platform stood between two dusty tinted windows on the left. An old movie poster hung on the water-stained wall: The Joe Louis Story. *America's Greatness was in his FISTS,* the tagline read, *The Screen's Big Story in his HEART!* A squat black man worked the speed bag in a ponderous rhythm while a Philco radio played "Boogie Oogie Oogie," by A Taste of Honey.

A short thin man in his early forties exited the office. He wore a checkered blazer with leatherette elbow patches and a brown fedora with faded salt stains peaking the hatband. "How you doing, fellas?"

"You Speight?"

"Exum's up in Chicago with a fighter," the man told my father. "Jack Cantrales. I mind the shop while he's gone."

Jack made me skip rope for a few minutes, then quoted a monthly training fee. My father shook his hand again and said, "Be back in a few hours, Eddie."

For the next two years I spent every free minute at Top Rank. As Exum Speight busied himself with the heavyweights, my training fell to Cantrales. Jack was an amiable bullshitter, always joking and free with advice, but later I came to realize he was one of the milling coves known to haunt boxing clubs, the "gym bums." Gym bums were pugilistic has-beens or never-wases—Cantrales's pro record stood at 3-18-2, his sole attribute an ability to consume mass quantities of red leather—who hovered, wraithlike, around promising fighters.

Gym bums were also known to squeeze a penny 'til it screamed, and Contrales was typical of the breed: he once slid his foot over a coin a kid had dropped, shrugged, and told the kid it must've rolled into the sewer.

It was a *dime*.

Near the end of high school Cantrales booked my first fight at Rosalita's, a honkeytonk border bar. My parents would've never allowed it had they known, so I squeezed through my bedroom window after lights out and met Cantrales at the end of the block. He drove a Chevelle 454 SS—car had get-up like a scalded cat.

"You loose?" he asked as we fled down the I-38 to Norias. June bugs hammered the windshield, exoskeletons shattering with a high tensile sound, bodies bursting in pale yellow riots.

"Yeah," I said, though I couldn't stop shaking. "Loose."

"That's good." Cantrales had recently switched his fedora in favor of a captain's hat of a style worn by Captain Merrill Stubing on *Love Boat*. Dashboard light reflected off the black plastic visor, according his features a malign aspect. "You'll eat this frito bandito up."

Rosalita's was a clapboard tonk cut out of a canebrake. Acres of cane swayed in the wind's grip, dry stalks clashing with a hollow sound, bamboo wind chimes.

Inside was dark and fusty. Hank Snow growled about some woman's cheatin' heart from a heat-warped Wurlitzer. Off in the corner: a canted plankboard ring, red and blue ropes sagging from the ring posts. I bent between the ropes and shuffled to the four corners, shadowboxing. A rogue's gallery of bloodsport enthusiasts swiveled on their bar stools. Someone called, "Looking sharp, kiddo!"

My opponent was a whippet-thin Mexican in his mid-thirties. White sneakers, no socks, a clean white towel around his neck. His hair plastered to his skull in black ropes. He looked exhausted. Mexican fighters often hopped the border on the night they were to fight, winding up at Rosalita's soaked from the swim and gashed from razor wire, sometimes pursued by feral dogs roaming the lowlands.

I took a hellish beating. The fight was a four-round smoker, each round three minutes long. Those twelve minutes stretched into an eternity, especially the final three, eyes swelled to pinhole slits and gut aching from the Mexie's relentless assault. The guy knew things about momentum and leverage I'd never learned in sparring sessions, how to angle a hook so it grazed my abdomen and robbed my breath, leaving slashes of glove-burned flesh. It was as though he possessed secret information about the exact placement of my organs, finding the kidneys and liver, drilling hard crosses into my short rib. I pissed red for days. Between rounds the bartender—who doubled as cutman— tended to my rapidly expanding face. He wore a visor, the kind worn by blackjack dealers, Vaseline smeared on the green plastic brim. He'd reach up and scoop a blob to grease my cheeks.

"You're breaking him down," Jack lied. "Stick and move, Eddie."

By the final round the Mexican looked slightly ashamed. He ducked punches nimbly, sticking a soft jab in my face or tying me up in close. A chorus of boos arose: the shadowy bar patrons were anticipating a KO. The only damaging shot I landed all night was a right hook to the Mexican's crotch. It wasn't on purpose: my eyes were so swelled I couldn't see what I was punching. He took the foul in good spirit, pulling me close until our heads touched, whispering, "*Cuidado,* lo blo, *cuidado.*"

Afterwards I sat on the trunk of Jack's Chevelle pressing an icepack to my neck. There was a tinny ringing in my ears and the moon held a wavering penumbra. I concentrated on not throwing up. Contrales handed over my fight purse: five dollars, management fee and trans-portation surcharge deducted.

"You were tight. Gotta let go with a few bombs or you get no respect. He laid your ass on the canvas five or six times, but you stood up.

Counts for something, right? Little bastard was sharp," Jack admitted. "A dead game fighter."

I nodded vaguely, not paying much attention, more concerned with how I'd explain my state to my folks.

"You fight, you lose. You fight, you win. You fight," Jack suggested, heading back inside for a fifth of off-sale Johnny Red.

The Mexican exited Rosalita's. He moved out into the cane, clearing the razor-edged stalks from his path with still-taped hands. Spokes of heat lightning flashed behind a bank of night clouds, whetting the foothills in crimson light. The fighter walked gingerly, no wasted movement. He stopped at a grove of palmettos and glanced up at a low bronze moon, orienting himself to the land before melting into the trees. I thought about the coming hours as he hiked to the border and scaled the fence, where perhaps a boat was moored amidst the cattails. He'd battle the Rio Grande's currents as they bore him to the far shore, then another hike would bring him to an adobe house in one of the fringing settlements. I pictured his wife and children: his wife's oval face and fine-boned hands, shafts of dawn sunlight slanting low-angled and orange through an open window to touch his daughter's sleeping eyes. The fantasy may've stood in sharp contrast to the abject reality—perhaps the man had nothing worth fighting for—perhaps all that waited was a lightless room, a bottle of mescal.

Looking back now, I do not believe that was the case. Reach a certain experience level, you don't fight without reason. You've seen too many boxers hurt, killed even, to treat matches as dick-swinging contests. Fighting becomes a job, stepping into the ring punching a clock. It's a pragmatic pursuit, opponents' equations to be solved using the chimerical physics of reach, height, spacing, leverage, heart. You'd no more fight outside the ropes than a factory lineman would work a shift for no pay. I entered my first fight for no other reason than to see if I *could*, testing what I thought I'd known against the unknown reality.

I lost because I was green, yes, but also because nothing was really at stake: my life wouldn't've been substantially better or worse, win or lose. The Mexican stepped between the ropes with the subdued air of a man entering an office cubicle. When he realized it was going to be an easy day he leaned back in his chair, kicked off his shoes. He didn't give the crowd what they wanted, didn't hurt me without cause. His job was to defeat his opponent, and he did. But he wouldn't be there without reason. He fought for the money, and for those he loved.

A family waited on the other side of that river. I know that now. I know what it means to fight for a reason.

The hallway's lit by forty-watt bulbs set behind meshed screens. The cement perspires, as do the oxidized copper pipes overhead. Rivulets of brown water spill from the joists. The place is a foreclosed steel-works factory. Corkscrews of drilled iron crunch beneath my boots. The air smells of mildewed rock and ozone. Up through the layers of concrete and wires and piping the crowd issues a gathering buzz that beats against my eardrums.

We fight bare-knuckle, or nearly so. A nostalgic few see it as a throwback to the days when barrel-chested dockhands brawled aboard barges moored off the New York harbor. It's not throwback so much as regression. A dogfight. No referees. No ten count. The winner is the man left standing. Rabbit punches and low blows, eye gouges, headbutts—I once saw a fishhook tear a man's face open, lip to high ear. Fighters score their hand wraps with sandpaper, soak them in turpentine, wind concertina wire around their knuckles.

I fight fair. Try to, anyhow.

I graduated high school in the spring of 1984. Excelling at English and Languages, I was accepted to Wiley College on a scholarship. That August I moved north to Marshall and spent three years living in my sister Gail's basement, studying and continuing to box. Gail's husband Steve was a journeyman carpenter and drywaller; he converted the unfinished basement into an apartment: bedroom and kitchenette, a small training area to skip rope and practice footwork. I'd squirrel myself away during midterms and finals, but otherwise spent my time reading in the family room, shooting hoops on the driveway net, or raiding the fridge. Gail occasionally tripped over my gym kit or spied a pair of hand wraps laid over the armrest of her favorite chair and pitched a fit, but for the most part we got along. Steve was a long-haul trucker circuiting between San Antonio and Sioux Falls. On my twenty-first birthday he bought a case of Lone Star and we sat on the back porch until the flagstones were littered with empties and we were howling at the moon.

With Steve hauling and Gail landing a teller job at Marshall First Trust, babysitting duties fell to me. My nephew Jacob was ten months old when I moved in. An inquisitive boy with a sweet temperament. The kid was forever crawling out of sight, disappearing around corners or behind curtains, knees pumping so quickly I was sure friction would singe the carpet. We'd play this game where Jake stuck his fingers in my mouth and I'd curl my lips over my teeth and bite down gently, growling; Jake would shriek—a garbled string of syllables, "eep-ooo-*ap!*" or "yee-*ack!*" or "boo-*ta*-tet!"—and pull his hand away. This went on for hours, until I became slightly nauseated by the taste of Jake's hand, a blend of sweat and mucus and the residue of whatever bacterial micro-sites he'd investigated that day. I remember the way Jake's gaze locked with mine, fingers inches from my mouth, his eyes glowing, positively *aflame,* as though to say—

"Look at the runt. Gonna get *creamed!*"

"Run along find your daddy, peckerwood!"

The spectators hurl other insults, but these two I pick up clearly. There looks to be a hundred or more, ranged around a barricade of sawhorses stolen from a construction site: bright orange, flashing halogen discs screwed to the horizontal beams. The intermittently blinking lights brighten the spectators' faces in ghostly yellows: a pack of bloodhungry crazies waving dollar bills. Moonlight pours through holes rusted in the roof, silver shafts gilding the crossbeams and glossing feathery shapes roosting in the latticework. A hypnotic sound underlies the hollering crowd: a distant, nearly sub-audible clash and cycle, the sound of long-derelict machinery shuddering uneasily to life.

My opponent is a dreadlocked kid two inches taller and forty pounds heavier than me. Goes by Nicodemus. Bare-chested, his arms are swelled, monstrous. Tribal tattoos crisscross the ribbed musculature of his stomach; ornate curlicues encircle his extruded bellybutton, giving it the look of a sightless eye. He turns to his cutman and says, "Who this, the shoeshine boy? Mus' be my birthday."

We meet in the center of the ring, where the cigarillo-smoking promoter runs down the stakes: a thousand cash to the winner, five hundred to the loser.

Nicodemus dry-gulches me while the guy's still laying out the stakes, a hard sucker punch glancing off the high ridge of cheek, splitting bone. The blow drops me to my knees. Chill static wind pours through my skull, electric snakes skating the bones of my arms and legs. Nicodemus shrugs and smiles, as though to say, *Hey, you knew the score when you stepped up,* then wades in swinging. Guess the fight's started without me. It's not uncommon.

I graduated in '87 and moved north to Pennsylvania. Having trained and fought steadily through college, I'd amassed a Golden Gloves record of 13-1. Teddy Hutch, an Olympic boxing coach, caught one of my fights and invited me to his training facility in Butler. The welterweight division was thin, he said; I could earn a berth on the qualifying squad. The program covered food and accommodation. His prospects worked at a local box factory.

I arrived in Butler late September. The trees and water, even the sky:

everything was different. The Texas sky was not completely blue; its colour, I've come to realize, was more of a diffuse lavender. The skies of Pennsylvania were a piercing, monotone blue; they pressed down with a palpable weight. The tattery, see-through clouds I'd known since childhood were replaced with thick cumulus formations. And the *cold*—me and a Hawaiian boxer named David Tua bundled ourselves in sweaters and jackets on the mildest of fall days, much to the amusement of the Minnesotans and Dakotans in training.

The prospects were billeted in a ranch house. The land behind fell away to a lake ringed by hemlocks and firs, rising to a wooded escarpment. We roused at five o'clock each morning and ate breakfast at long tables before donning road gear to run a three-mile circuit around the lake. Afterwards we herded into a school bus bound for Olympia Paper, where we spent the next nine hours ranged along canvas belt lines, driven half-mad by the pneumatic hiss of the fold-and-stamp machines. When the shift whistle blew we were driven to the Cyclone, a downtown boxing gym. We trained until eight o'clock before dragging ourselves to the bus, bolting dinner, and flopping into bed for lights out.

It was a rough life, and a lot of fighters couldn't stomach it: prospects came and went with such frequency Teddy considered installing a turnstile. But the regimen yielded results: I packed on ten pounds of muscle in eight months, and my cardiovascular endurance shot through the roof. My sparring partner was a Dixieland welterweight named Jimmy Carmichael. Jimmy had a peacemaker of a left cross; we beat each other black and blue in the ring but spent our days off together, catching the Sunday matinee and wolfing thick wedges of pecan pie at Marcy's on Lagan Street.

Jake visited that March. Steve was hauling a load up to Rochester and brought Jake along to visit. Steve dropped him off mid-morning, and we arranged to meet later for dinner. I was surprised how much

Jake had grown. His cheeks, framed by the furred hood of a new winter jacket, were flush and rosy.

"How ya been, jellybean?" I said.

"I been fine, pal o' mine," he said, repeating the greeting I'd taught him.

Jake was antsy following the long drive. We walked down to the lake. A low fog rolled across the frozen water, faint ripples thickening into groundmist at the tree line. We held hands. Every fir looked dusted in powdered sugar. Jake's hand slipped from mine as he ran ahead. He said, "I've never seen so much *white*."

The lake was a flat opaque sheet. A murder of crows congregated on a tree shattered under a weight of snow. The northern boys skated here on weekends; I saw the ruts their blades had left in the ice. Jake ran out, falling, sliding, getting up, running faster.

"Hey," I called. "Hey, slow 'er down, big guy."

I was raised in a part of Texas where the only ice was of the cubed variety. I'd only seen snow in Christmas movies. I mean, what did I *know* of ice? I knew it felt good pressed to the back of my neck between rounds. My five-year-old nephew ran heedlessly, hood tugged down around his shoulders, fine sandy hair and clean tanned skin brightened by the sun. What did he know of ice? Perhaps that it melted quickly on a summer sidewalk. Did he even know that much? We were both ignorant. But I should've known.

Nicodemus rushes across the ring, jackhammering his fists. He throws a series of haymakers so slow he might as well have telegraphed them last week; I feint from a kneeling position and hammer a left hook into his ass, nailing the sciatic nerve. Shrieking, he limps back. I struggle to my feet and bicycle into the open ring. From time to time someone shouts Nicodemus's name, and under that the distant hum of machinery.

He throws a looping right that I duck, rising with a short-armed cross to the midriff. He bulls me into a corner. I juke, try to circle clear, but he steps on my foot and hits me with an overhand right. Lips flatten against teeth, mouth filling with the taste of rust and bone. The air shimmers, shards of filigreed light raining down like shiny foil in a tickertape parade. I go down heavily under a sawhorse, staring up at a dark forest of legs.

I can no longer consciously recall the sound that ice made as it broke. Sometimes I'll hear another noise—the low crumple of a beer can; the squeal of an old nail pried from a sodden plank—similar in some way, timbre or pitch or resonance, and realize it lives somewhere inside me now. I remember the fault line racing out to meet him, a silver crease transecting the ice like a cracked whip. It seemed to advance slowly, a thin sluggish snake zigging and zagging; it was as though I had only to holler "Step back!" and it would rip harmlessly past.

Water shot up in thin pressurized needles from hairline cracks under Jake's feet. He lurched sideways, outflung arms seeking balance. The ice pan broke in half, plates levering up, a V of frozen water with Jake plunging through the middle.

I laughed. Maybe Jake looked silly going down, mouth and eyes wide, hands clutching at the broken border of ice that crumbled like spun sugar in his grasp. Maybe I could not conceive the danger: I pictured the two of us sitting before the fireplace in the big safe house, a blanket wrapped around his shoulders, a mug of hot chocolate, tendrils of steam rising off Jake's wet pants as they dried.

"Hold on, big fella," I said. "Do the eggbeater!"

My boots skidded along the ice. I overbalanced, fell down. Jake churned foam, clothes plumping with water. Everything seemed all right until I saw the fear and confusion, deep thin creases out of place on a face so young; I saw, with the dreamlike clarity that colors all memories of the event, molecular beads of water clinging to his cheeks and nose. I crawled forward, outspread hands distributing my weight. Jake splashed and kicked and called out in a reedy whisper, nose and mouth barely above water. Ice crackling under my hands and chunks of ice floating on the water and the trees of the near shore wrapped in transparent icy layers. So much *ice*.

He stopped struggling abruptly, just hanging there, eyes closed, water trickling into his mouth. Only his chin and the tips of his fingers floated clear. I reached the edge and extended a hand. The supporting ridge broke away and my chest and head slipped below the surface. Cold black water pressed against my eyeballs. I caught movement through the brown water and grabbed something—smooth and slim, perhaps a jacket sleeve—but the cold made my fingers clumsy and it slipped through. The lake shoved me back and forth, currents stronger than I'd imagined. Sinewy shapes turned over in the murk, shapes like seal pups at play.

I broke the surface snorting streams of water, wiping away cords of snot. I stared into the swirling blackness in search of movement, a leg kicking, fingers grasping. I plunged my arm in, stirring around, hopeful: a few strands of eelgrass draped over numb fingers. Not knowing what to do, I called his name. "Jake!" The word echoed uselessly across the flat expanse.

When my voice died away I heard it: a sustained resonant thump. I couldn't tell where it came from. The ice trembled. A dark form was pressed to the chalky sheet a few feet to the left, trapped beneath the surface. It twisted and thrashed, beating the ice.

I crawled towards the shape—crawled on my hands and knees like a fucking *infant*. Ice pocked with craters and boils from thawing and re-freezing. I saw a dim outline down there, a creature of crude lines and angles. The ice shuddered; fresh-fallen snow jumped off the surface, resettling. My fingers spread across the milky whiteness and ears plugged with frozen lake water, a frantic buzzing between.

I made a fist with my right hand and brought it down. The ice buckled, splintered, but held. Pain shot up my arm to the shoulder, a white-hot bolt. I raised the right again—my lead hand, the dynamite right—smashing the ice. It broke and my fist plunged into the darkness, grasping frantically, closing on nothing. A powerful current caught hold of Jake and he drifted sideways, beyond my grasp. Something passed through my fingers—a bootlace?

I tracked the shape beneath the ice. The freezing water on my arms crackled like dull metal. My teeth chattered and I called his name. Maybe I was screaming.

Passing beneath a patch of perfectly clear, glasslike ice, I caught his face through the scalloped sheet. Lips and nostrils robin's egg blue, the rest a creamy shade of gray. Cheek flattened to the ice, the buoyancy of flesh pushing him up. Eyes so blue, luminously blue, pearlescent air bubbles clinging to the dark lashes. A sinuous white flash below, silky curve of a trout's belly.

My right hand was badly broken: knuckles split and flesh peeled to the wrist, a lot of blood, some bones. I slammed my left hand down. The ice fractured in a radiating spiderweb. Water shot up through the fissures. My hand shattered like a china plate. Didn't feel a thing at the time. Jake stopped clawing, stopped thumping. His eyes open but rolled to the whites beneath the fine network of cracks. I hammered my left hand down once more, breaking into the icy shock of the lake. I snagged his hood but the hole was too small so I clawed with my free hand, breaking off chunks, razored edges gashing my fingers to the bone.

Finally the hole was wide enough for me to pull him through. A long swipe of mud on Jake's forehead, hair stuck up in rapidly freezing corkscrews. His nose broken and me who'd done it, smashing ice into his face. I gathered him in my arms and stumbled uphill to the house. "Please," I remember saying, over and over, a breathy whisper. "*Please.*"

Ernie Munger, a flyweight mending a broken rib, had spent a few summers as a lifeguard. He administered CPR while the cook rang for help. Munger's thick hands pumped the brackish water from Jake's lungs, pumped life back into him. Jake was breathing by the time the paramedics arrived. They snaked a rubber tube down his throat. Afterwards I stood by a large bay window overlooking the lake. The hole, the size of a dime from that distant vantage, was freezing over in the evening chill; tiny red pinpricks represented my bloody hand prints on the ice. The splintered bones pulsed: I'd broken forty-five of fifty-four.

I push off the floor and lean against a sawhorse, waiting for the teeth to align and the gears to mesh again. Nicodemus circles somewhere to the left, dancing side to side, weaving through blue shafts of shadow like animate liquid. Some bastard kicks me in the spine, "Get up and fight, you pitiful son of a bitch." Standing, I wonder how long was I down. Eight seconds? No ref, so nobody's counting. A pair of hands clutch my shoulders, shoving, the same voice saying, "Get out there, chickenshit." I strike back with an elbow, impacting something fleshy and forgiving. A muted crack. Those hands fall away.

Nicodemus advances and hits me in the face. He grabs a handful of hair and bends me over the sawhorse, pummeling with his lead hand. The skin above my eyes comes apart, soft meat tearing away from the deeply seamed scar tissue. Blood sprays in a fine mist. I blink away red and smack him in the kidneys. He pulls back, nursing his side. Knuckling the blood out of my eyes, I move in throwing jabs. Nicodemus's skull is oddly planed, a tank turret, deflecting my punches. His fists are bunched in front of his mouth, arms spread in an invert funnel leading to the point of his chin: a perfect opening, but not yet. Reaching blindly, he entangles my arms, pulling me to his chest. He rubs his hand wraps across my eyes and I wince at the turpentine sting. I snap an uppercut, thumping him under the heart.

The hospital room walls were glossy tile, windows inlaid with wire mesh. Jake lay in an elevated hospital bed, shirtless, chest stuck with EKG discs. Outside a heavy mist fell, making a nimbus around the moon and stars. Teddy'd visited the emergency ward earlier, taking one look at my hands and saying I'd never box again. I was on Dilaudid for pain, Haldol for hysteria. My mind was stark and bewildered. A machine helped Jake breathe. His father sat beside the bed, gripping his hand.

"Is he—will he be all right?"

"He's alive, Ed."

Steve'd never called me that before. Always Eddie.

"Is he . . . will he wake up soon?"

"Nobody can say. There was . . . damage. Parts shutting down. I don't know, exactly."

"We were . . . holding hands. He broke away. He'd never done that before. It was so strange. We were holding hands, then he didn't want to do that anymore. It's only human. I let him go. It was okay. I thought, He's growing up, and that's okay."

Steve smoothed the white sheets over Jake's legs. "The golden hour. It's . . . a period of time. Three minutes, three-and-a-half. The amount of time the brain can survive without oxygen. Only a few minutes, but the doctor called it the golden hour. So . . . stupid."

"I'm so sorry."

Steve didn't look at me. His hands smoothed the sheets.

I stalk Nicodemus, keeping left, outside his range. His eyes shot with streaks of red, their wavering gaze fixated on the darkness beyond me. I stab forward, placing weight on my lead foot and twisting sharply at the hip, left hand rising towards the point of his chin.

When I was a kid, a rancher with a lizard problem paid a dime for every one I killed. I stuffed geckos in a sack and smashed the squirming burlap with a rock.

When my fist hits Nicodemus it sounds an awful lot like those geckos.

The punch forces his jawbone into his neck, spiking a big bundle of nerves. My hand shatters on impact, bones breaking down their old fault lines. Nicodemus's eyes flutter uncontrollably as he falls backward. He falls in defiance of gravity, body hanging on a horizontal plane, arms at his sides, palms upraised. There's a strange look on his face. Not a smile, not exactly, but close. A peaceful expression.

Jake's twenty years old now. Comatose fifteen years. Were it not for a certain slackness of features he'd be a handsome young man. He grows a wispy beard, which his mother shaves with an electric razor. I've visited a few times over the years. I sat beside the bed holding his hand, so much larger than the one I held all those years ago. He smiled at the sound of my voice and laughed at one of our shared jokes. Maybe just nerves and old memories. Every penny I make goes to him. Gail and Steve take it because they can use it, and because they know I need to give it.

There are other ways. I know that. You think I don't *know* that?

This is the only way that feels right.

Nicodemus rises to one knee. He looks like something risen from its crypt, shattered jaw hanging lopsidedly, bloodshot eyes albino-red. Pain sings in my broken hand and I vaguely remember a song my mother used to sing when I was very young, sitting on her lap as she rocked me to sleep, beautiful foreign words sung softly into my hair.

He makes his way across the ring and I dutifully step forward to meet him. We stand facing each other, swaying slightly. My eyes swelled to slits and he moves in a womb of mellow amber light.

And I see this:

A pair of young-old eyes opening, the clear blue of them. A hand breaking up from sucking black water, fist smashed through the ice sheet and a body dragging itself to the surface. A boy lying on the ice in the ashy evening light, lungs drawing clean winter air, eyes oriented on a sky where even the palest stars burn intensely after such lasting darkness. I see a man walking across the lake from the west, body casting a lean shadow. He offers his hand: twisted and rheumatoid, a talon. The boy's face smooth and unlined, preserved beneath the ice; the man's face a roadmap of knots and scar tissue and poorly knitted bones. For a long moment, the boy does not move. Then he reaches up, takes that hand. The man clasps tightly; the boy gasps at the fierceness of his grip. I see them walking towards a distant house. Squares of light burning in odd windows, a crackling fire, blankets, hot chocolate. The man leans down and whispers something. The boy laughs—a beautiful, snorting laugh, fine droplets of water spraying from his nose. They walk together. Neither leads or follows. I see this happening. I still hold a belief in this possibility.

We circle in a dimming ring of light, feet spread, fists balled, knees flexed. The crowd recedes, as do the noises they are making. The only sound is a distant subterranean pound, the beat of a giant's heart. Shivering silver mist falls through the holes in the roof and that coldness feels good on my skin.

Nicodemus steps forward on his lead foot, left hand sweeping in a tight downwards orbit, flecks of blood flying off his brow as his head snaps with the punch. I come forward on my right foot, stepping inside his lead and angling my head away from his fist but not fast enough, tensing for it while my right hand splits his guard, barely passing through the narrowing gap and I'm torquing my shoulder, throwing everything I've got into it, *kitchen-sinking* the bastard, and, for a brilliant split second in the center of that darkening ring, we meet.

THE RIFLEMAN

LET ME TELL YOU, the pure shooter's a dying breed. We're talking pretty much extinct: think snow leopard, Komodo dragon, manatee. The dunk shot more or less killed the pure shooter: nowadays everyone wants to be a rim-rocker, shatter the backboard to make the nightly highlight reel. You got kids with pogo-stick legs leaping clear out the gym but these same kids *cannot* hit a jumpshot to save their life. Blame Dominique Wilkens, Michael Jordan, Dr. J. A few shooters still haunt the league, scrawny white riflemen hefting daggers from beyond the three-point arc; most Euros have a deft touch, skills honed in some backwater -vakia or -garia with no ESPN on the dial. A damn shame, because few things in life are as sweet as the sound a basketball makes passing through an iron hoop: we're talking dead through the heart of the net, no rim, no glass. Called a *swish,* that sound, but truly it exists somewhere beyond human description—if heaven has a soundtrack, man, that is *it.*

My son's going to change all that. Jason'll make it cool to be a pure shooter again; once he's chewing up the NBA you'll see kids practicing spot-up j's instead of windmill dunks. I take credit for that silky-smooth jumper of his: feet set in a wide stance, knees bent and elbows cocked at eye level, smooth follow-through with the wrist. We drilled for hours on the driveway net until the mechanics imprinted themselves at a cellular level. Read in the newspaper he went off for thirty-seven against Laura Secord High; those numbers'll attract scouts from Div I programs, believe-you-me. Jason's a Prime Time Player—a *PTP'er,* Dick Vitale would say, ole Dicky V with his zany catchphrases and kisser like a pickled testicle. My boy can *tickle the twine for two, baby!*

The Mikado's the only bar open on Saturday mornings. The TRW skeleton crew usually heads down after the shift whistle blows to knock the foam off a few barley pops. While I'm not *technically* employed there anymore I still like to hit the Mik for a Saturday morning pick-me-up, shake off the cobwebs and start the weekend on a cheery note. This particular Saturday it's about noon when they kick me out. I say "they" though in truth there's but a single bartender, a joyless moonfaced hag named Lola. I say "kicked out" but in point of fact I'd run dry and Lola isn't known to serve on the house. Once you reach a critical impasse like that, you'd best pack up shop.

The day bright and warm in a courtyard hemmed by the office buildings of downtown St. Catharines, the squat trollish skyline aspiring to mediocrity and falling well short. A warm June breeze pushes greasy fast food wrappers and pigeon feathers over the cracked concrete of an empty pay-n-park lot between a tattoo parlor and a discount rug store. Sunlight reflects off office windows with such intensity I'm forced to squint. Got to assume I'm drunk: downed eight beers at the Mik and polished off twenty ounces of gin watching infomercials last night. Haven't slept in days but in high spirits nonetheless, though I must admit somewhat alarmed by what appear to be tongues of green, gold, and magenta flickering off the tips of my spread fingers.

A trash-strewn alleyway to my left empties onto King Street. Catching human movement and the echo of up-tempo music, I wander off in that direction.

KING IS CLOSED OFF for a two-block stretch to host a 3-on-3 basketball tournament. Ball courts staggered down the road, three-point arc and foul stripes etched in sidewalk chalk. Mammoth speakers pump out rap music: guttural growls and howls overlaid with occasional gunshots and the clinkety-clink sound slot machines make paying off. Players sit along the curb in knee-length shorts, sleeveless mesh tops, and space-age sneakers, checking out the competition or waiting to be subbed in. The staccato rhythm of ball chatter underlies all other sound: *D-up! Get a hand in his face! My bad, my bad. You got that guy, man; you own him! Give you that shot—you can't stick that shit! All day, son, all damn day. And one! And ONE!*

Weave through duffel bags and water bottles and teams talking strategy, stop at a long corkboard to scan the tournament brackets. No names, just teams: Hoopsters, Basket-Maulers, Santa's Little Helpers, Highlight Reelers, Dunks Inc. If Jason was playing, he'd've given his old man a call, right? I went to every one of his high-school games, didn't I? I say "went," past tense, due to the incident occurring at a preseason game out in Beamsville. I say "incident," but I suppose I might as well say "brawl," that broke out when a few Beamsville-ians —and when I say "Beamsville-ian," I mean, more accurately, "inbred hillpeople"—took offense at my distinctive style of encouragement. I guess some punches were thrown. Well, the whole truth of the matter is that punches *were* thrown, first by me, then at me. Let me tell you, those bumpkins pack a mean punch—even the *bitches!*

Thankfully, when you're three sheets to the wind you don't feel a whole lot of anything. Coach Auerbach politely insisted I curtail my attendance.

Meander down the sidewalk checking out the games. The majority are tactless, bulling affairs: guys heaving off-balance threes and clanging running one-handers off the front iron, banging bodies under the boards for ugly buckets. It's really quite a painful ordeal for me: a classically trained pianist watching chimpanzees bash away on Steinway pianos. Stop to watch an old-schooler with Abdul-Jabbar eyegoggles and socks hiked to his knees sink crafty hook-shots over a guy half his age; the young guy's taking heat from his teammates for the defensive lapses.

The final court has drawn a huge crowd; can't see more than flickering motion between the tight-packed spectators, but from what little I do it's clear this is serious. A true student of the game can tell right off: something about those confident movements, that quickness, the conviction that lives in each and every gesture.

Push through the crowd and there's my son.

He's at the top of the three-point arc. Long black hair tied back with a blue rubber band, the kind greengrocers use to bind bunches of bananas. Apart from giving you the look of a pansy, long hair has a habit of getting in a shooter's eyes. But the boy refuses to cut it so one time I chased him around the house with a pair of pinking shears, screaming, *Swear to Christ I'm gonna cut that faggot hair off!* I was gassed at the time; you tend to do crazy things when you're gassed. He locked himself in the bathroom. I told him I'd cut it off as he slept. He passed the night on the floor, those hippie locks fanned out over the pissy tiles.

He takes the ball at the top of the key and bounces a pass to Al Cousy, a thick-bodied grinder on Jason's high-school team. Al's a bruiser with stone hands who's going nowhere in the sport. Way

I see it, the sooner he comes to grips with this, the sooner he can make an honest go at something more suitable: he'll make a great pipefitter with those strong mitts. However it works out, years from now Al can say, hunched over beers or gutrot coffee at some union meeting, he'd once played ball alongside Jason Mikan—yeah, *that* Jason Mikan.

Al pivots around his defender, gets blocked, shovels the ball out. Jason catches it a few feet beyond the three-point line, throws a head-fake to shake his defender, steps back and lofts a shot. The ball arcs through sparkling June air, a flawless parabola against a blue-sky backdrop, dropping through the center of the net.

"Nice bucket!" I call out. "Thattaboy!"

Jason looks over, spots me, glances away and claps his hands for the ball.

Watching that shot, the unstudied perfection of it, I think back to all the time we spent practicing together. Every day in good weather we'd be out on the driveway hoop, shooting until the sun passed behind the house's high peaked roof. Before Jason could quit he had to make fifteen foul shots in a row; he'd sink twelve or thirteen easy before getting the jitters. I even built a pair of defending dummies, vaguely human plywood cutouts with outstretched arms. These I mistakenly destroyed: stumble home less than sober and spy two menacing shapes in your unlit garage—who wouldn't kick them to splinters? One night I came back a little greased and dragged Jason out of bed. It was cold—had to knock a glaze of ice off the net—Jason there in his pj's and I chucked him the ball. *Every minute you're not practicing is a minute some other kid is. You got to* work, *son—hard and every day. Now can that fucker!* My neighbor Hal Lanier, beetle-legged and bucktoothed, sidled out onto his front stoop.

"Hey," he said. "You two mind calling it a night?"

"What business is it of yours, bud?"

Hal pulled a housecoat shut over a belly pale as a mackerel's. "Trying to sleep, is my business. Got your boy out here in his fuggin' jammies, screaming like a lunatic, is my business."

"Telling me how to raise my kid?"

"Telling you I got kids of my own trying to sleep."

"Why not come say that to my face, ya fat prick ya."

I'll admit to being a bit surprised when Hal took me up on this offer, crossing the frost-petaled lawn in his slippers to where I stood in my grease-smudged overalls, hitting me square in the face. Well! Down on the grass we go, rolling around chucking knuckles. *Shoot that goddam ball!* I kept screaming at Jason. *Fifteen foul shots before you go back to sawing logs!*

Jason's team is up 20-13 when he hits a fadeaway jumper from the elbow to win. The teams shake hands and head to the sideline, gathering duffels and water bottles. I trot over to Jason, who's speaking to a guy with a clipboard. For a moment I'm struck dumb with terror at what appears—and I feel a distinct need to stress this—what *appears* to be a cone of ghostly flame dancing atop the man's bald head. Whoa!

"Hey," I say a bit shakily, "great game there, kiddo."

"Yeah," says Jason, "thanks."

"This your father?" The fire on clipboard-guy's head is now mercifully extinguished. "Your son's a helluva player."

"Don't think I don't know it." I clamp a hand around Jason's neck, give a friendly squeeze. "Gonna redefine the game, this kid. Aren't you?"

Wincing, Jason shrugs out of my grip. "When do we play next?"

"Championship game goes in about forty-five minutes."

"Alrighty then," I say once clipboard-guy has wandered off. "What do you say me and you grab a bite to eat before the big game."

"I don't know. We were gonna set things up—defensive assignments, rotations, that sort of thing."

Dart a glance at Jason's teammates, big Al and lanky Kevin Maravich. "Boys don't mind if I steal this guy for a bit, do you?"

The two of them shrug in that mopey skeptical way kids their age have: as though, instead of asking could I take Jason to lunch, I'd suggested enrolling him in seminary college.

"Great! Have him back in time for the game. Honest injun."

WE HEAD TO THE MIKADO and find seats on the patio. Afternoon sunlight hits the scalloped glass tabletops, splintering in blazing pinwheels and fanwise coronets. Tempered light falls through the patio umbrella, touching the beaded perspiration on Jason's upper lip.

Lola's dog, a nasty-looking Rottweiler chained to the wrought-iron patio fence, yammers as its owner waddles outside.

"Back again, misser?" Lola's sun-blotting bulk towers above me, Lola tapping a toothmarked Dixon Ticonderoga against an order pad. "What'll y'have?"

"A Bud and a shot a rye. This fella'll have a Bud, too."

"He gots ID?"

"Dad, I got a game."

"Sweet Jesus, Lola, he's got a game!" Suddenly I'm angry—furious, really—at Lola for permitting my son to drink before a ball game. "Get him a Coke and a grilled cheese—you *do* grilled cheese, don't you?"

"Kin whip one up."

"Fine. Wonderful." Shake my head, disgusted. "He's got a *game,* for Christ's sake. The *championship*."

Lola shrugs and wanders off to fill the order. I say, "Hey, got any grape soda?"

"Nope," Lola says without turning back. "Coke and ging-a-ale."

I wink at Jason. "Never hurts to ask. Know how much you love your grape pop."

An inside joke of ours. A few years back Jason and some buddies had a pickup game going when I returned from a morning shift. Head to the kitchen for something to wet the whistle and on the counter spy a bottle of grape pop I'd bought earlier that week—*dead empty*. Don't know why, but this pissed the almighty hell out of me; guess maybe I'd been thinking about it at the drill press—a tall cool glass of grape soda, all purple and bubbly. Sounds ridiculous, but at the time I could've spat nails and thundered outside brandishing the empty bottle.

"Which one a you shits drank my pop?"

The driveway game ground to a halt, everyone standing about staring at their sneakers. After a moment Jason said, "I did, Dad. Hardly any left, really."

I stalked over and rapped his head with the bottle. Thin plastic made an empty *wok* off his skull.

"You drank it *all?* Couldn't leave a goddam glassful for your old man?"

"There wasn't even a glassful left." Jason rubbed his scalp. "There was like, only enough that it filled those dents, the, the *nubbins* at the bottom of the bottle. And it was flat, anywa—"

Hit him again—*wok!*—and again—*pok!*—and for good measure—*tok!* Silence except for big Al Cousy dribbling the basketball and the hollow glance of plastic off my son's head. Jason's eyes never left mine, though they did go a bit puffy at the edges, skin above his cheeks pink and swollen as though some horrible pressure were building there.

"It's not the grape pop," I said, intent on teaching my son a valuable life lesson. "It's the . . . *principle*. Now get on your horse—I mean *right now*—ride down to Avondale and pick up a fresh bottle."

Jason pulled his bicycle out of the garage. "Guys oughta head home."

"Yeah, why don't you boys skedaddle. Jason's got an errand to run."

He rode down the street round the bend. I stood rooted like a stump until he came back, bottle swaying in a plastic bag tugged over the handlebars. By then my anger had ebbed so I only swatted him good-naturedly and made him sink twenty three-pointers. Pretty silly, when you think back on it—I mean, *grape pop*, right? Which is why we can make a joke of it now.

Lola comes out with the drinks. Bolt back the shot of rye, suck down half a bottle of Bud, lean back in my chair. Feeling a little calmer, more inside myself, breathe deeply and smile.

"How come you didn't tell me about this—know how I like to watch you play."

"Sort of a last-minute thing." Jason cracks an icecube between his molars. "The other guy came down sick. Didn't want to, but they were in a bind."

"Well, good thing—woulda got creamed without you."

"Didn't *want* to," he says with emphasis. "They were hard up."

"Yeah, the whole tourney's below your skill level; you're too good for these chumps. So, any offers from down south yet? About that time of year."

"One, from Kentucky-Wesleyan." A shrug. "Like, partial scholarship or something."

"Kentucky-Wesleyan? But . . . they're Div II."

Jason stares out across the courtyard, telephone wires bellied under a weight of blackbirds. "Yeah, Div II. Maybe nobody's gonna come calling. So what? There's other things I could do."

"Other things? Like what?"

"I dunno . . . could be, like, a nutritionist or something."

"A nutritionist? What, with the carbs and proteins? The food pyramid and . . . oh god, the *wheat grass*? Don't be an idiot. This is just the start. You're gonna want to hold off for the best offer—and hey, might even want to declare straight out of high school."

"Declare for what?"

"Declare for what, he says—the *draft*, dopey. The NBA draft."

Jason shakes his head and for a split second I want to reach over and haul off on him. Instead I finish my beer and when Lola comes out with the sandwich order another.

"How's your ma doing?"

"Fine." Jason takes a bite of grilled cheese. "She's fine."

"Must be weird," I say hopefully, "the two of you roaming around that big ole house all by your lonesome."

"Not really."

Jason's mother and I are experiencing marital difficulties. The crux of the problem seems to lie in the admission I may've married her with an eye towards certain features—her articulate fingers, coltish legs, strong calves—that, united with my own physical makeup, laid the genetic groundwork for a truly spectacular ball player. She claims our entire relationship is "false-bottomed," that I ought to be ashamed for aspiring to create some "Franken-son" with little or no regard for her "feelings." She refuses to accept my apology, despite my being tanked and overly lugubrious at the time of admission. I feel this not only petty of her but verging on un-motherly, what with our boy at such a crucial juncture in his development.

"Who's gonna string up the Christmas lights this year, huh?" I ask, despite having gone derelict on this particular household duty for years. "You'll be away at school."

"Do it before I go, Mom asks me to."

Lola arrives with another beer. "Well, anyway, this'll all come out in the wash. Me and your ma just need some time apart. Lots of couples go through it, don't worry."

"I'm not worried."

Something in his tone gets my dander up: it's the tone of a truth-hoarder, a secret-keeper and now I really *am* going to smack the taste out of his mouth but my hand's arrested by the arrival of a pretty young thing who strikes up a conversation with Jason. Short but amply endowed—*built like a brick shithouse,* my old TRW crony Ted Russell would say—leaning over the patio rail in lavender tubetop, cheeks dusted with sparkling glitter, she says, "Hey there, cutie," in a high breathy voice. My son smiles as they ease into typical adolescent conversation: what so-and-so said about so-and-so, so-and-so's having a bush party tonight, so-and-so's an angel, so-and-so's a creep but drives a Corvette and all the while I'm staring—say "staring," but I suppose "leering" is more apt—at the girl, picturing her a few years down the road, that knockout body grinding up and down a brass pole or something. Leering at a ditzy cocktease no older than your son, a man is forced into one of two admissions: either (*a*) your son is more or less grown up, or (*b*) you're a lecherous perv.

"Look at my boy," I say, brimming with drunken pride. "All grown up and talking to girls."

"C'mon, Dad," Jason says nervously, as though addressing the drunken uncle gearing up to spoil a wedding. The girl, who up 'til now has treated me with the brusque inattention reserved for house-plants, seems baffled and somewhat sickened to learn Jason is the fruit of my loins: like discovering the Mona Lisa was painted by a mongoloid.

"Got to see a man about a horse." Swaying to my feet, I add, "Forgot to hit the bank. Spot your old man a few shekels, wouldya?"

Jason sighs in a manner that suggests he'd been expecting this all along. Reaching into his duffel, he lays a twenty on the table.

"That's a good lad. Knew your ma wouldn't send you out empty-handed."

"It's *my* money, Dad. I like, earned it. At my *job*."

"Sure you did, sonny boy." Tip him a wink. "Sure you did."

Stumbling through the patio doors, I hear the girl say: "So that's your dad? *Weird.*"

BATHROOM WALLS PAPERED in outdated concert flyers and old cigarette signs. Piss rises wicklike up the drywall in hypnotic flame-shaped stains. A fan of dried puke splashed round the base of the lone commode, dried and colorful gobbets. Disgusting, yes, but I cannot say with utter certainty I am not the culprit: the sequence of this morning's events remains hazy.

Relieving myself, my eyes are drawn to a snatch of graffiti on the stall: *For Sale: Baby Shoes. Hardly Worn.* Beneath this is written, *How about ten bucks?,* and under that a crude etching of a droopy phallus with what appears to be a flower growing out the pisshole. Stare up at a lightbulb imprinted with blackened silhouettes of charred insects, which for some reason remind me of the holographic shadows burnt onto brickwork at Hiroshima and Nagasaki. Standing there in the piss and puke and dim unmoving puppetshow thrown by the bugtarred bulb, a sense of grim desolation draws over me—a sensation of *psychological dread.* Through the smeared casement window phantom shapes dart and cycle, dark tongues licking beneath the warped frame. The stall presses in upon me, walls buckle-crimping like the lungs of some great primordial beast. A trilling voice invades my skull: *Weird-Weird-Weird-Weird-Weird.* Reel from the stall and in the crack-starred mirror glimpse my eyes punched out and dangling on sluglike stalks and there deep in the cratered sockets spy another pair of eyes, red and raw and slitted lengthwise like a cat's, peering back without pity or remorse.

The episode passes and everything's a bit cheerier when I get back outside. Jason and the girl are gone. Lola's cleared away the bottles and settled the bill. Pocket the change, leave no tip. The Rottweiler barks wrathfully—has it been trained to sniff out skinflints like those airport drug dogs? "Hush'n, Biscuits," comes Lola's voice from inside.

With a few minutes to spare before Jason's game, pop into the liquor store. A homeless man squats outside the door begging bus fare. Where's the guy need to get to so badly? He doesn't ask anything from me. Wander air-conditioned aisles, past cognacs and brandies and aged scotch whiskies, arriving at a cooler stocked with screw-top Rieslings, boxed Chardonnays and malt liquors. Settle on a smoky brown bottle, label stamped with a snorting bull: a plucky malt best enjoyed on those occasions one finds oneself a bit down at the heel. Paying the cashier with the coins my son hadn't bothered to pick up, it strikes me I may've hit a new low.

It's not kosher to drink in public so I hunt through the liquor store dumpster. An empty Big Gulp cup—bingo! A wasp inside, big angry bastard must've crawled down the straw to get at the crystallized globes of Orange Crush clinging to the waxed insides. It buzzes away as I pour in the contents of the brown bottle, re-fasten the lid, and step onto the sidewalk well pleased with this subterfuge. Sucking merrily on the neon pink straw, I pause to consider who else's lips it may've come in contact with. Could've been anybody, you got to figure—a bum's, Christ, some scabby diseased *bum*, cracked lips rich with fungal deposits and now I'm wondering if 7-Eleven even *sells* soda to the homeless, if they conduct a brisk trade with this sort of clientele, and while I come to the reasonable conclusion that no, they clearly do *not*, I cannot help but feel the earlier sense of lowness I experienced was merely a staging area, a jumping-off point for this profound, near-subterranean, even lower low.

A TEEMING THRONG rings the championship court. Shove through the mob with an air of boozy entitlement—it's *my son* they're gawking at, isn't it?—to find the game's already started. Jason's team is matched against a trio of blacks whose voices betray an upper New York lilt: "trow" for throw, "dat" for that, "dere" for there, "dear" for dare, so what you hear is *Trow dat shit up dere—go on, I dear ya!* Up from Buffalo with their dusky sunpolished skin, cornrowed hair and trash talk, figuring they'll take these pasty Canucks to school. Some bozo with a megaphone, the announcer I guess, does not call the game so much as cap each play with an annoying catchphrase: "Boo-*YA!*" or "Boom-shakalaka!" or "Dipsee-doo dunkaroo!" or "Ye-ye-ye-ye-ye-ye-*YEAH!*" or just "Ohhh, *SNAP!*"

The other team is up 7-4 when Jason takes the ball at the top of the key. He dribbles right and bounces a pass to Al Cousy on the low block. Al rolls off his man, elevates and fires a one-legged jumper that clanks off rim.

"Don't pass to stone hands!" I cry. "Jesus, son—use your *head!*"

The other team's point guard executes a smooth crossover dribble—an *ankle-snapper*—catching Jason flatfooted. Kevin Maravich shuffles over on helpside defense but the guard flicks the ball to Kevin's check, who dunks two-handed and gorilla-hangs on the rim.

"Biggedy-*BAM!*" hollers the announcer.

Jason keeps passing to his tits-on-a-bull teammates. Kevin gets blocked twice and big Al puts up enough bricks to build a homeless shelter. Their opponents dish out a constant stream of trash: *Don't go bringing that weakass shit in here, bitch—this is* my *house! Hope you got an umbrella, son—I'm gonna be raining on you all day! Boy, my game's so ill I make medicine sick!* The ref, a balding old shipwreck in frayed zebra getup, lets the Yanks get away with murder: pushes, holds, flagrant elbows. I give it to him both barrels.

"Hey ref, if you had one more eye you'd be a cyclops!"

"Hey ref, Colonel Mustard called—he said get a clue!"

"Hey ref, if your IQ was any lower someone'd have to water you!"

Spectators snorting and laughing, a beefy mitt slams between my shoulder blades and someone says, "Thattaboy—stick it to the man!" Take a haul on my drink and for a long vacant moment feel nothing but relentless seething hatred for the ref, the opposing team, Jason's teammates, anyone and everyone trying to stop him from reaching the goal he's destined for, stifle the gift that'll take him out of this rinkydink town, far from the do-nothing go-nowhere be-nobody yokels surrounding me.

The score's 13-4 and Jason hasn't taken a shot. He kicks the ball to Al who kicks it back, a stinging bullet hitting Jason in the chest. "What are you doing? *Take it,* man." Jason stab-steps his defender, gives him a brisk shake-n-bake, shoots. As soon as the ball leaves his hands, you know it's good. It passes through so clean the net loops up over the hoop and that *sound*—dear god, almost *sexual.*

"This guy's dialed in long distance!" the announcer brays.

Jason picks the point guard's pocket on the next possession, clears beyond the three-point arc, fires. *Swish.* 13-9.

"He's shooting the lights out, folks!"

The point guard muscles past Jason but Kevin gets a hand in his face and the shot misses short left. Al gobbles up the rebound and shovels it to Jason. The defensive rotation's slow and he gets a clean look from twenty-two feet, burying it. 13-12 and now the other team's a bit frazzled; "C'mon, naa," the point guard says. "D-up. We gut these bitches."

But it's too late: Jason's entered some kind of zone. Wherever he is on the court, no matter how tight the coverage, he's draining it. Running one-hander from the elbow—good. Fadeaway three-ball with a defender down his throat—good. High-arcing teardrop in traffic—good. In my head I'm hearing Marv Albert, longtime New York Knickerbockers play-by-play man and purloiner of women's undergarments: *Mikan takes the ball at the top of the circle, shakes his man, hoists up a prayer—YESSSSS!* Twisting circus shot around two defenders—good. Step-back three launched from another zipcode —good. The lead's flipped, 22-17; the Yanks' faces are stamped with grimaces of utter disbelief.

"This cat's got the *skills* to pay the *bills,* ladies and gentlemen!"

Throughout this shooting display Jason's expression never changes:

a vacant, vaguely disgusted look like he's sniffed something rank. He doesn't follow the ball after it leaves his hand, as though unwilling to chart its inevitable drop through the hoop. If you didn't know any better, you'd almost think he *wants* to miss. Scan the crowd for a familiar face, my shitheel supervisor Mr. Riley maybe—*See that, asshole? That's my son! My good genes MADE that! What did your genes ever make, Riley? Oh, that's right—a few stains on the bedsheets and a PUSSY TAX CONSULTANT!*

The game-winning shot's a doozy. Jason passes down to Al, who is blocked but corrals the ball and shuttles it to Jason. The other point guard's tight to his vest and Jason backs off, dribbling the ball high. Maybe it's just the malt liquor but at this moment he appears to move in a cocoon of beatific light: glowing sundogs and sparkling scintillas robe his arms and legs. He goes right but so does his defender, swiping at the ball, almost stealing it. They're down along the baseline, Jason's heels nearly out of bounds and he shoots falling into the crowd, a dozen arms outstretched to cradle him and as he's going down I hear him say, in a small defeated voice, "Glass." The ball banks high off the backboard and through the net.

"The dagger!" screams the announcer. "Oh lord, he hits the *dagger!*"

The crowd breaks up, drifting away in twos and threes to bars and parks and restaurants. A work crew dismantles the nets and sound equipment, packing everything into cube vans to truck to the next venue.

"Great game, son." Somehow I've managed to slop beer down myself so it looks I've pissed my pants. Try to pawn it off as excitement. "A real barnburner—look, you got me sweating buckets."

Jason's sitting on the curb with his teammates. "Yeah, guess it was a pretty good one."

To Kevin and big Al: "Lucky Jason was here to drag your asses out of the fire, huh?"

They don't reply but instead pull off their shoes and socks, donning summer sandals. Big Al's toenails thick yellow and thorny, curling over his toes like armor plating.

"What say I take you boys out for dinner?" I offer breezily. "A champion's feast."

"That's okay," Jason says. "Kev's parents are having a barbecue. They've got a pool."

"A pool? How suburban." Jam one hand in my pocket, scratch the nape of my neck with the other. "So Kev, where's your folks' place at?"

Kevin hooks a thumb over his shoulder, an ambiguous gesture that could conceivably indicate the city's southern edge, the nearest town, or Latin America.

"Could I tag along?"

Jason sits with his legs spread, head hanging between his knees. "I don't know. They sort of, like, only did enough shopping for, y'know, us three."

"Well, wouldn't come empty-handed. I could grab some burgers, or . . . Cheetos."

"You see, it's like, we kind of got a full car. Y'know, Al and me and all our gear and stuff. Kev's only got a Neon, right?"

"We could squeeze, couldn't we? Get buddy-buddy?"

"I don't know. Gotta do some running around first."

"I love running around. It's good for the heart."

Without looking up, Jason says, "Dad, listen, Kev's still on probation—his license, right?—so, it's like, he can't have anyone in his car who's been drinking. If the cops pull us over, Kev'll get his license suspended."

"Oh. Alrighty then." Stare into the sky, directly into the afternoon sun. Close my eyes and the ghostly afterimage burns there as a sizzling imprint, searing corona dancing with winking fairylights.

The boys gather their bags and waterbottles. Shake Kev and Al's hands, hug my son. His skin smells of other bodies, the sweat of strangers. Used to love the smell of his hands after practice, the scent of sweat and leather commingled. When I let him go the flesh around his eyes is red and swollen and it gets me thinking of that distant afternoon, grape soda and a sense of horrible pressure.

"Great game," I tell him. "You're gonna show 'em all one day."

He walks down the street, hitching the duffel up on his shoulder. Charting his departure, it's as though I'm seeing him through the ass end of a telescope: this tiny figure distorted by an unseen convex, turning the corner now, gone. Sun high in the afternoon sky, brilliant and hostile, beer's all gone and it's the middle of the day though it feels like it should be later, much later and near dusk and it dawns on me I've nothing to do, nowhere to be, the day stretching out bright and interminable with no clear goal or closure in sight.

NIGHTTIME AT THE KNIGHTWOOD ARMS subsidized housing complex. My bedroom window overlooks a dilapidated basketball court, tarmac seized and buckled, nets rotted from the hoops. Early mornings I'll head down and shoot baskets beneath a lightening sky, mist falling through the courtyard's arc-sodium lamp to create a cool glittering nimbus. Often someone'll crack a window in one of the overhanging units, *Knock it off with the damn bouncity-bounce.* Don't make much fuss anymore, just go back to my room.

Eleven o'clock or so and the bottle's almost empty when the phone rings.

"Hey," Jason says. "It's me."

"Glad to hear it."

"Yeah, well, wanted to talk to you about something."

Good news, I'm guessing: Duke, Kentucky, UConn. "Your old man's all ears."

"Well, it's like, I've decided to not play ball."

"You mean you're going to take the year off?" Try to remain calm. "Don't know that's the best idea, kiddo—gonna want to keep in the mix."

"No, I sort of mean, like . . . *ever*. I mean, *for*ever."

"Forever? Don't get you."

The mouthpiece is shielded. Jason's muffled voice, then his mother's, then Jason's back on the line. "I'm sick of it. Sick of basketball. Don't want to play anymore."

"Well," I struggle, "that's . . . sort of a childish attitude, son. I don't always like my job, but it's my job, so I do it. That's the way the world . . . *works*."

A sigh. "You know, there are other things in life. Lots of jobs out there."

"Yeah, well, like what?"

"I don't know," he says. "I was thinking maybe . . . a vet?"

"You mean . . . a veterinarian?"

"Uh-huh. Like that, or something."

"Oh. Well, that's . . . y'know . . . that's grand. The sick cats and everything. A grand goal."

"Anyway. Just thought I'd tell you."

"Yeah. Well . . . thanks. What say you sit on it a bit, Jason, let it stew awhile. Who knows—might change your mind."

"No, I don't think so. Alright, goodbye."

"All I'm saying is—"

But the line's already dead. Hang up and lie back on the mattress, stare out at the starblown sky.

When Jason was a kid I bought him this mechanical piggy bank. You'd set a coin in the cup-shaped hand of a metal basketball player, pull the lever to release a spring and the player deposited the coin in a cast-iron hoop. Jason loved the damn thing. Sit him on the floor with a handful of pennies: hours of mindless amusement. Every so often I'd have to quit whatever I was doing to unscrew the bottom, dump the coins so Jason could start over. The *snak-clanggg!* of the mechanism got annoying after the first half-hour and I would've taken it away if Jason wasn't so small and frail and I so intent on honing that fascination. There were other toys, a whole closetful, but he *chose* basketball. Right from the get-go. And yeah, I encouraged it—what's a father supposed to do? Guide his kid towards any natural inclination, gently at first, then as required. If that's what your kid's born to do, what other choice do you really have?

All I'm saying is, I'm no monster, okay? As a father, you only ever want what's best for your boy. That's your *job*—the greatest job of your life. All you want is that your kid be happy, and healthy, and follow the good path. That's all I did: kept him on the good path. I'm a great father. A damn fine dad. Swear it on a stack of bibles.

So my boy wants to be a veterinarian, does he? Well it's a tough racket, plenty of competition, no cakewalk by a longshot. Don't I know a guy out Welland way who's a taxidermist? Sure, Adam somebody-or-other, stuffs geese and trout and I don't know—bobcats? Ought to shoot him a call, see if me and Jason can't pop by, poke around a bit. I mean, you want to be a doctor, got to know your way around cadavers, right? It's the same principle. Adam's one easygoing sonofabitch; doubt he'll mind.

Yeah, that's just what I'll do. Finish off this bottle, hunt up that number, make the call. I mean, hey, sure it comes as a shock, but nobody can call Hank Mikan a man of inflexible fiber. When life hands you lemons, make lemonade. Life offers sour grapes, make sweet wine. A veterinarian, huh? Well, that's *noble*. Damn *noble*. And hey, money ain't half-bad either.

Let's finish this last swallow and get right on the blower. It's a long road ahead.

Like the shoe commercial says, right? Just Do It. Hey!

A MEAN UTILITY

MIDWAY THROUGH THE PITCH I pass a note to Mitch Edmonds, big kahuna of graphic design: *This is going good?* He grimaces and scribbles back: *If by "good" you mean heart-stoppingly BAD, then yes, everything's PEACHY.* Diarrhetic adjective use aside, I suspect Edmonds is correct. In fact, the pitch is veering towards a crash of Hindenburg-like proportions: feel the heat of compressed helium flames and charred tatters of zeppelin silk buffeting my face, hear Herbert Morrison's breathless voice screaming "Oh the *humanity!*" into a giant wind-socked microphone.

Supp-Easy-Quit is a stop-smoking aid in suppository form. The science is sound: the rectal arterial clusters, feeding directly into the larger sacral and iliac branches, are ideal nicotine-delivery channels. Yet the stone-cold fact persists: most smokers—most *human beings*—exhibit a distinct disinclination to propel foreign objects up their bungs. They'd rather chew Nicorette until their mouths seize with lockjaw, festoon their bodies with the Patch, Christ, insert *flaming nicotine wedges* under their fingernails. This hardwired predisposition renders the product a tough sell.

Don Fawkes, lead hand on the Supp-Easy-Quit account, aims a laser-pointer at a storyboard montage. "Okay," he says, "so here's this smoker who's trying to quit. He's in a smoky tavern—upscale, jazzy, bit of a speakeasy feel—tipping a few bevies, itching to fire off a lung rocket." Don believes his timely employment of hipster lingo is key to the middling success he enjoys. "So our man slips into the men's room and enters a stall, jazz music swells, he exits all smiles. Fade to black on the product logo."

The Supp-Easy-Quit reps—a power-suited Eva Braun flanked by a pair of lab-coated scientist pastiches—sit with arms crossed. The trio strike me as just-the-facts-ma'am types: their ideal commercial no doubt involves clinical footage of suppositories inserted into rectums, endoscopic cameras filming the dispersal of nicotine molecules into the bloodstream.

"Tell me: do you like it?" Don Fawkes, *Ignoramus extremus*, asks. "Do you *love* it?"

Fawkes's towering colossus of ineptitude fails to elicit any surprise or sympathy from me for two reasons: (1) last month Don single-handedly scuttled the Juicy Jubes kosher jujubes account, enraging a group of Hasidic entrepreneurs with the utterance of his ill-conceived tagline: *Juicy Jubes are Jui-y JUI-licious!;* and (2) a large chunk of meat is missing from my left calf, a chunk roughly correspondent to the bite radius of a Rottweiler named Biscuits. The wound is cleaned and dressed but the calf is a fussy area, a locus of veins and connective tissues—blood seeps through the bandages, pooling in the heel of my Bruno Magli loafer.

I was mauled two nights ago, at a scratch-and-turn dogfight held in a foreclosed poultry processing plant outside Cobourg. Dottie, a three-year-old pit bull and my wife Alison's darling bitch, was matched uphill against a hard-biting presa canario named Chinaman. Dottie was a ten fight champ with heavily muscled stifles and a bite to shatter cinderblocks; Chinaman was cherry but his lineage legendary with chest and flews capable of deflecting bullets. Betting skewed in Dottie's favor on account of her experience and ring generalship.

After Alison gave Chinaman a thorough inspection—the breeder a jug-eared hillbilly known to soak his fighters' fur in poison—the dogs were led into a chicken-wire pen. White worms of chicken shit dotted the floor, some with downy feathers stuck to them. The concrete was puddled with blood from the previous fight.

Dottie started out fast, butting her muzzle into Chinaman's chest and tearing a gaping hole above his right shoulder. Chinaman looked ready to buckle—it's the first critical injury that separates gamers from curs—but when Dottie went for his front leg he snapped at her skull, canines opening deep furrows across the bridge of her snout. Blood flowed down Dottie's chest and sprayed in her eyes. Alison gave a little moan. Chinaman's handler hollered, "Get at it, boy! Sic! *Sic!*"

The presa rushed hard and tried to pin Dottie against the pen. Dottie back-pedaled a few paces before fastening her mouth around Chinaman's advancing foreleg and ripping free a network of muscle and tissue. Chinaman kept pressing, chewing on Dottie's head; it sounded as if his teeth were raking bone. The crowd pressed around the pen, slapping the chicken-wire, stomping their feet. The smell was close and hot, sweetly animal.

The bell rang. Men with blunt baling hooks reached over the wire, digging into the dense muscling of the dog's chests, prying them apart. In the corner, I held Dottie while Alison went to work. After rubbing powdered Lidocaine into the dog's gumline to kill the pain, she chemically cauterized the facial wounds with ferric acid. Then she saturated a Q-tip with adrenaline chloride and swabbed the rims of Dottie's nostrils and ear holes, her anus. The dog's eyes, previously glazed, attained a clear focus.

The bell rang. Both dogs scratched the chalk line.

Dottie lived up to her reputation as a wrecker in the second. She butted hard into Chinaman's stifles, attacking that shoulder wound. Chinaman gave as good as he got, slashing at Dottie's dewlap, shredding it. At the eight-minute mark: a fibrous *snap* as Chinaman's shoulder broke. The presa was down to three legs. Dottie pressed her advantage, forcing Chinaman back, attacking the throat, a blur of snapping teeth, questing jaws, and bloody ropes of saliva as each dog angled for the killing clinch.

Chinaman managed to close his mouth around Dottie's muzzle, gripping her entire upper palate. The brittle splintering sound was unlike anything I'd ever heard. Dottie's spine stiffened and her claws tore at Chinaman's belly.

The bell rang. An acne-scarred teenager mopped up blood and redrew the chalk line.

Dottie's face was in ruins: bloody and cleaved open, shards of bone free-floating beneath the skin. Half her nose was torn off and her dewlap hung like tattered curtains. Alison debrided the worst wounds with hydrogen peroxide and Betadine before slicking them with mixed adrenaline and Vaseline.

"Pick your dogs up!" a man hollered. "That's enough. Enough!" The crowd jeered him.

"Maybe I should," Alison said. "Pick her up."

I'd've rather cut my foot off and eaten it! "Look at that one," I said with a nod at the presa, who was burrowing his head in the breeder's chest like it wanted to climb inside and die. "Bet you a steak dinner it doesn't toe the scratch."

Chinaman's breeder grabbed the dog by its neck and whipsawed it back and forth, growling, "Don't flake on me, you goddamn cur. Don't you fucking *flake*."

Before the bell Alison injected 10 cc's Epinephrine into Dottie's haunch. I felt the dog's fluttering heart rate normalize. Chinaman staggered from his corner, front right leg limp as a cooked noodle. The presa's muzzle was frosted white with Lidocaine.

Round three ended it. Dottie feinted at Chinaman's bum leg off the scratch and, in one deft move, rammed her skull into his good one. Forced to support his entire forward weight, Chinaman's left foreleg snapped. The presa toppled face-first, front legs splayed to either side, hinds scrabbling feebly. Dottie started clawing at Chinaman's eyes. Before long the baling hooks pulled her off.

After squaring all bets I was lugging Dottie through the parking lot—blood saturating her doggie blanket, dripping through the kennel crate's metal honeycombs—when this raspy barking kicked up from behind. I wheeled to see a huge Rottweiler bullrushing my blind side. It wore an inch-thick studded leather collar against which the striated muscle of its throat and neck pulsed. Links of twenty-gauge chain spat gravel between its legs.

I dropped Dottie and fired an off-balance kick. The rottie passed under my leg, clamping down on my calf.

Events unfolded at the narcotic pace of a fugue. My right knee buckled and I went down, blacktopped gravel dimpling the ass of my cotton Dockers. My skull caromed off the ground and everything whited out for a moment. Then I was struggling up, fists beating a frenzied tattoo on the dog's head as its square dark muzzle worried into the wound. Dottie pressed her busted face to the kennel's grate, growling low in her throat, bloody bubbles forced between her black eyes and orbital bone. The Rottweiler wrenched its head sideways, teeth sunk deep into the sinews of my calf, gator-rolling me across that chill November tarmac.

Five sausage-link digits grasped the underside of the rottie's jaw, thumb and index finger pressed to the axis where upper and lower palate met, forcing the mouth open. The woman restraining the animal was an eclipse of flesh clad in what appeared to be a pleated topsail, calves thick as an adolescent pachyderm's networked with bluish spider veins. A slimly ironic menthol cigarette hung off her bottom lip, defying all known laws of gravity.

"Bad Biscuits," she chastised the dog in a breathy baby-voice. "The manners on you. Why you want to go biting the nice man?"

Alison arrived in a blur of shawls and indignation. I noticed she poked her fingers through Dottie's crate before arriving at my side. Bright arterial blood pumped from my calf.

"Stop squirming," she told me, breaking out the peroxide and catgut to attend to the wound.

The woman waddled to her idling Cutlass Supreme. She opened the driver's door—sunblistered dashboard lined with neon-haired Treasure Trolls; bingo dabbers spilling from a sprung glovebox—swatting the dog inside. A shrewish, stoop-shouldered man sat in the passenger's seat, wearing camouflage fatigue pants and the kind of sleeveless white T-shirt favored by aged Italian gardeners.

"You can't," I said, reaching out to her. "Can't just . . . your dog *bit me!*"

She tucked her chin to her chest, setting in motion a rippling domino-effect of subsidiary chins. "Biscuits got a touch of the ringworm, misser. Gives him the cranks." Her look suggested I wasn't much of a dogman if I didn't know *that*. "Every one my babies is papered and rabies free. Don't need shots, promise."

"That dog should be destroyed!"

"I'm'n a *pretend* I didn't *hear* that, misser."

She jerked the door shut and fishtailed down the row of diagonally parked cars. Biscuits hurled his body at the Cutlass's rear window, barking wrathfully, white froth slathering the glass.

"Did that woman just . . . ?"

"Yes," Alison palmed me a vitamin K tablet to promote blood clotting. "Let's go."

"But you can't—"

"What do we tell the cops?" she said. "We were at this illegal dogfight and . . ."

"But we live in a polite society!" I was raving by now. "We operate under civilized rules!"

"Hush."

"I should bite *her*—bite that gargantuan . . . *ASS!*"

"Hush."

Halfway home Alison pulled off the highway. Dottie was emitting low wheezing sounds from the back seat, thrashing on the blood-thick blanket and tearing her stitches open.

We wrangled the kennel crate onto the rough shale of the breakdown lane. In the dead white of an arc-sodium streetlight I broke the kennel down, there being no other way to get her out. Alison held the dog's square head in her hands, massaging the neck and stomach, anywhere not gored. The medicinal smell of Epinephrine seeped out of Dottie's many cuts.

"Oh, Jesus. I can't bury another dog, Jay."

Alison touched Dottie's head, tracing her fingertips along the muzzle, kneading the expanse of slick fur between the ears. The dog looked up with sad, grateful eyes. Crickets chirped in long reeds bordering the ditch.

Near the end Alison injected Lidocaine into Dottie's temple, between the ring and index fingers on my left hand, which were cupped over the dog's tight-lidded eyes. Cars moved past on the highway, bathing our bodies in headlight glow. Dottie vomited blood. Her eyelids fluttered against my palm.

"I should've picked her up."

The dog started shaking then, the convulsions wracking her bones, radiating outwards.

"She wouldn't allow it," I said. "Dottie was a deep game dog."

"Are you loving it?" Don Fawkes repeats for the umpteenth time. "Tell me you love it."

But the Supp-Easy-Quit reps are clearly *not* loving it, a fact Helen Keller could've gleaned, but of which Fawkes remains blissfully unaware. Eva Braun jots in a faux-calfskin dossier with aggressive, slashing cursive while her lab-coated bookends eye Fawkes as they might a particularly offensive strain of bacterium smeared across a specimen slide.

Mitch Edmonds passes me a doodle: some guy with a gourd-shaped head in which a candle burns jack-o-lantern style, one eye twice out-sizing the other, pumpkintoothed and drooling, squiggly stink-lines and bowtie flies and a speech bubble reading: *You love it! You really, really love it!*

DR. CLIVE KETCHUM'S fertility clinic is located in a neocolonial-style office building at the corner of Steeles and Yonge. I mount the steps leading up to a narrow hallway with hesitancy. Took a Xanax at lunch, another on the cab ride over—feeling *no* pain.

Ketchum's waiting area resembles a film noir movie set: a large, dim, oak-paneled room with high ceiling, frosted-glass valances, a white sand ashtray under a no smoking sign. The receptionist is young, petite, and blond, with prominent tits and an air of having woken this morning knowing in advance every move she'd make for the remainder of the day.

"I have the five o'clock."

She consults the appointment book. "Mr. James Paris?"

I tip her a wink, resisting—barely—the urge to flex.

She leads me down a well-lit corridor into a spare antiseptic room. She gestures to an examination table and orders me to strip to my skivs before excusing herself.

I hoist myself onto the examination table. Butcher paper crinkles under my thighs. A large medical illustration adorns the opposite wall: *Scrotum and Contents*. It's all there: the superficial and external spermatic fascias, the tunica vaginalis, the epididymis and the testes, which, in this artist's rendition, resemble capillary-threaded quail's eggs. Disembodied tweezer-tips pinch and peel back to reveal strata of flesh and membrane and nerve.

Dr. Ketchum enters. The man's dimensions are those of a bowling pin, the majority of weight distributed to the hindquarters, and yet his body remains somehow insubstantial, as if stuffed with wadded newspapers.

He flips open a dossier, nodding, then shaking his head. "You've been doing the exercises?" He performs a series of spread-legged knee bends, arms veed in front of him like a high diver. Ketchum contends this maneuver—the "gonad agitator"—will promote sperm production and, in tandem with other, uniformly unpleasant exercises—the "urethral tube widener," the "scrotal exciter"—will have me shooting live rounds in no time.

"I've been doing them."

"It's strange."

"What?"

"Strange your sperm count hasn't increased since the start of your exercise regimen." He gives me a look. "It is my experience that men tend to baby their testes, usually as a result of early childhood trauma. But believe me when I say they're terrifically hardy organs. My advice is to really push yourself. Make those testicles *work* for you. Give them hell, as it were."

"I've been giving them . . . hell."

"Is that so?"

"It's been . . . a regular boot camp."

Dr. Ketchum chuckles perfunctorily. "Alright. The problem remains, James. Your scrotal sac is simply too *hot*. A blast furnace in there."

This is not new information. Five years ago, when our fledgling, lighthearted attempts at conception ended in failure, we blamed our lack of success on job stress, our recent relocation, a sheer lack of dedication to the task at hand. But as the streak lengthened, the finger of blame began to point wildly: the moon's cycles / Alison's low-protein diet / my pack-a-day habit / malevolent otherworldly forces. Alison visited a fertility clinic and, through a non-invasive, airy-fairy, casting-of-bones procedure I never truly understood, her womb was given a clean bill of health. Confusion and guilt propelled me to Dr. Ketchum's office, where a violently invasive, teeth-clenchingly painful process disclosed that my scrotum's core temperature equaled that of a steam cooker's. The few vulcanized sperm able to withstand the heat were reduced to heaving their exhausted flagellate forms against my wife's egg in the manner of bedraggled boat-people flinging themselves upon the impregnable walls of an asylum-denying nation.

Ketchum prescribed pills and herbal remedies, ordered the daubing of foul-smelling ointments and the quaffing of putrid teas. He suggested immersion in cold baths or icepack application to the affected region before intercourse. None of these measures proving effective, Ketchum advocated a strenuous exercise routine and . . . other tactics.

"Have you encouraged your wife to stimulate you anally? Gentle manipulation of the sphincter encourages more vigorous orgasms and promotes semen—"

"No, we . . . no."

Ketchum emits a robust, let's-not-be-prudish laugh. "Then by all means *try*. It's a natural, healthy sexual activity. Nothing peculiar or unmanly about it."

A fleeting image: Ketchum's naked, pinata-hollow body squirming delightedly under the anal ministrations of a faceless, tentacle-fingered woman.

"It's not that desperate."

"But your wife must be getting impatient."

"Alison's fine," I lie.

Sex has become a grim struggle punctuated by bizarre and superstitious rituals. While I lounge in bed with a bag of frozen peas thawing in my boxers, Alison discreetly checks her internal temperature against the magical twenty-seven degrees Centigrade ideal for conception. She has dressed as a French maid, a succubus, a cheerleader—*Ra-ra, hey-hey, fertilize that egg to-day!*—a schoolgirl, a milkmaid; the local costume shop conducts a brisk trade on my singular shortcoming. No sooner have I made my contribution than she's shoved me away, elevating her hips and bicycle-kicking her legs, body contorted into grotesque runic formations to aid my seed in "taking." Worst is the look on Alison's face as I come: a look of disquieting, anxious futility. *Not this time, tiger. You didn't bring the thunder.*

"Alison's just fine," I repeat. "We have other interests."

"Wonderful. It's important for couples with such issues to pursue outside goals." He flips the dossier shut. "Keep those exercises up—" a few more demonstrative deep-knee bends "—and don't forget the urethra-widening—" his eyes trail down to my calf "—good lord, James, what happened to your leg?"

ALISON'S FATHER owns a dairy farm on the outskirts of St. Catharines. When he spies a sick cow, he spraypaints an orange circle around the rear left leg. At night, when all the other chores are finished, he leads it to a brook running behind the house and shoots it in the skull. Once, when Alison and I were visiting at Christmas, he asked her to take care of a sick calf; it was cold and her father's arthritis was acting up. Alison asked did he keep his gun in the same spot.

Bundled in parkas and toques, we went out to the barn. Can't say why I tagged along, exactly, except perhaps morbid curiosity, or out of the misplaced notion she needed the moral support. The barn was dark and earthy, claustrophobic with the stink of livestock. Cattle snorted and heaved, expelling plumes of oyster-gray steam from their nostrils. We waded between their milling flanks, guided by bars of dusky sunlight pouring through the slats. A sponge-like tumor the rough size of a softball was tethered to the calf's jaw by a strip of skin. Alison shooed the youngster from its hiding spot beneath its mother's belly. The cow let it go without a fight, as if knowing it was sick, what needed to be done.

She led it down to the water, guiding it gently with a switch snapped off an elm tree. The calf's eyes wide and dark and dumb. The grotesque tumor bump-bumped against its throat. Early twilight hung suspended over the fields, patches of orange burning between the trees. Sparrows clustered on a snow-topped log lying in the middle of the brook.

Alison settled the shotgun against the calf's head. It flicked its ear, as though the muzzle were a fly it wished to shoo. I remember wind whistling down my neck and feeling terribly cold.

Alison cocked the hammer and calmly pulled the trigger. The gunshot louder than I expected, a rough bark rolling out across the clean snow-topped expanse. The animal went down silently. It half-stood on its front legs. The left side of its face was just . . . *gone*. I wanted to yell "Go down, just go *down*," the way a trainer would to an overmatched boxer. It fell over on its side in the shallows. We went back inside for hot toddies.

Half an hour after my doctor's appointment, I step through the front door of our house. From the upstairs nursery arises the plaintive clamor of pit bull puppies seeking attention—attention I studiously deny. Pass down a hallway hung with photos of champion pits chained to spikes pounded into browned patches of grass, mouths open and teeth bared, straining against their fetters.

Alison stands over the kitchen sink shaking water from a colander of diced zucchini. The cordless telephone is cinched between her shoulder and ear.

"No, no," she's saying, her tone that of a mother explaining a crucial fact to a particularly dimwitted child, "that is *not* the progression. Bulldog to German shepherd to Doberman pinscher to Rottweiler to pit bull. It goes *no further*. There is no evolution."

I place my hands on her hips and bring them around, fingers knitting over her bellybutton.

"No, I don't . . . no . . . that's in-*sane*." She twists out of my grasp, pressing the mouthpiece directly to her lips, as if this forced intimacy will convey the truth of her argument. "The presa canario is nothing more than a puffed-up bully. I mean, will a hundred-twenty-pound presa beat a pit? In all probability, yes. But a heavyweight boxer would pummel a flyweight—it's no contest. That's why there's weight classes . . . no . . . alright, yes . . . listen, I'm not going to argue." Alison hangs her tongue out. "Fine, if that's how you see it. All I'll say is, pound for pound, nothing beats a pit. *Pound* for *pound*, yes . . . okay . . . fine . . . we agree to disagree."

She jams the phone in its charging cradle and blows a raspberry at it.

"Who?"

"Nobody. Nothing. How was work?"

"Fawkes deep-sixed the Supp-Easy-Quit account."

"It's a tough product to market."

Alison always lets Fawkes off the hook. I took her to the office Christmas party last year and discovered the two of them in the copy room, sloppy drunk and giggling, photocopying asexual body parts: elbows, fingers, wrists, foreheads.

"And your day?"

"Oh, Dr. Scalise was being Dr. Scalise." Dr. Phillip Scalise, the cardiovascular surgeon at North York General, is thirty-five with the coarse-skinned face and dimpled chin of a *Look Who's Talking–*era John Travolta. Alison is his "all-time favorite" OR nurse. "During prep he was telling these awful jokes, just plain *awful,* and I shouldn't have been laughing but he's really just so silly sometimes."

I recognize this should bother me but, doubtlessly due to the Xanax I popped on the homebound subway, I find myself supremely nonplussed. "He's a silly one," I agree. "I'll go feed the dogs."

The sky's an odd color: a deep but muted red, the color of diluted grenadine. Someone a few houses over is doing yardwork: the staccato *chop-chop-chop* of a lawnmower rises above the pines. The training shed is set into the far left corner in the shade of a leafless maple. The maple is four feet wide at its base, thick lower limbs jutting almost parallel to the ground. I've often imagined nailing split two-by-twos into the trunk, a stepladder up to the boughs capable of supporting weight. I'd lay down planks and erect sturdy retaining walls, a corrugated-tin roof for rainy days, a rope-and-bucket dumbwaiter, maybe even a walkie-talkie link allowing for communication during those first nights of independence.

The shed is of solid prewar construction, dirt floor spread with Bardahl to keep the dust down. I take down a pair of ballistic-nylon gloves from a nail pounded into the doorframe and scoop Iam's Science Diet into steel tureens.

The chicken-wire pens house three fighters but now Dottie's gone we're down to a pair. Rodney is a four-year-old male, forty-seven pounds of bone and sinew and teeth and winner of five consecutive, most recently the first-round butchery of Grand Chief Negrino, a vastly overrated Neapolitan mastiff bitch. I set the tureen in front of him and, while he eats, first gently but with increasing force, punch the crown of his skull until he snaps viciously at my gloved hand.

"Good boy."

Matilda is the most aggressive fighter I've ever raised. Her nose is pressed to the chicken-wire, snuffling. She has a short, clean brindle coat with a pattern of gray stripes over a base coat of jet black. I stroke her sleek head and boxy muzzle, running a fingertip across the crescent-moon scars left after her ears were amputated. She licks the glove with her large pink tongue.

I slap her as hard as I can.

The blow doesn't budge her and then teeth flash, dense muscling of chest and flews flexes, jaws seize the glove in a bone-splintering grip and shake so violently it seems my shoulder will be jerked from its socket.

"Mat—aark! *Aaaagh!*"

I manage to drop the tureen inside her pen. Matilda immediately releases me and pads over to the kibble. I am struck, as I so often am, by the unstudied perfection of these animals.

Pit bulls are utterly fearless. It is a reckless, lunatic sort of fearlessness, a fearlessness suggesting the breed lacks any true conception of that emotion. Beauty exists in that fearlessness, and so the breed itself is beautiful. It is beautiful to watch your pit toe the scratch against a dog twice its size and note, in its posture and its eyes, the flat and unflinching assurance of victory. It is beautiful to hold a pit's wine-cask body between rounds, to take in its hideous wounds—ears bitten off and eyes crushed from orbit, compound-fractured legs, flesh stripped to the bone—and see nothing but a cold resiliency, an *eagerness*. These dogs truly believe they are invincible. They believe they will never die. It is beautiful to watch two pits at the end of a hard roll, lying in the pen's center or pressed up against the wire, slick with blood, blind and exhausted, licking one another with a shocking tenderness. The simple fact of their existence is its own beauty: there are creatures on this Earth upon whom the human frailties of pain, weakness, self-doubt exert no bearing.

Alison and I talk about our mutual fascination. Lately, it's about the only topic that doesn't lead to an argument. Sometimes she'll ask the question: *Should we be doing this?* I look at it like boxing: you train your fighter to the best of your ability, bring him along slowly, don't put him in against a murderer. "Besides," I tell her, "these dogs want to fight. They can't vocalize it, sure, but you can see, I can see. It's what they *do*." She'll nod slightly, say, "The way herding is what a sheepdog does, huh?" in a small voice that doesn't quite seem to believe. "Ex-*actly,* dear."

I walk back to the kitchen. The combined pain of my leg (Biscuits) and shoulder (Matilda) compounded by the ambient soreness resulting from ten minutes of urethral widening exercises has killed the Xanax buzz. I pull two T-bone steaks from the deep-freeze and set them on the counter to thaw. Then I retrieve bottles of rum and Crème de Banane from the cupboard, eyeball shots into a pair of wide-mouthed highball glasses, top them off with heavy cream.

Alison's in the nursery. Walls painted bright yellow, hardwood floor spread with sections of the *Globe and Mail*. Two mobiles: tinfoil baseball players shagging fly balls; tinfoil ballerinas pirouetting endlessly. A molded plastic chair with a dog-eared copy of Sun Tzu's *The Art of War* resting upon it, from which I often quote passages to the dogs: *In peace prepare for war, in war prepare for peace . . .*

My wife on the floor, surrounded by pups. They paw her in clumsy, exploratory fashion, climbing over her hips and breasts, capturing her shirt collar between their teeth and shaking their oversize puppy heads. I sit on pissy newspapers and offer her a glass.

"How was your appointment?" she says.

"Some different exercises."

Alison sets her glass down. A puppy commences licking the beaded condensation. "I was talking to someone at work," she says, "about artificial insemination. Interesting option—leaf through a donor book, choose a suitable candidate."

I imagine a houseful of miniature John Travoltas, or, worse yet, Don Fawkeses, running up and down the halls, sticky-fingered and greasy-haired, telling silly-awful jokes and asking if I love them. "I don't think we need to explore that option."

"I'm thirty-three, Jay," she persists. "Conception after thirty-five is basically a no-go."

A pup noses the toe of my loafer. I give it a boot, sending it skittering across the floor. "I'm thinking about scheduling a roll for Matilda."

"A roll? Now?"

I set my empty glass down and pick Alison's up.

"Mattie's barely a yearling," she says. "You haven't worked her properly . . ."

"She's the strongest dog I've ever seen. She'll crucify anybody."

"There's not an even-weight dog on the circuit she could be rolled against."

"I'd be matching her uphill."

"By how many pounds? Against *who*?"

I raise her glass to my lips. Our eyes meet over the rim.

"No way," she says with dawning awareness. "The Rottweiler that bit you is double her weight."

"Matilda will eat that mutt up. Devour him."

Alison cradles a puppy in her arms, kneading its baggy skin between her fingers.

"Stop coddling," I tell her. "Make a cur out of it."

The puppy takes her finger in its mouth, gnawing, slobbering. "Matilda's not ready."

"She'll . . . whup him."

"Roll with Rodney, at least."

"Matilda's ready."

She stands and walks to the window. With the night pressed against the window glass, the darkness reflects her face set in rigid lines. Alison doesn't have the sort of features that become more attractive with anger, the high Latin cheekbones or bee-stung lips that, when flushed, evoke a certain male stirring. She is much prettier when calm and accommodating.

"Matilda didn't bite you. It's not her fault."

"That's not what this is about!" I sway unsteadily to my feet, chest puffed with righteous indignation. The glass slips from my grasp and shatters on the floorboards. Puppies rush at the yellow mess. I kick at them, "Watch the broken glass, you little shits!"

Alison gathers double handfuls of newspaper and sops the spill. She's ditched the OR scrubs for a paint-flecked crop-topped shirt and a pair of cutoffs—her "bumming around gear," which she knows I find sexy in a slovenly, hausfrau-ish way. Her hair is combed out in feathered waves that I'd like to plunge my hands and face into. Her face seems suddenly pretty again, the face of the woman I married.

"Honey. Listen." I lick my lips and try to straighten my tie before realizing I'm no longer wearing one. "You know what? Hey, what— *hey,* what the hell was I thinking?" I'm in the boardroom, wheeling and dealing, soothing bruised egos, smoothing things over. "Matilda's not ready. You're absolutely right." Sell it, baby. *Sell it!* "We'll wait, okay? We'll just wait."

Her features soften into something approaching belief. "I think it's for the best . . ."

"Sure. Sure, I think so." I kneel beside her, picking up shards of glass. This triggers the discomforting memory of a fight we had months ago, a fight over . . . what? Finances, booze, assumed infidelities. The usual suspects. As the fight crested towards its predictable apex, I'd stormed into the den, plucked a blown-glass globe from the mantel—a gift from that honeydripping bastard Dr. Scalise, bartered from a legless peddler in Malta—and hurled it into the fireplace, where it exploded with a brittle tinkling sound.

"It's a good decision," she says.

"Sure."

"You think?"

"Sure I think."

SOMETIME THAT NIGHT, after a bout of energetic but futile congress, I have a dream. In this dream, I stand stark naked in the middle of a cavernous auditorium. The tiered stands are packed. Not with people—birds. Bluebills and meadowlarks, flamingoes and penguins, turkey vultures, toucans, sandpipers, pelicans, even a dodo. The sounds they make are disquieting: feathers rustling, talons scrabbling, beaks digging ticks from molting plumage. The aviary smell of them— dust and millet and caked shit—clogs my nostrils. I clear my throat, unsure of how to address this throng, yet convinced it is expected of me. Beady dark eyes, thousands of them, stare down.

"I'm sure you're wondering why I've called this meeting . . ."

Then my penis falls off. Not just my cock: balls, ball sack, pubes. The whole apparatus. My tackle doesn't drop so much as *float* to the ground in a series of oscillating parabolas, light as tissue paper, settling gently on the concrete. Touch my plucked groin with a trembling hand. The skin is pebbled, like the rind of an orange.

Every bird in the auditorium takes flight; the sound of their wings fills my ears like a stiff, storm-bearing wind. They swoop down, the flurry of their beating wings messing my meticulously styled hairdo. White gobs of guano pelt my face and chest. An army of birds descend upon my penis. I squawk, a birdlike sound, pushing through the feathery mob to recover it. A thousand beaks pecking, two thousand clawed feet raking, air thick with feathers. "That's mine!" I scream. A yellow goose with Xanax eyes hisses and bites at my fingers. A hummingbird with Tippi Hedren's face flies up my nose, flitting about behind my eyes. "No!" I scream pitifully. "I *need* that!"

The birds take flight *en masse,* flying up through a hole in the auditorium ceiling, vanishing into the vast pewter sky. Apart from the downy drifts of tail feathers, the floor is bare.

A BLACK SMUDGE marks the cement approaching the processing plant's loading bay doors. Years ago, after his Doberman bitch dropped a brutal roll to a wrecking-ball presa canario, some owner doused his dog with kerosene and set it on fire. The Doberman, leg-broke and missing skin from its face and haunches, ran in herky-jerk circles, biting at the flames climbing down her throat and igniting her lungs. She lay down, then lay still as a stone and burned to blackness on the concrete.

I step over the smudge and into the warehouse. Matilda's crate hangs at the end of my left arm, the dog dozing inside. Alison trails behind, lugging a diaper bag packed with narcotics, needles, catgut, gauze. She's here solely for Mattie's sake.

The morning after my bird dream, I told Alison in no uncertain terms that Matilda would be fighting Biscuits as soon as it could be arranged. She stared at me, toothbrush jutting from her mouth, lips frothy with paste. She shook her head, "I should have known." I said, "Hey, Mattie will kill that rottie!" and pinched the pudge girding her waistline. She slapped my hand away with a closed fist, called me a name. *Bastard? Fucker?* Her mouth was full of toothpaste.

Unaware of her opponent's trainer, the fat hillbilly—Lola Snape, the matchmaker told me—agreed to match Biscuits against Matilda. I wade through a crowd of dogmen, gawkers, and fight bums to the weigh-in. One guy wears a Russian fur hat and an electric-blue seersucker suit with hand-sewn bolts of red-and-purple lightning down each sleeve. He heels, on a shoestring leash, a peanut-sized pomeranian with a streak of red-dyed fur running skull to tail-tip.

Lola and her husband wait at the scale. She appraises me for a good twenty seconds before a flicker of recognition crosses her cow eyes.

"How's that leg, misser?" She pronounces leg as *laig*.

The weighmaster sets Matilda's crate on the scale. After subtracting fifteen pounds for the kennel, Matilda's official weight is fifty-three pounds.

I clip a lead onto Matilda's collar and draw her from the crate. Her body is a canine anatomy chart, every tendon group and connective ligature clearly visible beneath a thin sheath of skin. Her legs are roped with thickly dilated veins. She squats on her haunches and scratches behind her left ear, gaze never leaving the hulking rottie.

Biscuits tips the scale at a buttery ninety-three pounds. I am heartened to see his pendulous gut and bony forelegs, deficiencies I failed to note on our first encounter. His back and flanks are deeply scarred where he's been bitten, or more likely beaten. He growls at Matilda, upper lip rippling to expose canines the size and color of large cashews.

Their weights are chalked on a tote board, next to their records—Biscuits a surprising 11-1. The line is established at 3-1 against Matilda on account of her weight, greenhorn status, and murky lineage. The line excites a good deal of betting.

As we lead our dogs to the pen, Lola leans over and says, "Fat chance your little yapper's gonna beat my Biscuits." Days later, lying bandaged and in a hospital bed, a late-blossoming riposte of Churchillian wit will come to me—*You, madam, are the fattest chance I've ever laid eyes on*—but at the moment I simply entreat her to fuck off. She looks to her haystack-haired hubby in hopes he'll defend her honor, but the weevil-legged woodhick is engrossed by his gumboots.

"It'll be alright," I tell Alison, assuming she's noticed Biscuits's shortcomings.

"Whatever."

"Matilda will demolish him."

"Whatever."

We usher our dogs into the pen. I've got hold of Matilda's scruff over the chicken-wire; her body thrums like a high-tension powerline. A dwarfish man with phony hair rings the bell for round one.

The rottie comes out strong, thinking Matilda will be easy to stop in the first round, only Matilda isn't there. She feints left on Biscuits's lead-off charge, ducks under his advancing left foreleg, fastens onto the hanging meat of his abdomen. The bigger dog back-pedals madly, yelping, biting down at Matilda's thrashing head.

Lola hollering, "Get that little shit! Bite her! Get off, *get off!*"

The rottie twists his body sideways and Matilda tumbles across the pen with a chunk of Biscuits in her mouth. A rude bloody hole in the rottie's gut but he's still very much game.

The dogs square around as the crowd clusters close to the pen, leaning in for better views. Biscuits steps from left foreleg to right, then right to left, a boxer's shuffle. Matilda stands stock-still, mouth open, haunches quivering.

The rottie rushes again, crouched low, head tucked. Flashing teeth tear his ear to shreds before he smashes into Matilda's stifles, barreling her into the chicken-wire. Alison pokes her fingers through the wire, fingers clenched. Biscuits has Matilda pressed against the pen— Matilda pivots, lashing out with her hind legs, aiming for the gut-wound. Jaws come together, two or three splintered teeth skittering across the ground. With a level of cunning I wouldn't have guessed at, Biscuits fakes a strike at Matilda's throat, reverses and bites down on the rear right haunch. Matilda emits a shrill yowl.

"That's it, boy! Get at her!"

Teeth sunk deep into Matilda's flank, Biscuits drags her away from the chicken-wire. Matilda's body whips side to side, paws scrabbling uselessly. Alison's grip on the wire tightens as Biscuits shakes his head, neck tendons bunching. Blood pours down Matilda's brindled coat.

The bell rings. Men reach over the pen with blunted baling hooks to pry the dogs apart.

Matilda trots stiffly to the corner, rear right leg tucked close to her chest. I snap a muzzle on and grip her barrel chest as Alison goes to work. "Easy, Mattie baby," Alison whispers to the squirming dog.

She cleans away the blood and debrides the cuts with a mixture of hydrogen peroxide and rubbing alcohol. Peering down through the layers of meat, she winces.

"Severed veins."

"Do what you do."

After swabbing the deep tissues with a thick coagulant, she sprays the topmost layers with Granulex. Then she spreads the wounds' lips and cauterizes them with ferric acid. Matilda squeals against her muzzle. I glance at the other corner, where Lola runs a bead of Crazy Glue down Biscuits's ear before pressing the split halves together. The rottie's upper canines are busted to the gumline but he sports an enormous erection.

Alison swabs Matilda's nose with adrenaline chloride 1:1000 to jack some energy into her through the mucous membranes. When I remove the muzzle she nips at my hand.

Both dogs toe the scratch. The bell rings.

Biscuits slinks forward like a cat, protecting his gut. Matilda circles right, her bloodied flank resembling a port wine stain. The rottie cocks his head and goes for Matilda's throat. With blinding speed Matilda dodges back, the rottie's jaws snapping closed over vacant air, and counterattacks. Biscuits howls as Matilda's teeth open huge wounds on the right side of his face, skin folding down in a single flap, high cheek to jowl.

"Yes!" I holler. "Get him! Get *at* him!"

Matilda presses the retreating rottie, who is blinking to clear his blood-blind eyes; spectators at pen-side shield themselves from the flying blood. She hammers her head into Biscuits's chest and flews. The rottie casts his eyes around like a lost child.

"Eat him *up*, Mattie!"

Near the end of the round Biscuits worries his head inside Matilda's guard, bites into her chest, lifts the smaller dog up and smashes her to the ground. Matilda's skull snaps off the concrete and the sound of her ribs cracking is like a boot squashing a periwinkle. The bell rings.

Matilda staggers to the corner. Her left side is dented like the hull of a galleon hit by cannon fire. Blood drips in thin rills from her ears.

"She's bleeding inside," Alison says. "Those busted ribs are pressed up against . . ."

"Do what you do."

"Pick her up. Another round could—"

"Just *do* what you *do*."

"This is such bullshit. You are such bullshit."

She injects procaine into Matilda's ribs before tending to the dog's other wounds. I feel Matilda pushing against me, eager to get at Biscuits. She is in a great deal of pain, and could die shortly. All she wants to do is fight. I remember what the dogman from whom I'd purchased my first pit bull told me: *These dogs are bred for a mean utility. They are bred to fight and live only for the fight. It's all they know.* I wonder at a life so singular of purpose, a utilitarian existence no different from that of a hammer or shovel.

"Bad inter-cranial swelling," Alison says. "Blood's leaking out her eyes."

I use the adrenaline to swab Matilda's gums, her nostrils, her eyes covered with a thin film of blood and blinking uncontrollably. The dog's body strains mindlessly.

Biscuits drags himself to the scratch. His face, which Lola has unsuccessfully attempted to glue back in place, is a gummy mess.

The bell rings. Matilda goes for the rottie's leg but something's wrong, she can't see right, misses by a mile, jaw hammering off the concrete. Biscuits sidesteps, clawing at Matilda's eyes, ripping the forehead open. Matilda's turning a drunken circle, trying to draw a bead, unable to. She's yowling, but whether in pain or frustration I can't tell.

"Stomp it, boy!" Lola's yelling. "Stomp that mutt!"

"Pick her up, Jay. She's dying in there."

"She's a deep gamer. She'll be . . ."

The rottie flanks Matilda's blind spot—Christ, she's *all* blind spot—and mounts her, massive jaws clamped over her neck. Matilda's squirming, yammering, unable to move. Her bladder lets go with a stream of blood-red piss. Biscuits pins her to the concrete and lowers his body like he's taking a shit but he's not taking a shit, that red raw rock-hard dick—

"That's it, boy!" Lola, apoplectic. "Throw that little bitch your dirty *laig!*"

. . . and it comes to you in the sleepless witching hours, a question bracing in its simplicity: Do I deserve? *In the clean sane light of day such notions are so easily dispelled, but with dawn's awakening light filtering through the venetian blinds, quartering your face into corridors of day and darkness, the question takes on looming weight. What is essentially a biological question acquires critical moral import—a question of weakness so ingrained as to exert its sway on a cellular level. And you wonder if you are capable. Can you meet the world with fists raised, moving forward, fearless? All revolves within this. Advance. Retreat. Weakness. Strength. If you are capable, then so you are deserving. If not, not. At some point we all must answer to this. At some point we must stare it down. Am I capable? Do I deserve? She sleeps beside you, the woman you love, her steady exhalations raising the bedsheets by shallow increments, you thinking,* Do I? Do I? *and then . . .*

I'm launching myself into the pen, slicing my hands open on

snarled chicken-wire, tripping, stumbling, dragging myself up, calf stitches breaking open with a sick internal tear and the pain has me gagging but I throw myself at the rottie, shoulder-blocking it in the ribs and falling on top of Matilda, the crowd exploding in shocked disbelief, Matilda beneath me hot and tensed and shivering, whisper *it's okay, okay-okay-okay* and then the rottie on me, ripping at my rubber-bandy legs, at my neck, trying to get at Matilda but I turn into him, shielding my dog and Matilda licking my fingers and I look to Alison and the way she's staring at me, Christ, I haven't seen that look in years, the kind of look a guy can build on then baling hooks are out and digging into the dogs, digging into me and something explodes inside my skull, a combustive fireworks display, *boom, boom, boom,* starbursts and fractured light pinwheeling before the red curtain of my tightly shut eyelids as one pure thought loops through my fritzing, blown-apart brainpan: *so this is fatherhood.*

ROCKET RIDE

SOME CHICK in the fourth row's giving me the eye. Slim and pale with wide blue eyes, ass-length ponytail pulled through the back of her baseball cap, she sits in the shadow thrown by a woman wearing a straw hat on the verge of collapsing under a weight of plastic fruit. Her shockingly blue eyes meet mine, then skate across the show pool's surface. She's being coy about it, but I've seen The Look a thousand times.

I'm straddling the concrete wall dividing the wait pool from the show pool. Sunlight arcs over the amphitheater's zigzagged metal roof, yellow spears quivering the afternoon air. Stands packed with sunburnt tourists in their vacation finery: tank tops and flip-flops and sansabelt slacks, wifebeaters and board shorts. I spot a sallow-chested shirtless man: the unshakable maxim seems to be those with the most revolting physiques are inevitably those most keen to bare them. Blue inflatable dolphins, red seals, black-and-white killer whales bob amidst the crowd. Tinny upbeat music lilts from recessed speakers. Seagulls wheel and spiral against the unbroken blue sky.

The show opens with the sea lions. Their flatiron-sized flippers collide wetly, broken barks rebounding off the domed cupola. Trainers steer them through a standard routine: balancing striped balls on their noses and catching bright red rings around their necks until the act segues into a Keystone Kops–style chase, animals loping across the stage with trainers in fist-shaking pursuit. The action is punctuated by *boinks, tah-dahs,* and *wah-wah-waaas* supplied by the audio booth technician.

I sit cooling my feet in the pools. Sweat rolls down my neck, wicked by the collar of my wetsuit. Off to my left, a young girl in a wheelchair sits beneath the handicapped pavilion's wind-whipped awning. She looks maybe twelve, though could fall five years on either side: her disease makes parts of the body look worn, while others remain strangely undeveloped. The girl's father sits beside her, rubbing her arm. I glance down, depressed in an unfocused sort of way, and catch Niska rising through the water.

The orca's head crests the surface, sleek as a ballistic missile. Sun limns the contours of her black snout, thin golden traceries like the veins on a leaf. Her mouth yawns open, revealing teeth blunted with age and disuse. I reach down and slap her tongue—wet and bristled, like a piglet's hide—and feed her mackerel from a stainless steel bucket. She submerges for a moment before resurfacing, a gurgle issuing from her blowhole.

"Go on, you big hog," I say. "No more 'til showtime."

When the sea lions are finished, Kona's brought out from the opposite wait pool. He performs a few lackluster highbows then swims a lap around the pool, lashing his atrophied tail to the beat of "Feelin' Hot Hot Hot," by Buster Poindexter and the Banshees. Niska butts her snout against the metal gate separating the pools. She has a habit of rousing Kona's ardor, which, during shows, leads to a lot of "Mommy, what's that?" questions as Kona's thick, pink, six-foot-long cock spools out of its sheath like a bizarre Hindu rope trick.

When Kona's safely penned I crank a winch and raise the gate, ushering Niska into the show pool. I dive in after her. The cool water tastes of brine and chlorine. I blink the sting out of my eyes as Niska circles, body a rippled distortion beneath the waves. I feel the displacement of water as she rises, smooth and powerful, pushing me back. She surfaces in front of me, maw open. Breath like a fishmonger's floor, rags of mackerel hanging between her teeth. I catch my reflection—curly blond hair, dimpled chin, stubbled cheeks—in the black convex of one of her golfball-sized eyes.

I slap her tongue. "Let's do this thing, girl."

The Rocket Ride is the triple lindy of marine mammal behaviors. Anchoring your feet on Niska's snout, she takes you down into the water. Nearing the pool's bottom you arch your spine and surge towards the surface. Then, with a thrust of her tail, Niska launches you from the water. That you hit twenty feet is a given—Niska's feeling frisky, thirty's a definite possibility. At the height of your ascent perform a snap-pike before slicing down into the water. It's a shot of pure adrenaline: like being strapped to the nosecone of a Stinger missile.

Twenty feet underwater and the outside world disappears. Gone the crowd, the music, the birds and sun and sky. The water bitingly cold and pressure beating against my eardrums, hamstrings screaming as Niska propels me downwards. The pool basin rushes at me: flaking blue paint, thin serrate cracks, the shiny disc of a quarter some tourist must've prompted his kid to toss into the pool—make a wish. Brace my neck and arch my back and then I'm hurtling up through the water at phenomenal speed, lungs burning, a pearlescent helix of air bubbles corkscrewing up to the surface.

Niska's mouth opens. My left leg slips inside. Thigh raked down a row of teeth, shredding the wetsuit. Rocketing upward, faster now. My crotch smashes the crook of her mouth and something goes *snap*. Jam a hand into Niska's mouth and pry with everything I've got, her jaws a jammed elevator I'm trying to open. Whale gagging on the foot lodged deep in her throat, huge muscles constricting and relaxing. Bubbles swirling and ears roaring, mind panicked and lungs starved for oxygen, a bright flame of terror dancing behind my eyes and yet there remains this great liquid silence, all things distant and muted in this veil of salt water. A disconnected image races through my head: that famous black-and-white snapshot of a Buddhist monk sitting serenely in lotus position as flames consume him.

Immense pressure shatters my tibia below the hip. A wave of pain roars up my spine and through my neck, nearly tears my skull off. Open my mouth to scream and water rushes in, electric ozone taste choking my sinuses and then I'm breaking the pool's surface, hurtling up into the warm summer air, arms stretched towards the cloudless sky, gulls screeching, the syncopated beat of salsa music and the handicapped girl sitting beside her wide-eyed father, smiling an odd inscrutable smile.

I hit the water again and then I'm paddling like a dog, kicking but not really going anywhere. I'm not afraid—have never felt calmer in my life, in fact—but my body doesn't want to obey. It's so silly, almost funny. Why is everyone yelling? The water's red and the other trainers scream my name—*Oh god over here, Ben, over HERE!*—and I try to swim in their direction if only to shut them up but I can't, my body's all *fucked* so I end up paddling over to the wall. I try to get a grip on the wet concrete but my hands are sliced up, bloody, pinkie finger snapped at the knuckle and hanging like a half-opened penknife. Niska bumps my side, a gentle nudge and the screams intensify, ear-splitting decibels and I'm thinking, *Christ, will you people please shut up?* Prismatic bars of color streak my vision as I stare into the stands, where the girl who'd been eyeing me slumps with her face buried in the chest of the fruit-hatted woman. I remember the blue of her eyes—as though cut from the sky—and wish she'd turn them on me once more.

A cute but clingy trainer I'd pointedly ignored since fucking her late last summer tosses me a life preserver. Hook an arm through the blue plastic doughnut, towed to the pool's edge like a bead on a thread. Hands dig into my armpits and drag me onstage. All the color's washed out of things, the radiant reds, blues, greens, and pinks of the stage blended into neutral grays and then I see what's left of my leg, a shredded mess, adipose tissues encased in a yellow layer of fat, splintered bone shining in the crisp sunlight.

Niska swims slowly past. My leg hangs from her jaws, loosely flexed at the knee. Flashbulbs pop in the stands and I think, *That's not what they came to see,* but then maybe it is. My wetsuit's torn to the breastbone, peeled back in flaps to reveal tanned flesh, gym-sculpted abs, clean-shaven groin, my painfully erect cock. Brachial veins running like river systems under the elastic flesh, its size—6 ¾ inches: I'd measured, digging the ruler into my crotch for an added quarter-inch— grossly amplified, monstrous and hemorrhaging blood.

The cute trainer's lips move but no sound comes out. "I'm okay," I tell her, and smile. "It's o-o-kay, I'm . . . fine." She's crying, she's shaking her head. Overhead, a big pale sun burns without heat. I wish everyone would go away and leave me alone, wish I were somewhere dark and quiet and cool. My gaze drawn to a gap between the topmost seats and the amphitheater roof: calm ongoing sky reaching off to the horizon, remotely beautiful, all things in alignment.

Jesus, do something, do something . . .
Paramedics, move, move . . .

The leg, where's the fucking leg . . .
Quit pumping the plasma expander, his blood's thin as Kool-Aid . . .
These voices, even in the haze.

FIVE MONTHS LATER I'm in a VW Beetle driving down the QEW.
Snow piled along the highway-side and Lake Ontario a frozen white
stretch off to the north. I can just make out the slender spike of the
CN Tower rising beyond the Toronto harbor. Over the guardrails and
down the snow-covered shoreline, two muffled figures sit round a hole
drilled through the ice.

I sit in the passenger seat, cheek pressed to the window glass. My
right leg rests against the padded doorframe. My left leg is mostly gone:
a rude stump two inches below my crotch. The surgeons did a fine job,
considering: high-gauge stitches left a ring of baby-pink dimples, a
balloon knot of puckered flesh at the stub. I nearly died, or so I'm told.
The sacral, varicose, basilic, and femoral arteries merge in the upper
thigh, pumping a pint of blood a minute. I lost over a gallon before
the medics transfused me. From Niagara Falls, I was airlifted to the
Hotel Dieu in St. Catharines, where a team of surgeons operated for
two hours. Battleground surgery: a hundred years ago, some meatball
medic would've jammed a rum-soaked leather thong between my
teeth and slathered the stump with boiling tar. Thanks to today's
wonder drugs, I don't recall a damn thing.

I awoke two days later. The hospital room's every ledge festooned
with flowers in frosted glass vases, plush white teddy bears, balloon
bouquets bump-bumping in the AC flow. Condolences: family and
friends and co-workers, old high-school acquaintances, ex-girlfriends
softened by my pathetic state, a War Amps rep, the morbidly curious.
A summer intern conducted a brief interview for the *Standard*.

"Tell me what happened, in your own words."

"In my own words? A whale bit my leg off."

"I see." Scribbles on a notepad. "Did you see this coming?"

"What?"

"Was there, well, any . . . *hostility* . . . between the two of you?"

"Yes. I was envious of the whale's career."

"Is that so?"

"Insanely jealous, yes."

"Will you be suing?"

"Who—the whale?"

"Is that possible?"

"Get out of here."

Animal rights protesters held a rally on the hospital's front lawn. They toted placards bearing slogans: FREE NISKA and CAPTIVITY + MISTREATMENT = MURDER. They had a boombox playing "Freedom Calling" and a huge inflatable whale with shackles over its pectoral fins. My father got into a fistfight with the ringleader, a dread-locked grad student from the local university. They rolled across the grass throwing punches until a groundskeeper broke them apart. Dad got in one good shot: it landed with the sound of a hatchet halving a cantaloupe, splattering the protester's nose.

The car is my mother's. Slender and composed in jeans and a heavy sweater, silvery hair cut short in bob style, she sits ramrod straight with both hands on the wheel. Radio tuned to Light 98.1, Kenny G blowing a soulful sax. I reach over to change the station. She slaps my hand.

"My car, my music."

"Oh, god," I say. "Gonna slip into a coma, here."

"You'll survive."

My mother is a palliative care nurse. She passes each shift in a ward strung with shattered, hopeless, bedridden bodies, victims of voracious and uncaring diseases, kids with inoperable egg-sized tumors latched to their brainstems, infants born with horrible genetic defects.

As a matter of basic survival she's developed a professional detachment to the frailties, grotesqueries, and fateful idiosyncrasies affecting the human body. *Emotional scar tissue,* my father calls it. This brusqueness carries over to her family life. As a child, I dreaded the most minor cut or abrasion: she'd break out the iodine and cotton swabs for an unsympathetic clean and dress, slapping my hands away from the wound as I wailed. When I once complained of mild constipation, she insisted on giving me an enema. I recall leaning over the toilet, hands braced on cold porcelain and pants wadded around ankles, penis flapping between trembling legs as she inserted a greased plastic tube, followed by a spurt of warm, bung-loosening water. The whole experience was seriously . . . *oedipal.*

"What do you think about me running across the country, like Terry Fox?"

"You wouldn't make it to the end of the block. And don't compare yourself to Terry."

"Why not? He lost a leg, I lost a leg."

"Terry Fox had cancer."

"So what, you got to have cancer to do something noble?"

"It's a start."

"What if I donated all the money I raised to support the eradication of marine mammals? Fill the oceans with drift nets. Capsize oil supertankers. The *Extinction Foundation.* Once all the whales are gone we could get to work on the manatees."

"That's an awful sentiment, Benjamin. Just . . . *awful.*"

The highway cuts sharply west, spanning a narrow inlet splitting into a spider's web of iced-over streams. Back in high school, me and my friends took a rutted track to the mouth of the inlet, searching for chinook salmon that'd swim up the swollen tributaries to spawn. The spring runoff slackened and the streambeds dried up, leaving thousands stranded in shallow pools. They swam in restless, agitated circles, throwing themselves at the slippery mud banks. We'd tie triple-barbed hooks to our lines and jig them through the water. With a quick jerk, we'd snag a fin or a gill flap, a belly, a tail. The salmon were so plentiful it required no real skill at all. We hauled them thrashing to the shore and checked the sex; we squeezed the females' guts, emptying their eggs—orange globes in thick, briny liquor—into a gallon ice cream tub, for sale to a local bait shop.

One time my friend Joe hung a big female on a rotted fencepost; the fish had bent his last hook out of shape, and Joe held the thing's stubborn will to live against it. A few minutes later the fish was still bucking and thrashing. Joe picked up a stream-polished stone and chucked it. The stone struck with a heavy wet thud. The rest of us found rocks and hurled them. We hit the salmon's head and gut and fins, missing often, rocks sailing into the brush or bouncing off the post with a hollow *wok!* All of us laughing: the horsey, trollish laughter of teenage boys. Stones smacked the salmon's ugly sloped head, smashed its hooked jaw and gouged luminous flesh to reveal the stark contour of its skull. A shard of flint cut its belly and the pressure of our assault forced the pink of its gut through the slit. The post slick with blood and burst roe and incandescent scales winking in the pale spring sunlight. We became bored and returned to our rods. The fish continued to flop and flap, not quite alive, not entirely dead.

I think of these things. Casual brutalities, unthinking and profane. Think of them often.

DR. ALEXIS VITIAS's clinic is located on the seventeenth floor of the Hunts-Abrams medical complex in downtown Toronto. Mom gets my crutches from the trunk and trails me as I clump to the elevators. She attempts to straighten the hem on my jeans: with one leg rolled up and safety-pinned to my ass they don't hang right. I slap her hand.

"Jesus, stop touching me. It's not right."

"What's not right? I'm molesting you?"

"Christ, like you've got that Munchausen's syndrome or something."

"Don't be an idiot."

"You're one of those mothers who convince themselves their kid's sick so they can hold on to them. Soak toothbrushes in drain cleanser. Sprinkle arsenic in oatmeal. All kinds of sick shit."

The whole time I'm talking, she's tugging at my pants. "I'm helping you look presentable, Benjamin, not poisoning your breakfast. You wouldn't eat oatmeal, anyway—it's good for you."

"Munchausen's syndrome. A chronic case. One sick puppy."

"I don't care if you grow up."

"Sure you do. You've still got my baby foreskin in a jar of formaldehyde."

"I don't," she lies. Rifling her drawers for loose change as a kid, I found it tucked behind some balled socks: a wrinkly gray tube floating in a vial of piss-yellow fluid. Looked like a calamari ring. Years later, dad told me she'd bullied the doctor into handing it over. "You're imagining things."

"Imagining my ass. You keep my foreskin in a jar. A piece of your grown son's anatomy in a *Gerber babyfood jar*—"

"Settle down, you're getting all worked up—"

"—Gerber Split Pea and Carrot, you bizarre woman, would you please to Christ *stop touching me*?"

"Alright Mr. Hands Off," she says—then, with a sly tug as the elevator doors open, straightens the hem.

The waiting room's decor adheres to a design concept glimpsed on high-class porno sets: thick white carpeting, white calfskin sofa draped in a faux-leopardskin pelt, glass-legged endtables piled with glossy magazines. Vitias's receptionist sits behind a half-moon desk.

"I'm here for a fitting." Offer her a look I privately think of as the *Panty Melter*. "This horse needs a new shoe."

A pitying expression crosses the receptionist's face; perhaps she's trying to picture me before the missing leg and the extra forty pounds, result of four months spent in bed—the first month medically mandated, the remainder elective. This trip marks the first time I've ventured from my parents' house since what my mother refers to as The Mishap.

She consults her appointment book, frowns. "You're early." I get the sense I've committed a slight but shameful faux pas. "Take a seat. I'll find the doctor."

Dr. Vitias's body conjures up images of an ambulatory fire hydrant: thick and densely muscled, a vague flaring at his shoulders the only anomaly on an otherwise unvarying frame. Eyes the hue of antifreeze dart above the wiry unkempt beard of a Macedonian bull god. There is something in the palpitations of his tapered fingers indicative of a barely contained vitality, a *potency*, that he's constantly struggling to keep in check.

"Hello!" His exquisite right hand envelops mine, left gripping my elbow, shaking as though my arm's the pump-handle on a village well. "Here for a leg, yes?"

I acknowledge his brazen statement of the obvious.

"Okay, okay. Let me show you what I've got."

He leads us through a pebbled-glass door. I feel as though I've been ushered into a medieval torture chamber, albeit a sanitary and amply lit one. The room's dominated by a trio of lab benches strewn with all manner of equipment: chromium screws and shiny servo motors and stainless steel tools whose purpose I cannot fathom, a bolt of artificial skin threaded on a wooden dowel, curls and corkscrews of buttery latex overflowing the trashcan below. Two Rubbermaid bins: the first contains articulated fingers and toes, the second full of garishly painted finger- and toenails. An unfinished leg bent across the near bench, all pistons and hinges and metal tubes, skinless, cyborgean.

Artificial arms and legs dangle from the ceiling like pots and pans from a chef's rack.

"I take it you've had time to flip through our brochure." Hoisting himself onto a stool, Vitias swivels to face me. "Anything catch your eye?"

Badgered by my mother, I'd chosen the Campion P5 endoskeletal leg with titanium pyramid couplers, ballistic silicone sheathing, spring-load dynamic ankle. Vitias nods at my selection as a sommelier might at a diner's choice of vintage.

"Excellent, very nice." Rooting through a drawer, he comes up with a conical alloy plug. "This is the P5's female coupler. We attach it to the end of the tibia and, once everything's healed, you'll be able to snap the prosthetic on and off with ease."

"Snap on, *dum dum,* snap off, *dum dum,* snap on snap off—the Snapper." I snap my fingers. The joke's lost on them.

"Pay attention," my mother says. "This is important."

"On second thought, do you have anything in a peg?"

Vitias says, "A peg?"

"Y'know, a lump of wood—oak maybe, or ash. A pegleg. Like a pirate."

Vitias curls his lips into his mouth, nodding as though vaguely embarrassed. It's a variation on the look I've received from an endless cavalcade of friends and relatives and well-wishers: a remotely detached sentiment that, translated into words, would mimic the sappy schmaltz found in condolence cards: *With Deepest Sympathy and Sorrow for Your Loss.*

"A peg?" Vitias says. "Sure, we can do that. Some leather straps, maybe, lash it to your leg? Very swashbuckling."

"Stop being childish, Ben." To Dr. Vitias: "He's just being silly."

"My leg's gone, Mom. It's . . . shit. Whale *shit.* Why fake it?"

"But don't you want to look normal?" She's genuinely baffled. "Don't you want to . . . fit in?"

A wave of resentment rises within me, so all-consuming that for an instant the profile of my world, every angle and parameter, is etched in cold blues and greens. I reach for the nearest bin, dumbfounded with rage, shoving it off the bench's edge. Fingernails spill across the polished tiles with a roachsounding clatter.

"Stop it." Mom grabs my arm. "You're embarrassing yourself."

"Fuck . . . *you.*"

I've never spoken to her that way. Not ever. Her hand falls away, then rises, with the other to cover her face. She utters a wail of such resonant grief, loud and ongoing like a bestial moan, that it frightens me.

"Mom?"

She rocks softly. Again that deep animal moaning, horrifying in its immodesty, rising from behind her hands.

"Mom, I'm sorry. Mom, *please.*"

Dr. Vitias pinches spilled fingernails between his long delicate fingers, dropping them carefully into the bin.

WATCHING A LOT OF PORN these days.

Download it off the Internet to spare yourself the embarrassment of face-to-face purchase. Back in high school I drove my father's minivan all over town in search of an out-of-the-way smut peddler. A Korean deli received the bulk of my trade on account of its fine selection of filth and a proprietor who avoided all eye contact. I'd drive home in a lustful frenzy, boner pushing against my trouser leg, to jerk off in my bedroom or, if my parents were around, a locked bathroom. Sometimes I tried to achieve release without masturbating: flatten palm to crotch, cock skin stretched to a thrillingly painful tension, *will* myself to come. This required intense concentration, which my mother disrupted by banging on the door, enquiring if I'd drowned. Once, adventurous and low on funds, I bought a vacu-sealed four-pack for $6.99. Safely ensconced in the bathroom, I tore the plastic open and recoiled in abject horror: *Suckin' Grannies, 50 and Nifty, Old Farts,* a ratty paperback entitled *The Well-Spanked Farmgirl.* I beat off to a mildly erotic charcoal etching on the book's cover. The whole episode was anemic and dispiriting.

Now, thanks to the World Wide Web, a wondrous panoply of pornographic imagery is mere keystrokes away. It's amazing, the stuff that's out there: big tits and big cocks and big asses, Asian and Black and Latino, Lolita gangbangs, barnyard bestiality, pissing and shitting, fisting and spanking, catfighting and trampling, sites dedicated to corsets and chastity belts, to plush animals (*For those who truly love stuffed animals, in a PERSONAL way*), to ballbusting (*Hey, you Pencil-Necked Geek! Submit to Mistress Adrianna and she'll crush your puny weakling SACK!*), orthodontic braces, robots. *Balloon Buddies* features naked women astraddle giant sausage-shaped balloons; *AquaGirl.com* has smiling girls in scuba gear, diving bells, bathyspheres; *She-Wolves of the SS* pictures women dressed in Nazi regalia beating masked supplicants with riding crops; *Santa's Little Helpers* caters to those who get off on pointy-shoed, striped-stockinged midgets satisfying women of Amazonian carriage.

Off in a corner of my parents' unfinished basement, hooked to a spliced cable connection, I surf for hours. The flatscreen monitor reflects its jaundiced glow on my skin: slack and sallow, quivering rolls of fat girding my abdomen and overhanging the elasticized hem of my boxers. There's a fold-out couch beside the computer desk, spread with an old sleeping bag; come early morning I switch off the computer and crawl into the bag, sleeping off the daylight hours. Jerk off five, six times a day. Friction splits the skin, makes it bleed; wrap yourself in a sock and it's bearable.

My favorite site is *Xtreme Valkyries,* where musclebound women manhandle nebbish men. This one photo always gets me: a huge she-bear, muscled beyond all reason, hefting a skinny naked man above her head. And the guy's smiling, nuts squashed in this big she-bear's fist and he's *loving* it.

Utterly helpless. Emasculated.

THE WORDS *Unlimbited Potential* scrawled on a sheet of pink bristol board taped to the door of the Port Dalhousie Lion's Club, an arrow pointing down. Early June; first-birth mayflies buzz and circle the exposed lightbulb above the door. I park my motorcycle in the lot's rough gravel and ensure my prosthetic leg's snugly attached. The dynamic ankle squeaks: I'm supposed to lubricate it with silicone gel biweekly, but don't. Clear skies, Big Dipper tilting over Main Street.

Pause in the doorway. Rising up the short flight of stairs: voices and intemperate laughter, underlaid by the scratchy rhythm of a familiar country-and-western song. Consider leaving, but my shrink suggests I go. She also happens to write my prescription for Effexor and Elavil, two wondrous pharmaceuticals that, following the first dose, I knew I could never again live without.

So. Unlimbited Potential.

The Lion's Club is low-ceilinged with a warped parquet floor. A horseshoe of folding chairs rings a cheap plywood lectern. A folding table supports bowls of chips, a plate of macaroons, a metal coffee urn. All around are the hum of electric wheelchairs and the buzz of servo motors, the squeal of unoiled hinges, the thunk of false legs colliding with tables and chairs. I stare in stark horror at the fingerless, hand-less, armless, legless creatures shambling about. Those not resigned to wheelchairs have archaic prosthetics strapped to the truncated portions of their anatomy, fake limbs bent at perpetual angles. Others display their stumps with, by turns, a sense of downtrodden stoicism, strident pride, or weary indifference. Some are sunken and mottled around the eyes, the way tropical fruit goes bad and collapses. A great many strike me as hopelessly unsexed: with a few notable exceptions,

I cannot distinguish men from women. This revelation fills me with a vague dread.

I sit beside a thickset middle-aged man with a peppery weekend beard. He wears chambray work pants, dark blue, a heavy sweater despite the weather. The sweater, faded greens and whites in a Christmas tree motif, is in the final stage of decomposition: I am reasonably certain that, were I to look closely, its basic molecular structure would present itself to the naked eye. He glances over as I sit down, nods. It's entirely possible that he pities me as much as I do him, perhaps because I've elected to wear a shirt that was once form-flattering but now resembles a shiny black sausage casing stretched over the planetary bulk of my gut. Particularly revolting is the buttery belt of lard projecting between the bottom of my shirt and the hem of my sweatpants.

"First time?" A lemon-yellow prosthesis projects from the guy's right sweater sleeve. Looks like he's wearing a washglove except the fingers are melted at the tips. He's got a cup of coffee clenched between his legs, stirring with his left hand. Whitener floats on the surface in pale lumps, milky scum clinging to the cup's sides.

"First time," I say. "What's the deal?"

"Ah, a bunch of happy-crappy. Someone's gonna step behind that podium and yak for a bit, we're all gonna pretend to be interested, that person's gonna cry, we're gonna clap, drink our coffee, go home. Christ, most of us are only here on our shrinks' say-so."

"Same here."

"Oh, yeah?" The guy perks up. "What're you on?"

"Elavil and Effexor."

"The good stuff. Lucky dog."

"You?"

"Fuckin' Prozac. Might as well give me Flintstone vitamins."

We introduce ourselves. He's Gil, a long-haul trucker from Stoney Creek. Twice-divorced, kids on the East and West Coasts. He tells me that between alimony and child support, he's barely got two pennies to rub together.

"And just the other day some bastard stole my new prosthesis. I'm back to the old one." He lifts his fake arm, which looks pretty trailworn. "Had a nice new unit—articulate digits, ribbed sili-skin, even little fake hairs. Guess I fell behind on the payments because a repo man crawled through my bedroom window and swiped it off the nightstand. Can you imagine—repo'ing an amputee's *arm?* We're talking ten shades of *low,* man. So," he nods at my prosthesis, "how'd that happen?"

I suppose it's standard protocol to discuss such matters, the same way AA members swap tales of epic benders. "That was you?" Gil says when I tell him. "I read about it in the papers. They ran that photo. Man, it was . . . *gruesome.*"

Taken by an opportunistic shutterbug, the photo graced the pages of the *Toronto Star,* the *Standard,* the *Globe and Mail,* a few syndicated dailies. An unfocused middle-distance snapshot, it conveys a sense of great activity—of *frenzy.* I'm laid out on the wet stage, sunlight reflecting off the show pool's surface. Though parts of my body are obscured by the milling trainers, the stump is clearly visible. In the far left-hand corner, Niska's shadow curves beneath the water.

I cut out every copy of the article I could find and taped them to my bedroom wall. While I was out at a doctor's appointment, my mother tore them down.

"Same kind of thing happened to me." Gil raises his yellow melted hand. "Shark, thirty yards off Indian Rocks Beach in Clearwater, Florida. I'm out past the break where the water's calm, just paddling along. Then something's rubbing up under my legs, thick and rough: felt like I'd been run by a power sander. I caught a brown flash a few feet down and knew I was in *mucho* trouble. Tiger shark, most likely. Vicious fuckers. Stripped flesh from the elbow down; *gloved* me, that being the technical term."

A young woman sits beside him. Blond and strikingly beautiful, firm well-formed breasts straining against a white linen blouse. Looks about twenty, though she could be younger. The ghost of a harelip scar is visible when she smiles. She appears to have no arms.

"Gil," she says, "introduce me to your friend?"

"Friend?" says Gil. "Just met him."

She says, "Heidi Giroux."

"Ben Jones. Nice to meet you."

Heidi smiles again, making me think of a girl I'd treated shabbily. *You rotten-ass bastard* were her last words to me. We broke up over the phone, two thousand kilometers between us and the insult didn't register, didn't sting. In fact, I liked the sound of it, the way it tripped off her tongue. *You rotten-ass bastard.*

An utter shipwreck of a human being shambles to the podium. He appears to be composed entirely of diverse plastics and latexes, wood, possibly carpenter's putty. A pincer-like mechanism constitutes his left hand. His right leg is a tapered peg. I'm unsure whether his state is the result of a single catastrophic accident or a series of unrelated minor misadventures. A horrendous farming mishap? A fraternity prank gone horridly awry? The mind reels. He speaks in gulps and gasps, sentence fragments clearing his lips in a metronomic, hypnotic cadence.

"There were times . . . I thought . . . why not just . . . end it? But with the love . . . and support . . . of my wife . . . my kids . . . the grace . . . of God . . . I go on. What else . . . can anyone . . . do?"

The man cries. We applaud. Mingle. Disperse.

Afterwards Heidi and I sit on the gate of Gil's Chevy Sierra while he hunts the glovebox for rolling papers. To the south, down a soft slope, night waves lap the shores of Martindale Pond, slapping the hulls of tethered rowing skulls. By the domelight's glow, I see Heidi is not entirely armless: a pair of stubs project from her smoothly sloped shoulders. She smells of vanilla perfume, a brand favored by high-school girls.

Gil materializes bearing a joint of herculean proportions. He sparks the tip and sets it in the crook of Heidi's mouth. She takes a decidedly unladylike toke, expelling bluish smoke through her nose.

"Himalayan Gold," Gil says. "Buy it from a guy in Texarkana and smuggle it over the border in a box of clementines. Drug dogs can't sniff it."

Gil plucks the joint from Heidi's mouth, takes a hit, passes it. Potent stuff: a shiny metallic bubble expands inside my skull, dense and bright with colors. Cars pass on Main Street, the growl of motors swelling, receding. From Old Port Dalhousie comes the intermittent screech of teenagers scarring the tarmac in juiced-up musclecars. A mosquito hums against Heidi's neck. I slap it. "One here, too," she says, eyes falling to her chest, where another mosquito rests on the comfortable swell of her breast. What the hell—slap that fucker, too.

"Do you ever think about it?" Gil's weaving side to side. "Karma?"

"Gil," Heidi says, "please."

"No, I'm serious. Not saying I deserved this, exactly—who *deserves* to get their arm tore off, right? Then again, maybe I did. Sit and think on it awhile and you realize, yeah, of course you deserve it—*conceivably*. Some unkindness or cruelty or selfishness, doing the wrong thing when the right thing was too hard or didn't suit your purposes, hurting someone just for the rip of it, 'cause it made you feel like a big man. Great Wheel of Karma, man. All comes around."

"I call it bullshit, Gil. Pure bullshit."

Gil shrugs, unfazed at my skepticism. "When something awful happens to you, can you chalk it up to bad luck, crossed stars, wrong place, wrong time? Not me. As a human being, you've got to believe there's a *reason*. Catted around on my wives, wasn't always there for my kids. A tiger shark took my arm thirty yards off the white sand beaches of Indian Rocks. A bit harsh, sure, but all things seek balance. Tit for tat. Did I deserve it? Could be I did."

"You can't possibly believe that."

"Why not? Comforting, in a way. Square your debt and start again, fresh."

"It's ridiculous. What about all the people who suffer horribly for no reason? What about . . ." Cock a thumb at Heidi. ". . . her?"

"You don't know what I deserve," she says. "You don't know me at all."

"Okay, okay, then what about . . . starving children? What about kids born with warped spines, or . . . or *retards*. Explain them."

"Not claiming it's an easy theory to defend. Just my belief."

"Yeah, well, it's the stupidest fucking thing I've ever heard."

Gil raises his artificial hand to his lips. The roach glows between those yellow fingertips, blistering the plastic. "A few years ago, this elephant, Tyke, was killed by the Toronto police. A performing elephant, right, with a traveling circus? Got loose after a show. Cops boxed it in with their patrol cars and opened fire. It hadn't hurt anyone, but I guess it could've. Took two hundred rounds to put the thing down. They shot it in the trunk and belly, its ears and face, trying to put a slug in its brain but its skull was so thick the bullets were driven flat. I remember blood on that gray skin—so *much* blood. It went down on its front knees, head bowed like it was surrendering. The cops reloaded and kept shooting."

"So what?" An intense rage gathers, only slightly offset by the mellowing effect of the dope. "What the *fuck* does that have to do with anything?"

"So who's to blame?" Gil says. "The cops? They were doing their job. Tyke? Scared, mistreated animal. What I'm saying is, when I saw the photo of you in the paper I thought of that elephant shot to death on the street. Karma, man. Universal and everlasting."

"What are you *talking* about? I had nothing to do with that. You don't know the first thing about *me*."

"Don't know nothing about nothing, man. Speculation, is all. I gotta go."

He climbs into the truck, keys the engine. The final bars of Warren Zevon's "Werewolves of London" rattle from the truck's stereo. Rolling down the window, he waves goodbye with his fake hand, pulling away.

"Go . . . *fuck!*"

Taillights brightening, the truck slows. I ball my hands into fists, loosening them only when Gil gooses the gas pedal and turns onto the street.

"What an *ass*hole."

"He gets that way when he's high," says Heidi.

"Are you two close?"

"We smoke up after the meetings. I guess we're friends."

"Whatever. I'm leaving."

"Give me a lift?"

"I drove my bike, and I'm pretty high. Might kill us both."

"Who cares?"

"The depth of your nihilism shocks me."

HEIDI LIVES outside Welland, a township near the Merritville Speedway. When I was a kid my father took me to the Speedway to watch Baja buggies tear around a dirt oval, nitrous oxide funnycars, demolition derbies. I remember the cool autumn air thickened with stirred dust, Dad buying beer for himself, Orange Crush for me. I drive slow down back roads, taking it easy on the curves. Heidi leans against the backrest, powerful legs wrapped around my waist. Midges and moths splatter the helmet's faceshield. The soft heat of Heidi's body, her breath on the hairs of my neck.

The house sits at the base of a wooded valley. Pickup trucks in the blacktopped drive. Smells: woodsmoke and pinesap. Sly noises in the fringing trees: raccoons, maybe spring turkeys.

Heidi slides off the seat. "Sit a minute?"

She leads me to a wicker swing on the porch. A motion-sensor halogen snaps on and I note, in that stark sudden light, just how beautiful—and how young—she is. My prosthetic leg collides with a porch rail and she says, "Shshsh. You'll wake my folks."

We sit on the swing. Heidi's body presses close to mine. I know nothing about this girl: her age, her hat size, if she is an honorable person, whether she's ever been happy and in love. It's been this way many times before, anonymous and meaningless, but what once seemed ideal now fills me with a profound melancholy.

"How did it happen—your arms?"

"Tragic cheerleading accident. Do you really want to know?"

"I guess not, no."

"Of course not."

Then Heidi's kissing me. She is very adept, very *knowledgeable*—a surprise. She draws my tongue into her mouth as though her intention is to consume it. Her arm stubs dig into my breastbone.

And as we sit in that queer half-embrace on the porch I experience a vision of such clear unflinching intensity it takes my breath away: the two of us sitting on this same porch years from now, surrounded by children. Armless, legless, unfinished children wobbling around on artificial legs and crawling on stumps and swinging from the porch on shiny hook-hands, grinning and babbling and lurching about. I'm dandling a toddler on my knee and realize that—horrifically, insupportably—the fucking thing has a prosthetic *head:* milky white latex draped over curved steel slats, hair shining with the false luster of a doll's, roaming marble eyeballs socked in its fake face, whining servo motors teasing the corners of its mouth into a wide smile and in that darkness gears meshing, pinions spinning and winding. And while I recognize the scenario is an impossibility I push her away.

"What's the matter?"

"Nothing. I have to go."

"Do you have a girl? It's okay, I don't mind. Don't go, it's fine."

I'm shivering now, I'm trying to stand.

"What's wrong, Ben? Did I do something wrong?"

"No. Yes. You have . . . no fucking arms."

"You . . . *asshole!*" She flinches away from me as though I'm the bearer of some deadly equatorial disease. "You're not better than me!"

"I know." Clomping down the steps sickened with myself, with her, the whole pathetic scene. "I *know*."

Key the bike, open the throttle. Heidi's yelling now, her face pink with strain. Although I cannot hear her over the engine's roar, I can guess what she's saying.

You rotten-ass bastard.

Blast out of the valley like a house on fire. Bury the needle, tach redlined, 170K in the passing lane. The sky a smooth black dome, cold and starless. Cut onto the QEW, accelerate up the Niagara overpass. Catch a whiff of burning rubber and figure it's a tramp steamer or garbage scow plying the Welland Canal until I see flames and realize my leg's on fire. I set the prosthesis too close to the tailpipe and now latex is burning merrily, a greasy skirt of fire robing my hips. I gear down and slap at the flames, picturing my broken-necked body propped against a concrete bridge support, clothes burned away and flesh melted from the heat.

The image isn't entirely unpleasant. Sort of funny, actually, in a semi-tragic way.

Jam my hand down my pants, pop the coupler. Leg tearing free, bouncing across the street-lit tarmac over the retaining wall.

Plummeting three hundred feet, extinguished like a burning match-stick in the darkly flowing water.

I'VE TAKEN TO screwing with people in online support chatrooms.

Sign in under a phony name to retain your anonymity. Online, you're nothing more than a screen moniker, a disease, an addiction, a sickening frailty, a set of reduced values. It's amazing, what's out there. More amazing is how maddeningly supportive everyone is. I've joined groups for Albinism (CASPER82: Know what I miss most, guys? The sun. The warm, bright sun); Narcolepsy (MR.ZZZZ: So I says to Jim, I says to him, I says akcifaacvggggggggggggggggggg); Breastfeeding (CHAPPEDNIPS: My nipples get so dang sore. ☹ It would feel really nice if another woman rubbed them, preferably in slow, concentric circles. ☺); Compulsive Gambling (CARDSHARK: Bet I can beat my addiction faster than any a you chumps. I'll book you 5-to-1 odds); Retirement (MOTORHOMER: Don't you sometimes feel, lying in bed late at night, that life is basically empty and devoid of all meaning without a job?); Dementia (NAPOLEON55: Which one of you slippery motherfuckers stole my slippers?), Gulf War Syndrome (VOICESINMYHEAD: Look down at your best friend's face and all you see's a pile of GOO); Chronic Fatigue Syndrome (DOZY: Let's just forget about this wacky syndrome and take a nap); Cold and Flu (MA'SCHICKENSOUP: You are the wimpiest bunch of candy-asses I've ever met. It's a fucking *cold,* for Christ's sake!). Pepper my posts with emoticons, smiley faces and frowny faces and winking smileys. Smiley faces acting as a short-hand for grief, commiseration, love, hope, redemption.

Lately I've haunted Friends of Bill W, a group for recovering alcoholics. Tonight I'm CONSTANTCRAVINGS.

STONESOBER: Welcome aboard, Constant!

BETH54: Welcome, Constant. How long have you been a friend of Bill?

CONSTANTCRAVINGS: Thanks, Stone and Beth. ☺ Me and Bill have been acquainted three weeks now.

STONESOBER: Bill's a good man. He changed my life.

BETH54: Mine, too. He'll change yours, Constant.

CONTANTCRAVINGS: I hope so. Pretty rough going at the moment. ☹

STONESOBER: Gotta be strong. Gotta *live* strong.

CONSTANTCRAVINGS: Sometimes, alone here in the dark, I get to thinking about how good a beer would taste. A cool frosty one sliding down my throat, all bubbly and golden. Man, that would hit the spot.

BETH54: Put those thoughts out of your mind. Stay strong in your beliefs.

CONSTANTCRAVINGS: Wobbly pops. That's what my buddy Franky calls them. "Hey, man," he'll say, "let's head down to the Hitching Post, blow the foam off a few wobbly pops." I wonder what Frank's doing, right now.

STONESOBER: Better off without him. He's an enabler.

CONSTANTCRAVINGS: We used to have canoe races. Remember those? Line up five glasses of draft beer, those little 8-ouncers, drop a peanut in the last one. First guy to chug all five and swallow the peanut was the winner. I loved winning. Gave me a real sense of accomplishment.

BETH54: We remember canoe races, Constant. Change the subject, huh?

CONSTANTCRAVINGS: Scotch, too. God, I do love my scotch. That smooth brown goodness rolling over my tongue, into all the nooks and crannies of my mouth. That delicious, nutty, cask-mellowed taste.

STONESOBER: What are you, Constant, an ad writer for Bushmills? lol!

CONSTANTCRAVINGS: Man, I know they call it Demon Alcohol, but it's always seemed somehow angelic to me. Makes things more . . . bearable, I guess is the right word. The world's just a little bit brighter, a little softer. You know?

BETH54: Sigh. Good luck, Constant. [BETH54 has exited chatroom]

CONSTANTCRAVINGS: Oh, sweet baby Jesus. My wife, the ridiculous old prune, she collects airplane booze. Those little bottles, right? And I see now she's lined her collection on a shelf above the computer. Christ, they're all here: Johnny Walker Red, Absolut, Crown Royal, more. Dozens of little soldiers lined in a row. Lord, I'm all shaky and sweaty. Maybe just one . . .

STONESOBER: Don't do it, man! It's not worth it!

CONSTANTCRAVINGS: I just cracked the seal on a bottle of Captain Morgan's. My word, that smell. I'm in heaven. It tastes so damn GOOD. It's even better after not drinking for so long. Like being a virgin again! Hey, Stone, won't you join me? ☺ Must be some booze lying around your house — in the toilet tank, maybe? Under the sink?

STONESOBER: Good luck, Constant. I'll say a prayer for you.

CONSTANTCRAVINGS: Say a prayer for yourself, killjoy! Have a drink and lighten up!

[CONSTANTCRAVINGS, you have been banned from this forum]

I'M SITTING IN A CORNER BOOTH at the Concorde, a strip club near Clifton Hill. I used to come here with my high-school buddies, all of us toting fake IDs. We'd sit along pervert's row, laughing and hooting, superior in our youth and wide-open future and potential to do great things.

On the raised parquet stage, a topless chick spins disinterestedly round a polished brass pole. A woman in her mid-forties stands in the red glare of a *HOT NUTS* vending machine, naked save a pair of pink heels. She's eating barbecued peanuts from a plastic cup, pinching them between fingernails that must be two inches long. It's the most oddly revolting sight I've ever laid eyes on.

I'm drinking Sauza tequila: empty shot glasses on the table, ashtray filled with wrung lemon wedges. The darkness and smoke favor the strippers, whose faces are made for mood lighting. In their younger years, many of them worked the pole at Mints or Private Eyes but, bumped by the influx of new meat, they've carted their sagging anatomies and failing looks here, a final stand before the street corner.

A new girl steps through the tinsel curtain to a smattering of desultory applause. Blood-red spotlights disguise the needle tracks on her arms but do nothing to hide the seam of a C-section scar curving from bellybutton to bikini line. A guy sitting up front whistles sharply, the way one seeking a dog's attention might.

A woman slides into the booth. At the tail end of her career, pencil thin lines where her eyebrows should be, a broken nose that's healed badly. A sarong wrapped around her waist, which I suppose could be either a token gesture at modesty or a means of concealing some gruesome defect.

"Drinking alone, baby?"

"Looks that way."

"Want some company?"

My response is noncommital and she slides closer. She wears the brand of perfume strippers prefer; I wonder if there's a communal atomizer they all share.

"I'll suck your cock for fifty dollars." She laughs crazily, as though I'd told a rakishly indelicate joke.

"I don't even know your name."

"Sharday. What do you say, hon?"

"Let me have another drink."

"How 'bout getting me one, too?"

Suitably fortified, we sneak out the back door. A clear autumn night and the sky spread with stars, remote and numberless. Sharday leads me across the parking lot to a row of motel rooms. Her room is small but neat and smells of carpet freshener. Framed photos of two young boys on the nightstand; she turns them face-down before easing me onto the bed. Bills change hands. She unbuttons my jeans, tugs them down.

"What's that?"

"A fake leg." I assumed she'd noticed the replacement prosthesis in the club. For a moment I think she's going to call it off, as though amputation's contagious and she doesn't want to risk it.

"How did it happen?"

"War wound. Desert Storm. Some brown bastard cut it off with a sword. Those wiggly looking swords."

"A kirpan?"

"Sure . . . one of those."

Sharday slips a condom over me with the clinical disinterest of an ER nurse. She works with a brisk, businesslike air, humming a familiar tune I can't quite put a name to.

"Is it okay?" she says. "Feel good, hon?"

"It's . . . fine."

"Something else you want? It's cool."

I tell her to tuck her arms behind her back so that, from my perspective, it'd look . . .

"Like I have no arms?"

"Yes," I say. "Like that."

She does as I ask, but I can't look at her. Lean back on the bed, stare at a ceiling covered in a constellation of water stains. One resembles a suckling pig, another some breed of tropical bird. Stare at Sharday's bobbing skull, those dark roots growing out of her scalp. A bedspring pokes through the threadbare mattress, jabbing me in the spine. Music seeps through the wall from the other room: "Let My Love Open the Door," by Pete Townsend. The song is followed by another and another, then "The Things I Do for Money" by the Northern Pikes is playing.

"Awful sorry, sugar. I'm dancing in a minute."

She pulls the condom off and tucks me back inside my boxers. No refund is offered. I clip my leg on. Sharday leads me outside.

"Gonna be okay, hon?"

"Thanks for trying."

She pecks me on the cheek then sets off across the lot, the *click-click* of her heels echoing off the graffiti-tagged walls. I walk out to the street. Cars packed with teens cruise past on Ferry, looking to pull a

U-turn and head back down the Hill. A wire-mesh rack propped beside the Concorde's door, stuffed with brochures for local attractions: Castle of Frankenstein, Skylon Tower, Hollywood Wax Museum, Colonel Tilliwacker's Haunted Lemonade Stand. In the top right corner: a glossy blue brochure, killer whale leaping beneath the hub of a brilliant rainbow. *Everyone Loves Marineworld,* spelled out in inch-high bubble script.

A CAB DROPS ME OFF outside the front gates as early morning stars bleed into the lightening sky. Ticket booths boarded up, closed for the season. Head to the trainer's entrance, kicking through drifts of crackling leaves. My key still works. In the prep area fillet knives hang on a magnetized strip above a block of frozen herring thawing in a metal basin. The odor of chlorine and gutted fish; the bark of penned sea lions. Step through another door onto the stage.

Security lamps burn on the amphitheater's perimeter, casting a silvered sheen on the water. Cross the stage, past props silent in their wrap of shadows. A paddle wheel turns with a steady trickle of water. Birds roost on a bridge spanning the show and wait pools. Peel off shirt, remove shoes and socks and pants, uncouple my leg. Late September wind buffets what's left of my body. I break out in gooseflesh.

The whale was captured in a drift net off the coast of Siberia. Sectioned from her pod, hooked to a fifty-ton winch, dragged aboard a Russian freighter. She spent three weeks cradled in a body hammock, hosed down with salt water. A crane lifted her through a moonlit sky and into a new world: 90" × 60" × 30", glass and concrete. I was the one who fed her. Taught her. Kept her alive. I came to believe she belonged to me, the way land or a car can belong to a person. I forgot that every time I entered the water I belonged to her, and the moment I remembered was the moment it ceased to matter.

Ease myself down by the pool's lip, dangling my leg in the water. Niska swims at the far end, dorsal fin cutting the glasslike surface. Air jets from her blowhole, a shimmering spume lit by the stark white lights. Cup water and lift it to my mouth, relishing that salty sting. The pool dark and fathomless, dropping into forever. As a child I suffered this recurring nightmare in which the floor of my bedroom turned liquid, bed bobbing on the placid surface. Peering over the mattress, I saw shapes wheeling and surging in the inky water, primordial Lovecraftian horrors with scales and blunt teeth. How far down did that darkness stretch: through the Earth's core, out into space, to the edge of the known universe? The distance from the foot of my bed to the open door was perhaps five feet—I could clear it at a leap. But if I were to slip . . . ?

Push off the concrete ledge, move out into the pool. One-legged and overweight, I cut an ungainly path through water so frigid it robs my breath. Niska's head turns, a languid sweep. Her body describes a slow half-circle, starlight rippling over the contour of her dorsal ridge. I tread water, cold pressing against my ribcage. Catch my reflection in the pool's dark mirror. No fear or indecision in my eyes and for that I'm thankful. Nothing to be done for it, now. There is only acceptance, and a hope that, in those slender moments separating what is from what may be, there might be understanding.

I once spent the night with a girl picked up at a downtown bar. I can no longer recall her name, her smell, the color of her eyes. She lived in an old building facing St. Paul Street, backing onto Twelve Mile Creek. The bedroom overlooked a wooded dell, creek running swiftly behind. Early that morning I woke to the sound of voices. I sat up and went to the window. Three figures stood in the half-light. Down along the woodline, where it was too dark to make out ages or faces: vague outlines, rough movements and angles. Two larger figures had the smaller boxed in. They shoved the person to the ground—a woman;

you could tell by the pitch of her voice. One of them fell on top of her while the other stood off to one side, head sweeping side to side. Predawn sunlight streamed through the window, picking up a patina of dust on the venetian blinds. I went to the kitchen and rooted through the drawers, laying my hands on a butcher knife. When I returned the two on the ground were rocking rhythmically. The other one said something—*Give it,* or maybe *Give 'er*—and laughed. I couldn't quite grasp what I was seeing. I gripped the knife so tightly the grain of it lingered on my palm for hours afterwards. Then I slid it under the boxspring and slipped into bed, curling my body into that nameless girl who never stirred.

Maybe that's how she wants it, I thought. *Maybe there's an arrangement.* A span of dark time went by, punctuated by a single low moan. It wasn't any of my business. *She'd scream if she needed help.* Birds chattered in the trees, and below that, the sound of endlessly rushing water. *Someone else will notice. Someone else will commit.*

And what becomes of it all? The brutalities and insincerities, the callousness and selfishness, wrongdoings real and imagined, the acts of inaction, the fear, regret, guilt? Doesn't just go away, that much I know. Gil had it right: a balancing act takes place every minute of every day, a silent tally, each act carrying its own discrete weight, its own transformative power.

And do we ever really know where we stand? At this moment, in this breath—which way the scale tips?

Square your debt. Start over fresh.

The whale surfaces. Mouth slightly open, light glinting on the points of her teeth. You're breathing heavily, held up by pure adrenaline. Run a hand over the smooth cone of her snout. She gurgles low in her throat, angling her head to expose the soft seam of her mouth. Stare into that huge black eye, search for some sign of recognition.

"I'm tired, girl." You slap her tongue. "So let's do this thing."

Taking your signal, Niska moves out into open water. She describes a quickening path around the pool, past the handicapped pavilion where, some million years ago, a young girl with an inscrutable smile watched you rocket into blue summer sky. Niska's dorsal fin dips below the surface. Give yourself over to the current, its power and possibilities. A locking sensation, all things in balance. Moon an unblinking eye and beyond it a million stars, around which revolve untold worlds.

Water surges beneath you, a thrilling push. Tiny bubbles trail to the surface, bursting with a fizzy club-soda pop. You hear yourself say, "I'm so sorry," though to whom or for what reasons you will remain forever unsure.

ON SLEEPLESS ROADS

GRAHAM LOVED the way his wife moved. While out walking he used to fall a half-step behind, just to watch. Her hips—but more than that. Legs, arms, the faint bob of her head. The way it all came together, the way it *meshed*. She loved to dance with her long black hair tied up on top of her head. She wore a moonstone on a leather thong that glimmered in the soft swell of her throat when the light from a mirror ball caught it. Seeing her like that, a snatch of song always came to him: *My girl don't just walk, she unfurls*. The photos Graham kept in his dresser gave a sense—weightless, beyond gravity—but didn't do justice to the way she once moved.

She didn't move that way anymore. Her limbs jerked erratically or not at all. Her body shook, an abiding shiver. *Bradykinesia*, the doctors called it, caused by a lack of dopamine in the brain. She'd lost all sense of equilibrium: when she fell she did so heedlessly, the way a chest of drawers pushed from a second-story balcony falls. Pills with names like Sinemet and Comtan and Requip. Sometimes she didn't take them. At first it was an act of defiance: she'd sit in a kitchen chair facing the wall, fingers white around the armrests, teeth clenched and muscles bunched along her jaw. Now it was an act of exploration: she wanted to see how strong the disease was, sense its power, her own powerlessness against it.

"Like slowly going blind," she once said. "Better to be born that way, don't you think?"

When things got really bad Graham held her down. Her wrists escaped the gentle manacles of his fingers, fists striking his chest with a resonant thump. Her body held a mindless strength: as though he were grappling with a possessed bundle of sticks, those brooms in *The Sorcerer's Apprentice.* Only her steady gaze, those blue eyes darkened indigo by the drugs, expressed understanding. He'd jam a leg between hers, thigh pressing her hips. At these times he'd recall those days when she'd visited his bachelor apartment—TV on a milk crate, cinderblock bookshelves—making out on his sagging futon, his leg between hers and the friction of denim on denim, eyes half-closed and her voice whispering, *Yes, like that. Just . . . like . . . that.* He'd look down at her body, her *now*-body, the flailing limbs and skeletal rattle of her teeth and yet always those eyes, that calm indigo gaze.

"I'm heading out, Nell."

She was sitting in a recliner beside the television tuned to an old episode of *The Beachcombers.* A book lay open on her lap. She tried to turn the page. Soon Graham turned it for her.

"You're not watching this?"

"S-suh-seen it a-ah-already," Nell said. "Relic steals Nick's l-l-logs in t-thuh-this one."

"Relic's always stealing Nick's logs. Turn it off?"

"It's uh-o-okay. Something to luh-luh-listen to."

A sheen of sweat on her face, glittering her skin like frost in moonlight. She was always sweating: the drugs, mainly, and her body never truly at rest. Still gorgeous. She'd never lose that. When Graham first saw her, the words *Nordic beauty* came to mind: those blue eyes and high cheekbones. He'd pictured her face framed by a white fur hood, a range of snow-topped mountains rising in the distance.

Graham set The Plunger on the hassock beside her recliner. He'd bought it—a saucer-sized disk connected to a phone line running to a jack in the wall—at a medical supply store. When pushed, it automatically dialed 911 to dispatch paramedics. They didn't have the savings to hire a private nurse while he worked. So . . . The Plunger.

Graham kissed his wife. The warmth of her lips, that faint tremble. He checked his watch: 11:00. Night pressed to the living room window and beyond that a few stars, very faint, very beautiful.

"See you in the morning."

"B-buh-be c-caref-ful."

The clean raw air of the late October night left a taste of winter at the back of Graham's throat. Snow fell through the arc-sodium glow of a nearby streetlamp, flakes touching his hair and melting in streams down his neck. He opened the door of a '95 Freightliner tow truck— the words *Repo Depot* stenciled in blue above the fender—keyed the ignition, and pulled out onto the street.

He worked at night. Safer that way. As a rule, people didn't react favorably to having their possessions spirited away—their ugly sides tended to present themselves. Graham worked while the city slept. Ninety-five percent of the time, he avoided confrontation.

The remaining five percent . . . those were interesting times.

He'd been slapped, punched, kicked, stabbed, smacked on the head with a blackthorn shillelagh. A .22 round lodged behind his left kneecap, a .40-caliber round stuck in his clavicle, ass and thighs pocked with rock-salt scars. He'd been bitten: dogs mostly, though once by an incensed deadbeat. In the late '70s he repo'd a tractor left overnight in a fallow field. At the first rumble of that Cummins diesel engine the farmhouse lights snapped on. Moments later the screen door banged open and the entire family was racing at him like the hammers of hell. A man, a woman, two kids dressed in sleeping flannels. They carried shovels and mattocks and pitchforks; the woman hefted a wheat scythe that wouldn't have looked out of place in the Grim Reaper's skeletal hands. As he worked the clutch feverishly, Graham had a dim inkling of how Frankenstein's monster must've felt, hounded by maddened villagers. The man hurled the pitchfork. A tine punched through the heel of Graham's boot, severing some muscles and nerves. His limp was faint, but noticeable. Not bad for twenty-five years on smash-and-grab duty. A lot of repo men had caught worse.

He drove through the city's industrial outskirts, past oil refineries surrounded by razor-wire fences and lit by a stargazer's constellation of halogen bulbs. He merged with the Trans-Canada Highway, hooking around the city's northern flank. Flat frost-white fields, fences, barns, the knuckled swells and dark contours of the distant hills beyond. Some feral creature—a coyote possibly, maybe a wolverine— slunk across the frozen fields. The Freightliner's 8.8-liter diesel engine sent a steady vibration through the cab. Johnny Cash sang about Fulsom Prison blues. Cattle asleep in the pastures, plumes of steam puffing from their nostrils. A low autumn moon cast a burnt orange glow over oak and birch.

Any thrill associated with his profession had long since worn off. It was different when he was young. Back then, he had it down to a cold science: five seconds to slide a slimjim between the driver's-side window and rubber lip, another five to pop the lock; thirty seconds to get at the ignition switch—he wore motorcycle boots with steel heels: one deft kick and the assembly snapped right off—another ten to jam a Phillips screwdriver down the ignition collar. In less than a minute any car in the city was his.

The tally of his repossessions over the years was impressive. '82 Lamborghini Countach, midnight black, sticker price a quarter-mil. Vintage '57 Chevy, candy-apple red with lozenge headlights, glasspack muffler, Great White tailfins. Many years ago, when they were dating, Graham flew Nell to Cape Cod to repossess a houseboat. They sailed it down through Bridgeport to New York, where Graham returned it to the dealership. Not just vehicles: coin collections and silverware, Royal Doulton figurines, a nineteenth-century Japanese musket. He'd shimmied up a rusted drainpipe to snare an antique weather vane in the shape of a codfish, hotwired a '77 Harley Softtail in the parking lot of a biker bar, squeezed through a half-opened window to reclaim a funerary urn.

For a few soul-deadening months he'd repossessed medical equipment: electric wheelchairs and cases of dialysis mixture and sphygmomanometers. He even nicked some poor soul's prosthetic arm. Nell was in and out of the hospital those days. The initial diagnosis was brain parasites: they were eating the lining of her brain so it pulled away from the inside of her skull, causing seizures. Graham suffered terrible nightmares: he found himself inside Nell's head, shrunk to microscopic size on the teeming surface of a brain eaten away to the size of a chimpanzee's by parasites—eight-legged tick-looking creatures with needlish mouths—and Graham powerless to stop them (this was better than the dream in which *he himself* was a parasite feasting on the jelly of his wife's brain). The tests weren't covered under their health plan, so Graham was forced into the ghoulish line of work to clear a few extra bucks. As soon as Nell was diagnosed with Bradykinesia, he begged off the assignment.

THE HOUSE WAS A dilapidated bungalow with an eccentric roofline, chipped marigold siding, front yard strewn with unraked leaves. The wooded cul-de-sac was located in a quiet neighborhood in the city's north end. In the bordering yards, the outlines of bikes and skateboards could be seen under a powdery dusting of evening snow.

Graham backed up the narrow drive and killed the engine. He double-checked the reclamation papers, dimmed the domelight, grabbed his toolbox, and swung down from the cab.

The truck was a Dodge Ram dually, V-10 engine, chrome running boards and rollbar. Graham fished a set of keys from his pocket—no need for slimjims or coathangers these days; dealers kept key-casts for every vehicle sold—and unlocked the driver's door. The steering wheel was bolted with a red Club lock. Graham rooted through the toolbox for the canister of Freon. He sprayed the assembly, enjoying the sound it made: rapidly freezing water. Frozen metal shattered with the tap of a hammer. After checking the VIN number on the dash, Graham keyed the ignition—a brief blast of Dwight Yoakam's "Takes a Lot to Rock You" before he found the stereo's volume knob—and, dropping into neutral, rolled the truck down the driveway until its rear wheels were set in the tow jack's sling.

He'd nearly secured chains around the rear axle when a man stepped out the front door. The porch light was off and he moved silently, materializing from the spiderweb of shadows thrown by a leafless maple tree.

"What are you doing?" he said. "You're . . . you're thiefing my truck."

Graham bent over his toolbox, grabbing the second canister he always carried: mace. Sometimes it was the calmest ones who ended up causing the most grief. He looked the guy over: short and thin with the sort of engorged belly Graham associated with starving Ethiopians, wearing a pair of camouflage pants and a T-shirt the vague color of boiled liver. His whole body was canted awkwardly to one side: right shoulder sagging, left shoulder hiked nearly level with his ear, the odd plane recalling a teeter-totter.

"I'm not stealing anything, and I'm sure you know that, Mister"—
a quick glance at the reclamation papers—"Henreid. Do this quiet as
I can, try not to wake the neighbors, okay?"

Henreid stood on the unkempt lawn, a sullen grimace stamped on
his face. It never ceased to amaze Graham how people reacted: as
though he were an agent of a shadowy agency whose heinous modus
operandi was to bring misery upon hard-working, law-abiding,
god-fearing folk. Surely Henreid knew this day was coming, unless
he'd ignored the threatening letters and phone calls. He'd likely been
expecting this for a while, but, true to the nature of such people, had
hoped, with the unwarranted anticipation of a death-row inmate, to
receive divine reprieve in the form of a bank error in his favor, an
unexpected windfall bequeathed by a dead aunt, a butter-fingered
clerk slopping coffee on his payment records, absolving all debt and
responsibility.

"I'm only a month or so behind. Can't you let it slide? I'm good
for it."

"I got no say in the matter. Sorry."

Henreid disappeared inside. Graham crawled under the truck
chassis, doubled the chain around the axle, clipped it to the sling.
While he worked the winch motor, lifting the Dodge's two-ton frame
off its back wheels, Henreid reappeared with a child.

"Say hello to the nice man, Charity."

The girl was dressed in a blowsy violet nightgown, protuberant
belly swelling the fabric, rubbing sleep from her eyes. She looked at
Graham and smiled, maybe because a child's natural instinct was to
do so, maybe at her father's coaching. Her teeth were in awful condition: jagged and bucked, lapping one another like the shingles on a
shaker roof. She was the kind of woebegone child one couldn't help
but forecast a grim future for—eating lunch on the schoolyard's
fringe, dateless on prom night—a girl earmarked for a lifetime of bitter

experience, the inescapability of which enveloped her in a diffuse aura of melancholy.

"He's taking away Daddy's truck," Henreid went on. "Now Daddy won't be able to drive you to school, or . . . to the ice cream parlor."

"The city's got a great school-bus system, sweetheart," Graham said to Charity. "And it's better to walk to the ice cream shop. Good exercise."

The girl's eyes held a faintly panicked cast, likely for no other reason than her father had woken her in the dead of night to converse with a burly stranger. Her arms found their way around Henreid's waist, head burying into his paunch.

"I know, sweetie, I know," Henreid said. "Maybe if you ask the man, ask him *reeeal* nice, he'll let Daddy keep his truck."

"I can't do that, Charity." Graham's eyes were fixed on Henreid. "You might want to ask your Daddy why he's driving such a spiffy truck when he could spend a few bucks to put some braces in your pretty mouth."

"Hey, don't you talk that way—got no damn right!"

Graham raised his hands in the manner of a surrendering PoW. "You're the boss. Come up with the truant payments, your truck's back at the dealership."

He stepped up into the tow truck's cab. The engine caught with a full-bodied rumble, the diesel *tik-tik-tik* breaching the dark silence. Graham pulled out onto the street. Henreid and his daughter dwindled to morose specks in the rearview.

THE SNOW LET UP, leaving the streets slick with a brilliantine shine. Graham drove through quiet neighborhoods, postwar Normandy houses banded by hawthorn hedgerows interspersed with modern flat-roofed structures that stuck out, as Nell might say, like cocktail olives on an ice cream sundae. In the early morning hours the streets seemed remote and unreal, a dreamscape envisioned by someone of limited imagination. The only sign of human life glimpsed through the windows of all-night diners and coffee shops, a rogue's gallery of sunken-eyed loners and insomniacs, men and women who'd reached the end of their tether and hadn't quite realized it.

The first time Graham noticed his wife shaking, they were dining at an Italian restaurant. Waiting for their meal to arrive, Graham heard a sly tinkling: his wife's hand trembled atop her cutlery, knife fork spoon arrayed neatly upon a white tablecloth.

"Honey, you're shivering."

Nell glanced at her hand, flattened her palm to the table. "Drafty in here."

Graham agreed it was. A few minutes later, her hand shook again. Nell jammed it between her legs and pressed her thighs together. When the food arrived, she couldn't hold her fork. In desperation she clutched it in her fist, the way a child might. She set it down with a clatter and ran a hand through her hair, that hand quaking badly, laughing, saying, "Silly, silly, silly," under her breath.

"Are you alright?"

"Yes, fine. Just . . . stress. Work's been hectic. It's so damn *cold* in here."

Graham placed a hand on Nell's arm. Her body vibrated faintly, a deep-seated tremor originating at the very heart of her. Graham's childhood home had been within earshot of a busy railyard. As a precaution, his father taught him to place his hand on the tracks before crossing: if the track trembled, it meant a train was near. That's how Nell's arm felt: a section of track trembling before an approaching locomotive.

"We should go home."

"I'm okay." She smiled, then lowered her eyes, as though embarrassed. In that moment, Graham knew she'd suffered with this for some time—a few days, a week, a month?—without telling him. Tough, proud, foolhardy woman. "Finish your dinner, Graham. It's getting cold."

The Dodge dealership hung suspended in a wash of halogen light. Showroom garlanded with plastic flags the shape of baseball pennants, fluttering faintly in the night wind. Two prices soaped on the windows of cars and trucks, a slash run through the higher one, suggesting the salesman, in a fit of improvident and potentially bankrupting bonhomie, had elected to cut his customers a rare deal.

Graham unlocked the impound lot's gate and nosed the Freightliner through, parking Henreid's truck between a Ford Bronco and a Jeep Cherokee. He dropped the keys in the nightbox. The next job was on the other side of town. A mobile home. He poured a cup of Nutrasweet-laced coffee from a silver thermos and set off southwards.

After Nell was diagnosed with Bradykinesia, their relationship changed. A distance developed between them, expressing itself in small ways. They didn't touch one another as much, where before they always squeezed shoulders, patted bottoms, held hands. Graham knew this was because Nell didn't want him to feel her shaking; after one particularly ugly argument, he'd entered into unwilling accord. They passed hours together in silence, where before they'd discussed every daily triviality—again, this was at Nell's instigation, as she was self-conscious of her worsening stutter.

A pall of futility hung over their marriage. All the things that had seemed so imminent—financial security, children, ripe old age—were no longer. They felt as though the future had been misrepresented, falsified. They fell to contemplating all those things not done, things they'd always believed there would be time for, later. All the vaguely instructional clichés by which they'd conducted their lives—Hard work pays off, Good things happen to good people, Someday our ship will come in—were worthless in the face of this mindless, devouring disease.

Graham prayed. Not having grown up in a religious household and ignorant of all things devotional, he composed prayers like business letters, each no more than a veiled Faustian pact: *Dear God, if, in your infinite wisdom, you can see your way clear to cure my wife, feel free to take ten—no, fifteen—no, twenty years—off my life, or give me leprosy or strike me with a lightning bolt. Please consider my offer, I think you'll find it a fair one, amen.*

THE HOUSE was a rambling two-story: latticed mullions on catherine-wheel windows, meticulously landscaped lawn, shrubs swaddled in canvas and bound with twine. It backed onto a man-made lake, one of several in the city: pulling up, Graham glimpsed water through gaps in the foliage, moonlight glancing off ribbed waves. A lip of light spilled beneath the garage door; every so often, that lip was darkened by the shadow of a passing foot.

The motorhome, a late model Chinook Summit, was parked at the end of a wide interlocking brick driveway, parallel to the garage. Standing in the RV lot, the owners had no doubt imagined rambling, cross-country journeys, sultry nights parked on lake shores lit by a harvest moon—just like in the sales brochure. Of course job, family, and other obligations rendered their freewheeling fantasies just that, resigning the motorhome to its current role as a repository for dust, cobwebs, and shed maple keys. Graham repossessed many such luxury impulse items: Sea-Doos, bass boats, catamarans, executive nautilus equipment. The owners seemed to think since they weren't actively using these toys, they should be spared the onus of paying for them.

The camper door hung ajar. Graham picked his way through the cramped living space, puzzled to find signs of active habitation: his penlight swept countertops littered with empty potato chip bags and crushed beer cans; the kitchen table and captain's chairs held hamster cages; a twenty-five-gallon aquarium sat on the floor, next to a chicken-wire cage scattered with brown feathers. The predominant smell was of cedar shavings, and below that the ammoniac odor of rodent piss.

Graham slid behind the wheel and dropped the gearshift into neutral. The camper rolled down the drive's smooth grade, Graham pumping the brakes gingerly. He wedged blocks of wood under the tires and slid under the RV's bumper, squinting up into the dark topography of linkages and drive shafts, wiping beads of coolant off the radiator grille to stop them dripping onto his face.

He'd clipped chains to the axles when the garage door began its rattling ascent. A square of grainy yellow light fell across his legs. He peered out from under the front wheels at a pair of advancing shins.

"Ah, jeez," a voice said. "Coming to take your pound of flesh."

Graham hauled his ass out from under the hood, fists balled. He took one look at the guy and relaxed: tall and willowy, dressed in a kelly green track suit with a badly pixelated photograph superimposed on the sweatshirt. The overall impression was of lightness, airiness: the man seemed constructed from featherweight space-age polymers. His pinched features bore an expression that reminded Graham of those lab-coated scientists in 1950s Movietone filmstrips.

"My final possession spirited away in the middle of the night." The guy threw his hands up helplessly. "This is it—the end of James Paris! The end, I tell you!"

Graham wondered what it was about property seizure that gave rise to soliloquies so melodramatic they'd embarrass a threepenny hack.

"Relax, Mr. Paris. It's no big deal."

"Says you, no big deal." The man smelled as though he'd spent the night marinating in Bushmills Irish whiskey. "You got what's left of my life chained to the bumper of your truck."

Up close, Paris looked older than Graham had initially thought: skin wrinkled and crepey around the eyes and mouth, shiny over the cheekbones. Whether this was true age or a temporary haggardness brought about by recent events was unclear. Graham saw the photo on Paris's sweatshirt featured two pit bulls. The names Rodney and Matilda were printed below in block letters.

"Mr. Paris . . . "

"James, call me James."

"Graham. You're behind on your payments, James."

"I know, Graham. How much—a month? Two?"

"I don't know for sure."

"How'd you know where to find me? Isn't even my house."

"We have our ways."

"Alison must've called the dealership. She won't be satisfied until I'm under a train trestle, eating Alpo. The woman wants me ruined." Paris pronounced ruined as *roon'd*.

Ex-wife, Graham figured. He'd filled the role of distribution agent in more than a few bitter divorces, ensuring both parties got exactly what the settlement stipulated. Surveying his own modest possessions, he often wondered how much of it he owed to the avarice and spite of men and women who once pledged 'til death us do part.

"Would you mind giving me a minute to gather my stuff?" Paris said. "I've got a few things in the camper and—oh, you little *brat!*"

A small lumpy shape wobbled across the driveway, making a bee-line for the canvas-wrapped mulberry trees. Paris stumbled after it, slippers skating across the wet flagstones. He fell on top of the ungainly creature then rose to his knees, cradling a furry bundle to his chest.

"Swear, can't turn my back for a minute," he said. "The rest of them are fine, but this one, he's too curious for his own good."

Paris held a guinea pig. Brown, with a white stripe running down the center of its vaguely bovine face, eyes like glossy black BBs set on either side of its skull. It sat serenely in Paris's cupped palms, hairless paws resting on a curled finger, warbling and blinking its eyes.

"No end of frustration." Paris stroked the animal with thumb and pointer finger, shaping the fur on its head into a mohawk. "He's a good boy, still. Come inside?" He nodded towards the garage. "Just for a minute? I won't hurt you."

Graham smiled: he outweighed Paris by a good seventy pounds. Peering into the garage, he saw video recorders set on tripods, white umbrellas angled on poles, a boom mike suspended from a roofbeam.

Graham followed Paris into the garage. A miniature set lay sprawled across the floor: strips of sod interspersed with bristly thatches of alfalfa and gnarled bits of driftwood. Tiny houses scattered about: one shaped like a boot with a thatched roof and a window cut in the heel, the other a white cottage with a sagging roof and water wheel. A drift of popcorn lay beneath a magnifying glass rigged to a stick driven into the sod. The enclosure was hemmed by a chicken-wire fence.

An assortment of avian, amphibian, and rodent life roamed the pen. A mouse's pointed white head poked from the cottage's shuttered window. A frog perched atop a chunk of granite, the elastic bladder of its throat expanding and contracting. A duck slept off in the corner, beak buried in its feathered ruff. A painted turtle stood facing the boot-shaped house, head telescoped from its shell on a long wrinkled neck.

Paris set the guinea pig down on the grass. It scurried over the turtle's shell into the boot.

"Where's my star?" said Paris, scanning the ground. "Where's Sammy?"

A twitching pink nose emerged from the pile of popcorn, followed by a round furred face. The hamster—brown and white, black-tipped ears—gripped a kernel of popcorn in its paws, chewing in the rapid, gluttonous manner of such creatures.

"Will you look at that." Paris ducked behind a camera, angling the lens. "I've been begging him to do that all night!"

He left the camera rolling and went over to the workbench, where a half-empty bottle of Bushmills sat. He poured a respectable two ounces into a white mug; rooting around under the bench, he came up with another mug, and, after wiping it clean on his sweatshirt, filled that too.

"Like herding cats." He handed Graham a mug. "I end up burning two hours of tape to get the shot I need. Got to work at night, too, since most of these guys are nocturnal."

The mouse crawled out the cottage window, nosed its way through a patch of alfalfa and entered the boot. A distressed squeak. The guinea pig's head appeared out the top of the boot, pushing up the conical thatched roof: it appeared to be wearing a coolie hat, the type worn by Vietnamese rice farmers.

"What are you up to here?"

"Are you kidding?" Paris seemed genuinely upset. "It's *Riverside Tales!*"

"The TV program," Graham said, confused. "The . . . the children's show?"

"Of course, the children's show. Well, not *exactly*. There were some, let's say, obstructing *legalities,*" Paris waved his cup in a dismissive arc, "that, well, caused me to change the focus from series continuation to a stand-alone effort in the spirit of the old series."

"You mean a knock-off?"

"Homage, Graham, *homage*. See, there's *Sammy* Hamster," he pointed, "and *B*P the Guinea Pig, *Marian* Mouse, *Scholarly* Old Frog, Turtle—they're all here!"

Graham remembered the show about a group of animals living along a river. Each episode, some problem arose—a flood or a blizzard, one of the guinea pig's wacky inventions gone awry—that the river-bank denizens would solve. Though childless himself, it was the sort of sweetly instructive program Graham might encourage kids to watch.

"You're the creator?"

Paris shook his head. "Nah. I'm up late a few weeks back, watching the tube. Three, four o'clock in the morning—nothing but infomercials and test patterns. I came across this old children's show, *Riverside Tales*. I'm thinking, four in the morning—what kid's watching this? Anyway, seemed like something I could pull off. Head to the pet store and buy the cast, right? No SAG, no unions, no agents, none of those hassles."

Two dishes sat in a corner of the pen. One held sunflower seeds and barley pellets; the other was empty. Paris slopped a thimbleful of liquor into the empty dish. "A rare treat," he assured Graham. "Helps with performance anxiety. Anyway, the show went on hiatus years ago. This," he said with a boozy sweep of his arm, "is *The New and Improved Riverside Tales!*"

"You're a film producer?"

"No, ad executive. *Was*, should say. Ever seen the commercial for Blastberry Crunch?"

"You mean the breakfast cereal? The one with the, oh, the giant talking berries?"

"Colonel Blastberry, right, and the Berry Patrol. That was my campaign. I wrote the jingle that played over 'Ride of the Valkyries.'" He sang in a low baritone: "*Colonel Blastberry, Colonel Blastberry, Colonel BlastBERRY, nutritious and brave!*"

"So why are you doing this?"

"I was *fired*, is why. I'm stone *broke*, is why. I'm living in a *camper*, is why. My ex-wife is a bloodsucking *vampire bat*, is why." Paris's face contorted. "God, I don't even live in a camper anymore!"

"What about your house? Why don't you sell it?"

"I told you, I don't live here. I'm house-sitting for friends. I gave Alison everything: the house, the car, the dogs. Were it legal for that sea hag to suck the very air from my lungs, believe me, she would."

"I take it you're angling for a film grant."

Paris nodded. "Rented the video equipment, sunk the last of my savings into this set, these critters. Talking Custer's last stand, here."

"I don't remember a duck," Graham said, with a nod towards the slumbering mallard.

"That was my idea. Dillson Duck. He's comic relief." Paris shook his head. "He's not working out."

The hamster wandered over to the water dish and lapped the booze. It shook all over like a wet dog shaking itself dry.

"That's the spirit, Sammy," said Paris. "Hey, would you mind doing me a tiny favor before leaving with my camper and, y'know, the final shreds of my dignity?"

"What's that?"

"I'm on the last scene, here. In this episode, BP built a popcorn machine." Paris indicated the magnifying glass tied to a stick. "The machine caused some problems, but they've been resolved. So, now, the *denouement*. Good triumphs, evil is thwarted—"

"Evil? It's popcorn."

"What? I know it's popcorn. It's a *metaphor*." Paris enunciated slowly, as though addressing the recipient of a frontal lobotomy. "The popcorn represents evil, metaphorically speaking."

"Ah."

"Music swells, harmony abounds, the riverside animals clasp hands in the spirit of friendship and love." Paris stifled a belch. "All that crap. Fade to black."

"What can I do?"

"Well, I've got to get these guys together in one shot. They need to be . . . *frolicking*." He clapped his hands briskly. "So! Could you handle the camera while I motivate the talent?"

"I can handle that."

Paris herded the animals around the popcorn with a pair of plastic spatulas. For the most part, they seemed resigned to their roles:

Scholarly Old Frog burrowed into the white drift until only the green-black humps of its eyes were visible. Dillson Duck quacked morosely and went back to sleep. Turtle tucked his head into his shell and wouldn't show himself for love nor money. Sammy— slightly intoxicated by now—became amorous with Marian Mouse; his advances coldly rebuffed, he bit her.

"We got some . . ."

"Yeah, I see." Paris brushed a cluster of dark pellets off the popcorn."Goddamn turd factories." He opened a jar of peanut butter, dipped his finger, offered it to the rodents.

"So that's how you make it look like they're talking?"

"You bet. They love the stuff. Sticks to the roof of their mouths. Drives them bananas."

Marian, BP, and Sammy sat around smacking their lips. It really did look as though they were having an animated, albeit distracted, conversation.

"That's a wrap," Paris said. They'd spent the better part of an hour, filled two video cassettes, killed the bottle of Bushmills. "Iron out the bugs in the editing room."

Graham glanced out the window, moon hanging low and fat over the lake. "I've got to go." He didn't want to leave. The booze suffused him with a mellow glow, softening every angle, inspiring a pervasive goodwill towards all creatures great and small.

"Yes, we've both got business to attend to. Suppose I'd better head to the dump and gather the makings for a shanty."

Paris hunted a cardboard box out from under the workbench, setting the animals inside.

"What are you doing?"

"You're taking my home, remember? Their home, too."

"But . . . you can't abandon them." Graham was horrified Paris would set the box out on the curb for tomorrow's garbage pickup.

"They're your responsibility."

"Relax," said Paris. "Come with me."

THE BACKYARD SLOPED DOWN to a thin stretch of sand along the lake's shore. The sky held a livid pallor, the onset of dawn. Snow piled along the banks. Waves lapped the shoreline.

Paris walked down to the water. The animals congregated inside the box, preening, scratching the cardboard. Paris set the box in the sand, heeled off his shoes, removed his socks, rolled up his pantlegs. He tucked the dozing duck under his arm and waded into the lake.

"Cold," he hissed through his teeth. He waded out until the water touched his knees, setting the duck down. "You're free. Rejoin your mallard brethren."

The duck swam towards Paris.

"No! Go away. You're free, don't you get it? Free!"

Paris trudged back to shore, leaving the duck to swim in aimless circles. He plucked Turtle and Scholarly Old Frog from the box.

"Boys, it's high time you became men."

Graham sat on a boulder near the water. He didn't say anything—wasn't his place to. Paris laid the animals down on the coarse sand. The frog hopped into the water, an inky blur lost amid waving strands of eelgrass. The turtle dipped a tentative foot into the water. Satisfied, it swam out into the lake. The dark convex of its shell cut a slow path through the water, starlight bent upon the dome.

Paris stretched out on the sand. Breath puffed from his mouth, white and vaporous. Graham stirred the toe of his boot through the sand in a figure-eight pattern.

"They'll be okay, won't they?"

"I don't know," said Graham. "Winter's coming."

A series of shrill squeaks arose from the box as Marian Mouse's unsullied character was again challenged by a boorish Sammy Hamster.

Turtle's shell described a lazy arc through the water, looping back towards shore.

"Cuts people's chests open. What he does for a living."

"He who?"

"Guy sleeping with my wife. She's a nurse, he's a cardiovascular surgeon. Looks like John Travolta, and not *Saturday Night Fever* Travolta—*Look Who's Talking* Travolta. It's depressing." Paris took a deep breath and let it out slow. "Sometimes I think about walking into the hospital, into the operating theater, punching him. Right in his swarthy face. I bet he wears gold chains under his OR scrubs—a *lot* of them. I think, y'know, like maybe it'll solve something, right? Answer something. But then I think, hey, this is the way she wants it. She's happier now, right? I know that."

"Maybe you should be happy for her, then."

"It's just, I thought I'd be happy, too. I wanted to be free, unfettered. All I could think about. A fresh start, hey?"

"Sure," Graham said. "Sure, I know."

Sleeping away the daylight hours, Graham's most persistent dream was one in which he repossesses a car, but, instead of driving to the impound lot, keeps driving. The car is a '63 Corvette Stingray convertible, cobalt blue. Sitting behind the wheel, he senses his personality shift to that of the car itself: growling and aggressive, the loudest, meanest dog on the block. All the perceived shortcomings that haunt his waking self—a lack of true intellect, a feeling he could've done better—evaporate like water dripped on a searing engine block. The city of his dream is such as he's never seen before: he drives dusty laneways strung with adobe huts where dusky-skinned children chase lean hens through open yards, past imposing Kashmiri towers bellying in the shape of onions at their peaks, greenwater canals clogged with sleek gondolas.

He arrives at a house that, despite its unfamiliar architecture, he instinctively recognizes as his own. The front door opens, Nell stepping into the clean mid-afternoon sunlight. Barefoot, wearing a short summer dress. She moves haltingly, trembling, arms outstretched in search of an elusive balance. Then a magical thing happens: hairline fissures run down her arms and legs, thin and twisting like cracks in granite. Her face shatters, the fractured portions—high arch of cheek, fluent plane of brow—flaking off, skin curled and like burnt paper. Her expression does not change, though her eyes lighten to a brilliant shade of blue. Graham thinks of a Russian doll, of a chrysalis birthing some strange new-old and beautiful thing. She skips lightly down the path—oh, the way she *moves*. Her beauty is so merciless it exists nearly in the abstract. And though he knows, deep in those chambers of heart and mind that never truly sleep, this is only a dream, he still holds an unshakable belief in its possibility.

Other times, driving the streets at night, his restless mind slipping in and out of focus, a different dream comes. He repossesses another car. This one never takes a concrete form: four wheels, bland and nondescript. A getaway vehicle. He drives through the city as he knows it: redbrick houses and beige apartment complexes with squares of light burning in odd windows, darkened parks, pockets of ugliness and despair overlooked by distant snow-capped hills. He pulls up to the house he and his wife have shared for twenty-five years, idling at the curb for a long empty second. He sees Nell's trembling silhouette in the front window. Then he sets the car in gear and pulls away, turning the corner at the end of the block, the red eyes of those taillights dimming, gone. He does not know where he is going, doesn't quite accept his own dream logic. The vision dissolves—he often snaps out of it with an audible yelp—and in its wake all that exists is a cold and resolute self-loathing.

"Nobody really holds anyone," said Paris. "You only hold someone as well as you're able and you're only held as much as you'll allow. In the beginning, you know, that's where the excitement lies: the uncertainty, right? The . . . *fear*." Paris turned to Graham and smiled. He had a way of smiling that made Graham sad. "Don't you think it'd be nice if life was like the Riverside? I've been thinking about it a lot. Everybody works together. Everybody gets along. There's love, sure, but not the kind that breaks people in half, wrecks things. Puppy love. Nobody gets hurt. Everyone's just . . . friends. It'd be good, I think. A good life." He laughed, the stiff barking noise of a small dog. "I'm an idiot."

Turtle swam back to shore. It stood in the shallows, staring, with ancient pondering eyes, at the box it'd been plucked from.

"Silly thing." Paris walked down to the water and picked the turtle up, returning it to the box. It seemed content to be back, its existence delimited by those four off-brown walls.

"Where's the frog?"

"Think you lost him."

"He'll be okay. He's resourceful."

Paris waded out into the lake, where Dillson swam in meandering circles. "Get your feathered ass over here." At the last possible moment the duck took flight: a splash of water, a dim flapping of wings, a plump shape fleeing across the moon's face into the first ashes of light to the east. Paris stood in water up to his knees, shaking his head. High above, a jet left its gauzy contrail on the lightening cupola of sky.

"Maybe this is the way it happens." Paris did not elaborate.

"Maybe so. Listen, I'm not gonna take your camper."

"Really?"

"I came, you weren't here. That's my story."

"Hey, man, thanks."

"It's temporary. Agency'll send someone else."

"I only need a week to cut the episode."

"You should be okay. Can't stay here, though."

"Right. I'm a no-good deadbeat." Paris's quasi-criminal status appeared to energize him. "I'm on the lam. Bonnie and Clyde."

He came out of the water. "I really hate to do this, seeing as you've exceeded your good Samaritan quota for this week, but I've got to ask you one last favor."

BEAMS OF PREDAWN SUNLIGHT filtered over the horizon, touching the hoods of parked cars, the windows of office buildings. Moon still visible, a pale hub above the hills. The city hung suspended between darkness and day. Early morning dog walkers and paperboys went about their business with an air of reluctant obligation.

Graham drove silent suburban streets, a meandering route home. He loved this time of day, everything clean and fresh and full of possibility. A cardboard box sat on the seat beside him. Hamster, mouse, guinea pig, and turtle slept quietly inside. All four were touching, drawing heat from one another, bodies expanding and contracting as they breathed. Two cages and an aquarium stacked in the footwell, next to a sack of cedar shavings, another of barley pellets. He pulled into his driveway, hefted the box, and went inside.

The television was on, muted, tuned to another episode of *The Beachcombers*. Nick was hollering at Relic, presumably for stealing logs. Nell lay on the recliner. Even in sleep, her body shook fitfully.

Graham switched the TV off. Sparrows congregated on the backyard picnic table, brown bodies staggered in ranks like Confederate soldiers. He thought of the first time he'd seen Nell, at a high-school dance. A slim beautiful girl standing in the splintered light of a revolving mirror ball. She danced alone, swaying her hips and snapping her fingers to the beat. He was stunned when she asked him to dance. He wondered if it were a joke to amuse her friends, not really caring if it was in his desire to be next to her. He remembered her eyes in the malarial heat and darkness of the high-school gym, glittering blue, pupils wide and dark. The sparrows took flight *en masse,* a dark flurry of bodies vanishing over the rooftops.

"H-H-Honey?"

Nell was awake, rubbing her eyes.

"Just me. I didn't mean to wake you."

"Wh-wh-what's t-that you g-got?"

Graham set the box on the armrest. "Some new friends I made last night."

He set the guinea pig on Nell's lap. It burrowed into the loose folds of her sweater, warbling contentedly.

"I h-had a g-g-guinea p-pig when I w-whu-was a kid."

Graham placed the remaining animals on different parts of his wife. They roamed the prone topography of her body: the backs of her hands, swells of her arms, crook of her neck.

"T-tuh-tickles," she said. "W-wh-where w-wuh-will we put these g-guys?"

"We'll find room."

In the mellow half-light of the den, the animals made a nest of Graham's wife. Marian Mouse nuzzled through the soft curls of Nell's hair. Turtle sought the valley between her breasts, paused as though awaiting permission, then eased down. Nell petted BP's head, the guinea pig happy to receive any attention.

Her hand hardly trembled. It hardly trembled at all.

A distressed squeak from somewhere below. Graham scanned his wife's body: no hamster. It must've slipped between the seat and back, down into the guts of the recliner.

"Stay as still as you can," he told Nell, kneeling beneath the leg rest and lifting the green corduroy flap, exposing the chair's inner workings. The hamster was caught in a V of metal struts forming the recliner's levering mechanism. Each strut was attached to a heavy spring quivering with the movement of Nell's body. The hamster hung helplessly, stunted legs kicking the air, eyes bulging comically.

"Please," Graham said, reaching a hand towards the shivering creature. "Please, Nell, please stay still."

FRICTION

My name is Sam. I'm a sex addict.

Welcome, Sam.

Thanks, all of you. So, when did I first realize I had a problem—that's the question, is it? Guess it'd be in my teens; fifteen, maybe sixteen. Standing in a bodega in the city where I grew up, only place you could find Black Bart licorice gum—remember that stuff? This woman came in for cigarettes. She wasn't remarkable in any tangible way. I recall her elbow. The, um, inside of it—crook of her arm, really. When she reached over the counter to pay you saw these downy hairs, a raised blue vein and I wanted to touch that spot, smell and taste it. Crazy, but I wanted to shrink myself, atomize like those scientists in *Fantastic Voyage*, view things on a cellular level. I wanted to know everything about it—not her, you understand, I didn't care about her history or goals or fears, any of that. Just be intimate with that unthinking portion of her. That was the first time I felt that way—my whole world collapsing in a single gesture or stimulus. Same way Hank Aaron must've felt swinging a bat for the first time, Ray Charles tickling those ivories. So this is it, huh? My life's purpose. Crush homeruns. Write great music. Obsess about a woman's elbow. Oh. To some the wheat, others the chaff. But you make do, right?

I'VE GOT THE GIRL bent over a glasstop desk with her ass in the air, my hands on her hips, thrusting diligently. Her name's Caitlin— no, Kitten. Glass fogged under Kitten's armpits and her nipple rings produce a glasscutter clink on the tabletop. She's blowing Wayne and every so often pauses to exhort me to Fuck her, Fuck her hard, Fill her up, Harder, Faster, Make her cum, et cetera. Klieg lights hot on my skin and a cameraman between my spread legs, zoomed in for an insertion shot. Give it a little swizzlestick action and Kitten moans at this pedestrian maneuver. Wayne's leaning forward, red flushmarks across his thighs caused by pressure from the table. An eagle spread-winged across Kitten's lower back, red rose clutched in each talon.

"Give it to me," she says. "Give it to your little *whore*."

"Cut!" The director barks. "Take twenty, people."

Break for a set change. The cameraman slots a fresh tape into his handheld, the sound tech adjusts his levels, a gopher swabs the desktop with Windex. Towel wrapped round my waist, I consult the craft table's meager offerings—mesh sack of oranges, box of Triscuits, brown-looking bananas—select an orange and sit on the sofa.

I'm peeling the orange and stuffing rinds between the cushions when a girl sits beside me. She approaches from behind, barefooted, easing herself down stealthily as though her intention is to catch me unawares. Moderately tall, maybe five-six, long legs, narrow waist, high breasts. Naked as a jaybird. Untucking the towel, she takes me in her hand.

"Thanks," I tell her, sectioning the orange.

"Just doing my job. Want some oil or anything?"

"That's okay. You got a soft touch. Not like the last fluffer—like pulling weeds."

"There are those who believe I have healing hands."

The girl's eyes swim with gold flecks like you'd find floating in a bottle of Goldschlager and she's looking off across the set, into darkened corners filled with dusty props and costume racks. The boom mike guy sits on an overturned milk crate, watching. She laughs softly, though at what I'm unsure.

The orange is dry and gross, like a pulp-sucking vampire's been at it. "Want some?"

"Hands are sorta full, here."

"My name is Samuel. Sam Chancey. And yours is . . . ?"

"Do you really need to know, Samuel Chancey? I mean, would it enhance any of this?"

"No," I say. "Well, I mean, *possibly*. Who knows? Just like to know, is all."

"And I'd like to fuck Douglas Fairbanks. Ain't gonna happen."

"Okay, well then, are you new—like, to the city?"

"What's with the small talk? We're way past that stage—I'm in your pants already." She snorts out her nostrils like a pissed-off bull. "What are you, one of those touchy-feely New Age types? Bet you got healing crystals in your nightstand."

"Don't even know what's in there. Toenail clippers and Dristan nasal spray, I think."

This gets a laugh and I ask her where she's from. She takes my hand and draws it between her legs. "Make yourself useful." She's wet—I mean *sopping*—and I'm rubbing her pussy gingerly, then faster. Her face pinches up and she makes a noise like she's stifling a sneeze, orgasming twice in rapid succession. "Okay," she's whispering, more to herself than me. "Okay, okay, oooo-*kay*." Breathing heavily, splotches of color on her throat, clitoris the size of a pomegranate seed. She butts her chin against my shoulder, opening her mouth to orgasm again; when she pulls away thin crescent-shaped divots, the imprint of her teeth, are visible in my flesh.

"Thanks." A slight shudder. "That was pretty alright."

"You're not that hard to please."

"I'm hypersensitive. There are drugs, but I don't take them."

"Drugs to do what?"

"Y'know, like, dampen the sensation. Anyway, don't like them. Like my entire body is packed in cotton batten or something."

"Who wants that?"

"I know, right?" She kicks a thigh over mine, hooks her foot around my calf, draws my legs wider. "Sure, it'd probably make things better in the long run, but we are who we are."

"You betcha." My winning smile. "Warts and all."

Wayne Harvey sits on the sofa. A silverhaired veteran, women love my co-star's gallant demeanor: he treats starlets as though their maidenhood remains unsullied. Overlooking the bowlegs and turkey wattle, he's quite dashing: the Jimmy Stewart of hardcore porn. The fluffer takes him in her other hand.

"I thank you for your efforts, milady," Wayne says. "But I'm afraid your kindly ministrations will have no effect."

"Why—what's the matter?"

"Wayne's penis is broken," I inform her.

He shoots me a sour look. "True, Samuel—if crudely put."

It happened a few years back. Wayne was in a solo scene with this acrobatic little blonde: she was jerking and bucking and practically doing the loop-de-loop. Wayne was sweating buckets and holding on for dear life, now she's riding him, Wayne's thrusting up to meet her and the gal's biting her bottom lip begging for more but they come together awkwardly and something just went *snap*.

Shocking but true: you can break your dick. A fibrous sheath, the *tunica albunginea,* surrounds the tubes and blood vessels; when erect, the sheath is stretched tight and hard beneath the skin. Severe trauma can rupture the *tunica*: roughly the same force it would take to, say, bust your nose. The medical term is a penile fracture—though doctors familiar with the injury use the euphemism "bent wick."

I was standing off set and heard this awful noise: the closest compari-son I can manage is the sound of a drumstick torn from a roast turkey. Then the girl's screaming and Wayne's hopping around hollering. His cock hung buckled at this hideous jackknifed angle and the taut skin kept it bent, no way to release to the pressure. The tip a dusky eggplant bulb and a fearsome hematoma, this dark grape-sized bubble, swelling along the break. There's poor Wayne staring down at his mangled unit, black as blood sausage, squeezing it at the root as though that might help. I'm not going to lie: it was pretty fucking revolting.

Thankfully this story has a happy ending. Unable to summon a screenworthy erection, Wayne underwent IPP surgery—Inflatable Penis Prosthetic. The urologist made an incision at the base of Wayne's penis and threaded an expandable bladder up the shaft, then another incision in the testicular sac to deposit a pump the size and weight of a triple-A battery. A hole drilled into his hipbone anchored the prosthesis; the sundry tubes and wires were tucked behind his abdominal wall. Damn thing works like a charm: Wayne pumps up and wades on in, then deflates and lounges around until it's time to re-inflate for action. Porno's Six Million Dollar Man.

"Are you sure?" the fluff girl asks him. "Really, I don't mind."

"Well, if it's no bother." Wayne smiles. "But please view my lack of arousal as an expression of my physical limitations, not a comment on your skills."

The two of them fall into an easy repartee, the sort Wayne excels at: meaningless and lighthearted, subjects ranging from recent movies to stale jokes to articles he's read on some humanitarian topic: Save the

Monkey-Eating Eagles, Liberate the Goatherds of East Timor, Thalido-
mide Babies March for World Peace, et cetera. She even laughs at
Wayne's ghastly puns: *I once knew a bailiff who moonlighted as a
bartender, my dear. He served subpoena coladas.* Get the girl off and she
won't even pay attention to me—how's that for gratitude? My nose is
distinctly out of joint.

Before the final scene we experience what might be charitably
described as a "technical malfunction." More pointedly, Wayne's prosthesis . . . well, *explodes.* The guy's pumping up, cock rising steadily,
then this panicked expression crosses his face and he's scrabbling at his
crotch crying, "Sweet lord!," clawing at his balls and I'm wondering is
he looking for the pump in there, an off switch or something and his
cock's just *monstrous,* I mean red and swollen and Wayne's staring
down with an expression of sick dread then this *pop,* not loud exactly
but percussive like a pistol fired under wet sand and his cock—Christ,
it *expands* and Wayne's on the floor screaming bloody blue murder
and there's this noise like when you blow up a balloon and let go except
it's coming out his *pisshole.*

"Man down!" hollers the director. "Jesus, man *down!*"

Wayne's rolling around with his eyes rolled to the white, mouth
open but no sound coming out. Two minutes ago you're cracking one-
liners and detailing the plight of East Timorian shepherds; now your
penis is curled like a fishhook and blood's leaking out. It's a funny old
world.

The fluff girl kneels beside him. "Call an ambulance!"

I snatch Kitten's cellphone—she's actually *talking* to someone as all
this goes on—and dial 911. "God, man—are you okay?"

The way Wayne's glaring at me—*yeesh,* if looks could kill. Of course,
I've now found myself on hand at both his penile catastrophes. Could
he think I'm somehow responsible—a voodoo doll? A miniature wax
penis stuck full of pins?

When the ambulance arrives the attendants look puzzled, then, after a quick examination of the set and its players, get the idea. They heap cold packs onto Wayne's groin, strap him to a stretcher.

"Look on the bright side," the cameraman says. "Makes for a dilly of a lawsuit."

The fluff girl insists on accompanying Wayne to Emerge. I offer to tag along but the attendants won't allow it. As the ambulance pulls away she's staring wistfully out the rear window—who's she looking at, if not me?

My name is Sam. I'm a sex addict.

Welcome, Sam.

Thanks, everyone. So, what have I lost—that's tonight's question? Everything, I guess you could say. Job, family, security. The normal life. Not that you'd find it surprising. The support of such systems requires some sort of a . . . *veneer*. A veneer of normalcy, right? Repeat the mantra: Happy family, happy family, happy family. But the secret was doing more damage than the truth. Told my friends, my boss, my co-workers. Full disclosure; the unobstructed facts. Four hundred sexual partners over the past five years, nameless and unremembered. What else can you do? Beg forgiveness. Grovel. I was demoted but kept my job. My wife and I entered counseling. Inside I realized it couldn't last. The person I was desperately trying to be—the husband, the family man—was a fraud. I'm incapable of that change. It's not that I'm weak or spineless: the process of transformation demands you become a *whole new person*. I'm not saying change is impossible or that you or you or you won't make a clean break; I sincerely wish it for everyone. But it's simply not in me and I won't apologize. Right now it's about learning how to cope, make my way as best I can without hurting anyone. That's why I do dirty movies: no commitment, no lies, no guilt, nobody gets harmed. Love and responsibility do not factor into the equation. Like those signs you see in national parks: *Take only pictures, Leave only footprints.*

EARLY EVENING by the time we wrap. A crease of sunset lines the horizon, interrupted by the high rises of downtown: buildings I'd once travailed in, wheeled and dealed, buildings I'm now effectively banned from. Bright pinprick spires burn in foothills beyond the city, derricks venting sour gas, flames frayed by a south-blowing wind. A pale crescent moon sits like a toy boat in the gap between two dark mountains. Across the road an empty lot hosts abandoned shopping carts, old tires and castoff watertanks rusting in the nettles, a junked car with garbage bags taped over its shattered windows. A huge scavenger bird with a raw boiledlooking head perches on the car's spavined roof: a buzzard, though to the best of my knowledge such creatures are not native to this part of the planet.

Take a Phillips screwdriver from my glovebox, remove the license plates from Wayne's Buick Century, screw them to my Chevy Cavalier. A dastardly deed but Wayne won't catch any heat: got to figure he'll be laid up for a week. Ironclad alibi. Settle behind the driver's seat, doff my trousers, arrange a layer of Kleenex between my spread legs. Rev the engine, pull out of the lot.

This old Western movie crystalized it for me. Black-and-white, which generally I cannot abide. There was this cowboy and his horse, a Palomino. The cowboy doted on his mount—fed it apples and sugar cubes, brushed cockleburrs out of its mane with a wire comb. Towards the end they're on a wagontrain trekking through the Sierra Madres when the horse is slowed by a split hoof. The cowboy jams his pistol to the horse's eye and pulls the trigger. *Why'd you do that?* the wagonmaster says. *Thought you loved that horse.* The cowboy spits and says, *Nossir, but I do love horses. That is to say, I cherish the nature of horses— hardworking, reliable, docile. But* alla them *is that way. Can always find y'self another horse.*

Now, it's conceivable to cherish the *nature* of women, right? They're beauteous and supple, willing to accommodate the man who knows how best to stroke them. But that's on a whole: you might feel nothing on a case-by-case basis. *A sex addict's relationship is with sex, not people.* For addicts it's crucial to break any object of desire down to its base elements: tits, asses, lips, hips, cocks, cunts. The process of dehumanization is like a *moral imperative.*

I dearly cherish the nature of woman.

Cruise streets in the gray twilight, past decrepit rowhouses and shops with gated windows, homeless persons and lean winter dogs hunched at the mouths of go-nowhere alleys, a boarded church cloaked in the shadowy overhang of tall maples, through cones of lamplight casting their blue nocturnal glow, on over a swing bridge spanning the blighted waterway. Mammoth construction cranes stand still as obelisks against the quilted sky. Difficult to shift gears with my pants rucked around my ankles.

Scan the sidewalks but fail to spot a suitable candidate: here a bagwoman, less human being than agglomeration of filthy ponchos trundling a shopping cart with a frozen wheel; there a chick resembling an ambulatory fire hydrant, bull-dyke by the looks of it, hieing a chowdog on a length of heavy-gauge chain. Real slim pickens. Call my pal Danny Dewson; we co-sponsor one another through Sexaholics Anonymous.

"Hey. It's me."

"It's you," says Danny. "How goes the battle?"

"Gotta be honest with you . . ."

"Honesty's the best policy, Samuel."

"So here it is: I'm cruising. Right now, cruising."

Silence on his end. "Are you, like, past the point of no return? Stripped and ready to rip?"

"Cocked, locked, ready to rock," I tell him.

"Oh, man." Danny clicks his tongue. "Oh, man-oh-man. Where are you?"

"Corner of Bonita and Empress. Between the peepshow theater and that rub-n-tug joint."

"Sure, near that bar with the room in the back." Danny's fingers drum the wall beside his phone. "Listen, you probably ought to just let yourself go on this one, okay? You can fall off the wagon every once in a while, so long as you hop right back on."

This is exactly what I need to hear. "Everyone cheats a little now and then, isn't that so? I mean, it's not the end of the world, is it?"

"Of course it isn't," says Danny. "Of course not."

"And hey, not like I'm committing a mortal sin or anything."

"Well I'm really not up on all that, Samuel."

"But you think it's okay? This one time?"

"I'm gonna greenlight you, here."

"Bless you, Danny. Bless your heart."

"Stay strong, brother."

The moment I hang up she's walking down the sidewalk—we're talking *on cue*. Materializing out of thinned mist like an apparition, some vaporous half-glimpsed angel, not entirely real. Wearing tight blue jeans ripped at the knee and some sort of fur-trimmed coat. Too far to make out exact features but that's not critical.

Pull alongside her, roll down the window. "Excuse me? Excuse me, miss?"

She checks up and hunkers down on the sidewalk. At this unforgiving range her face does not hold up: teeth shot to hell and this oddshaped growth, a *carbuncle* I guess you'd say, growing out the side of her nose.

"Lookin' for somethin'?"

"Well, you see, I'm sort of lost." It's a struggle to keep my body still, I'm masturbating so furiously. "Do you know the way . . . to the highway?"

She leans forward, resting her wrists on the windowframe. "That what you're really after, cowboy?" Her eyelashes are clotted with pebbles of mascara and the furred collar of her coat smells like a drowned rodent—Christ, she's not making this easy. "Let's not pussy-foot around."

"Well, maybe we can work something out. If you could just . . . lean a bit closer . . ."

She thrusts her head through the window, face inches from mine as though this forced intimacy might somehow seal the deal and I surrender control with a moan, splashing the steering column as a feeling of absolute peace floods through me, ecstatic well-being of a sort experienced only by Buddhist monks and perhaps tiny infants—*enlightening* peace. I'm beset by these heartwarming thoughts towards this woman, dreams of a good life and healthy future, happiness and love but this mini-satori is fleeting and I'm overtaken by a sense of futility known to few on earth, brought about by the inconceivability of these dreams for this woman or myself or anyone really, staring through the windshield at a night sky spread with stars, the conceivable worlds couched in those dark sprawling spaces between the light host to alien lifeforms possessed of such nobility and decency as I will never even fathom, and this sense of incalculable desolation draws about me, I who remain so trivial, insignificant, tenuous, and specklike.

Among addicts, the act of release frequently triggers feelings of ecstatic euphoria followed by periods of profound remorse, paranoia, and depression.

"Well," the woman assumes in a pragmatic tone, "you're not a cop." Her eyes narrow to feline slits. "Really should charge you for that."

"Thanks." Slip the gearshift into first, work a crumpled twenty out of my pants pocket, toss it on the street and pull away. "Sorry about that."

"Hey, anytime . . ."

There are over three trillion nerve receptors in the human body. Fully seventy percent are located in erogenous zones. This is what you're fighting. Every minute of every day. It's an uphill battle.

My name is Sam. I'm a sex addict.

Welcome, Sam.

Lisa, my wife—ex-wife—and a six-year-old daughter. Met Lisa out East; went to the same college. She had this air like she'd swallow you up and blow you out in bubbles if you strayed too near. I mistook the effect she had on me for love. She could've had anyone. She chose me. I don't love her, but I do *care*. If she were penniless, I'd support her. If she were dying I'd give her blood, a kidney, whatever. Her mistake was believing it was within her power to change me. My daughter, Ellie . . . I love her deeply. Looking at her I realize I'm still capable of that. When I think of her in idle moments, it's always some mundane task—brushing her teeth, tying her shoelaces. Silly, day-to-day stuff. I never allow a week to pass without seeing her, calling her, letting it be known how much I care for her. I used to wish the love I felt for Ellie were somehow able to . . . *stretch*, encompass more people. But it can't, and that's okay. I once believed my heart was somehow impoverished, but now I recognize it's no larger or smaller than the next man's—my heart is simply different.

THE HOUSE IS AN awkward duplex with swayback roof, mullioned windows, a single-car drive. We used to live in a big house on the ritzy side of town back in the Days of Yore, epoch of the Steady Job and Frequent Promotions and Healthy Bank Balance, also the Weekly Business Junkets and Late Nights at the Office and Dirty Dark Secret.

Lisa answers my knock in a housecoat, hair wet from a bath. In the darkened family room the TV casts flickering luminescence on the walls.

"Hi there. Hoping maybe I could see Ellie for a bit."

"What are you doing here?" My ex-wife crosses her arms over her breasts. "You get Ellie every other weekend, you know that."

"Well, yeah, of course, but I was hoping maybe a few minutes . . ."

"You stink, Sam."

"Do I?" It's genuinely upsetting I failed to recognize this. "Oh, jeez. Could I wash up?"

Lisa purses her lips. I consider the single worst act I'd committed during our marriage. Probably the time I returned from a whorefilled weekender, gave her the clap, then halfheartedly argued she'd given it to me. Yeah, that's the one.

"I wouldn't ask but I'd really like to see her. Half an hour and I'm out of your hair."

She steps aside. "Okay, for a little while. But clean yourself up."

In the bathroom scrub at a stiff patch on my jeans then dry off with Lisa's Conair. Unzip my fly and push the blowdryer into my pants until the heat becomes unbearable and switch it off. In the medicine cabinet find a bottle of perfume and give myself a liberal spritzing.

My daughter sits on the sofa watching a kids' show. In the room's muted light she appears somehow insubstantial, a flickering hologram of herself.

"Hey, kiddo."

When she smiles I see she's lost a baby tooth, upper left canine. "What're you doing here, Daddy?"

"Seemed like the thing to do at the time." Sitting beside her, the cushions compress in such a way that Ellie's body tilts into the soft crook beneath my arm. "What ya watching?"

"The animals talk." Her body shrugs against mine. "They live on a river. The guinea pig's funny."

On the TV screen a mob of industrious creatures—hamster and mouse, turtle, a duck—cavort in a drift of popcorn. The guinea pig's voice reminds me of Jimmy Cagney: *Youuu doity raaat! Youuu kilt my bruddah!*

"You smell like a girl," Ellie says and for a moment I'm filled with a dark and predatory dread until I realize she's talking about the perfume.

"Spilled some of your mom's smelly stuff on me. You don't like it?"
Another shrug. "Okay, I guess."

I settle my arm around her shoulders and squeeze. Feel the movement of her chest and try to match my breathing to hers, our lungs expanding and contracting in perfect synchronism until I fear hyperventilation. We watch in silence; I'm content to simply be near her, drinking in her warmth and calm as a camel does water for a long desert trek.

Lisa comes in with a tray of milk and Fig Newtons. When she hands me a glass our fingers brush and she pulls away as though burned. Ellie finishes one cookie and reaches for another.

"No more," Lisa says. "Too much sugar before bed gives you nightmares."

"I like nightmares," my daughter reasons.

The program reaches a heartwarming conclusion, riverbank denizens throwing a party. The hamster's zipping around in a miniature motorboat, shiny black eyes bugged out in abject terror. Sitting with my daughter's head rested in the crook of my arm watching the rodents frolic all I can think about is female genitalia, a sheer wall of vaginas like some sort of cliff, furred pussies, shaved pussies, blond and black and ginger-haired pussies, and I'm standing at the base of this forbidding structure stark naked wearing a pair of blue-tinted skigoggles and then I'm climbing, grabbing onto labias for purchase, searching for sure handholds in the loosest ones, jamming toes and fingers into moist slits wishing for crampons or a bag of talc. Ellie shifts against me and I'm trying desperately to think of anything else, marigolds–seahorses–merry-go-rounds but nothing works, I'm stuck with the pussy-cliff, scaling its slick alien veneer like an intrepid mountaineer tackling the perilous northface ascent on K2.

What kind of person harbors such thoughts? I mean, really, what *kind*?

Addicts are frequently beset by bitter self-loathing in response to erotic fantasies over which they exercise no control.

"Well," I say, "about time I hit the dusty trail."

"Stay," Ellie says. "*VeggieTales* is on next."

Giant talking cucumbers. Yes, just what the doctor ordered.

"I'd better not, honey. Got to get to my meeting. See you this weekend, 'kay?"

Give her a big hug. Crumbs on her top lip, breath smelling of milk. Lisa follows me to the door.

"You're good with her, Sam. I'll give you that."

"What can I say. I love her, I guess."

She smiles in a way that makes me sad. Perhaps intuiting something, she asks, "What are you thinking about?"

Scaling a cliff of vaginas.

"Oh, nothing."

"C'mon."

"Well, okay . . . I was reading this book the other day. There was a character who . . . well, he screwed watermelons. At night he'd cross into his neighbor's melon patch, cut a hole in a watermelon with a penknife. The Moonlight Melonhumper. And I guess I got to thinking it wouldn't be so bad, would it—balling melons? Grow some in your backyard or just, y'know, keep a few on hand. Whenever the urge struck you could slip away and take care of business. What I'm saying is, it'd be possible to lead a normal life." A brittle laugh. "Humping watermelons. Jesus Christ, Lisa, wish that did it for me."

"Is this something they advocate in your group?" she says. "This kind of . . . frankness?"

"Sort of. I'm not certain."

"Well," she says stiffly, "goodnight. I'll drop Ellie off Saturday morning."

It's 8:45, giving me fifteen minutes to make group. Crossing the front lawn the cellphone buzzes in my pocket. It's set to vibrate on account of the pleasant shiver it sends up my balls; I've been known to slip it into my underwear and ring myself from payphones.

"It's me," says Danny Dewson.

"It's you. How goes the battle?"

"Well, Samuel, I'm gonna level with you—"

"Always pays to keep things on the level."

"Right. So here it is: I'd really like to stick my . . . *rod* . . . through this . . . *hole*."

"Where are you?"

"That peepjoint off Sanford. Between the second-run porno house and the strip club."

"Right, a ways up from that place with the secret knock." Unlock the car, settle into the driver's seat. "I think it's okay this time. As setbacks go, it's minor."

"That's true, isn't it? Not like I'm some kind of devil for wanting to do this, right?"

"Of course you aren't, Danny. Of course not."

"And hey, there might not even be a girl on the other side, right?"

"Sure," I tell him. "Who *knows* what's on the other side."

"So you think it's okay? This one time?"

"Gonna give you a free pass."

"Hey, that's super, Samuel. Just super."

"Stay strong, brother."

My name is Sam. I'm a sex addict.

Welcome, Sam.

Nothing extraordinary. My dad was a freelance contractor; Mom a teacher. I can only imagine their sex life was normal, maybe a bit dreary. It wasn't like Dad would've beat me had he caught me masturbating; Mom didn't breastfeed me till I was fifteen. Hope I don't come off like an asshole, but I think the Deep Dark Secret rationale is a crock. Don't know why I am the way I am, but it doesn't boil down to one particular event or deep emotional scar. No one's to blame. Some people are built differently, that's all. The problem I see is when we stand against our nature, try to be someone else. The whole martyr mentality makes me sick—the nobility of suffering, to hurt is to love, all that bullshit. Somewhere along the line it's become fashionable to be who we're not, squeeze ourselves into cubbyholes, spend our lives in abject misery to disguise our basic selves. Hey, if your nature is selfless, giving, honorable, open, unabashed, forthright, decent or whatever great —wonderful, bully for you. We're not all built the same way. Doesn't mean we're degenerates.

SEXUAL COMPULSIVES ANONYMOUS gathers Tuesdays in the Louis Riel Library's conference room. I frequent several groups: Sex and Love Addicts Anonymous (Wednesdays in St. Peter's parish hall), Sexaholics Anonymous (Friday afternoons at the Live and Let Live Club), Renewal from Sexual Addiction (Sundays at First United Methodist). Every once in a while I'll spot a familiar face on the street or in a restaurant and realize I am part of a secret cabal, a roaming addictive underclass inhabiting this, and every, city.

Nod to the librarian, eyeing her legs, weave my way through periodical racks and paperback carousels and newspapers threaded on wooden dowels to the conference room. The room's decorated in a Thanksgiving motif: shellacked gourds and ears of maize, pie-plate turkeys with tissue paper tails. Table scattered with crayons and children's books left over from the Reading Buddies program: *Digging Dinosaurs*, *Where the Wild Things Are*, *Sadako and the Thousand Paper Cranes*. The usual suspects: Baney Jones and Owen and Bette. Seat myself beside the fourth person, who I'm surprised and more than a little excited to find here.

"Hey," I say to her. "How's Wayne? He going to be alright?"

"He'll be fine," the fluff girl answers in a whisper. "Ambulance guy shot him up with morphine so he wasn't feeling much of anything. I'm going to check back on him tomorrow."

"Great news. Maybe I can come with?"

She shakes her head. "Don't think so. Wayne isn't your biggest fan."

"Why—what did I ever do?"

She cocks an eyebrow.

"Are you insinuating I *wished* Wayne's dick would break? That I somehow *rigged* his penis to . . . *explode?*"

"Mr. Chancey." The addiction counselor is maybe twenty-five, recent college grad with this high breathy voice like he's got a penny-whistle lodged in his throat. "If you could save your conversation for the break. Bette, please go on."

Bette O'Neal is a large woman: I believe the euphemism is *Rubenesque*. She's a dual addict: an overeating nymphomaniac.

"Well, okay, so I'm at my son's high-school basketball game, alright? He's seventeen, a senior. The ah, the point guard or something. So they're playing and it's a close game, five points, around that and I'm in the stands which're crowded but not too crowded—not a playoff game or like that." Bette sips from the liter bottle of Pepsi she's brought. "There's this guy on the other team—*boy* I guess I should say, but who knows? What's the legal age nowadays?"

"Eighteen." The counselor's name is Joey. "The legal age of adulthood is eighteen."

"Oh. So okay, maybe *legally* he's a boy, but a lot of it depends on maturity and . . . like, upbringing, doesn't it? Not like I actually *did* anything—I mean, physically speaking. Anyway this guy, boy, whatever, he's tall and lanky and . . . lithe I guess, which I know'd usually describe a girl or like a cat but this boy, he really was *lithe*. I'm sitting there in the stands totally *consumed*—can't take my eyes off him, the way he's running up and down the court. The gym's got that smell you get when guys or gals or people, just any old people, find themselves in close contact. Like sweat but I don't know, *deeper* than sweat. Know what I'm talking about?" A few people nod and Bette says, "So I'm staring at this boy and touching myself. Brought a coat on account of the chill and lay it across my lap. Strange but I didn't imagine fucking, his hands on my tits, my mouth on his cock, any of that—just watching him run and jump was enough. The biggest turn-on was his youth: he was young and clean and probably disease-free, which, even though I wasn't fucking him I still felt was, y'know, a *plus*. Orgasmed five times real quick, like a string of firecrackers going off." Sip of Pepsi. "That was my week."

"Thank you for sharing, Bette." Joey'd winced every time Bette used the words *fucking, cock,* or *tits.* "While it's commendable you didn't act on your urges, you must admit such behavior is not socially acceptable."

"Ah, lay offa her," says Baney Jones, a sixty-three-year-old serial exposer.

"I'm not *on* her, Mr. Jones," says Joey. "We're trying to create a supportive and honest environment. That means critical appraisal of—"

"Ah, your mother wears army boots!" Baney slaps a liverspotted palm on the table. "You're giving her the gears! Reading her the riot act!"

"It's okay," Bette says. "I'm a big girl, sweetheart; I can handle it."

Baney tugs a plaid-pattern porkpie hat tight over his skull, shooting Joey a glare from beneath the brim. Joey elects to move on. "Owen, is there anything you'd like to contribute this evening?"

Early twenties with a mop of sandy-reddish hair, Owen Traylor's a tragic case: working a summer construction crew on break from college, he was struck—*impaled,* is I guess the right word—with a length of rebar: it split the left side of his head behind the eye and the pressure forced a portion of Owen's brain through the wound. Thankfully the hospital's got a crack neurosurgeon on staff who was able to patch Owen's skull in a grueling ten-hour procedure. He's damn lucky but something's still jakey in his noggin, a few mis-crossed wires because Owen's blowing his load *all the time*. We're talking fifteen, twenty times a day. Riding the bus, say, or shopping for deli meats at the supermarket and blammo—Mount Vesuvius. Poor bastard wears adult diapers but the constant convulsions have turned his abs hard as granite. Owen's not an addict so much as a neurological anomaly but attends regular as clockwork, and if it helps him, hey, that's peachy.

"Went on a date the other night," he says. "Sandy, that girl in my sociology class."

"You handed round a photo, didn't you?" I ask. "Black hair, right? Green eyes?"

"Ah, yes," Baney says. "Fine bosoms, as I recall. High and proud."

"Right," Owen goes on, "that's her. She's real smart and talented— she painted my portrait, did I tell you?—and, I don't know, just, oh you could say, *great*. She's got a fantastic laugh and I'm not a funny guy, not naturally, but still I'm always trying to say something to crack her up."

Joey taps his ballpoint pen on a legal pad. "Is Sandy aware of your physical handicap?"

"It never came up." Owen shifts uncomfortably in his orange cafeteria-style chair. "We been seeing each other for a month or so, on and off. The other night things got, well . . . *intimate*."

Everybody leans forward perceptibly. Baney says, "*Now* we're down to brass tacks."

"Mr. Jones," Joey warns, "please."

"So we're at her place watching TV on the couch. One thing led to another and . . ."

"How did one thing lead to another?" Bette wants to know. "Don't skimp, Owen. Don't give us the ole *dot-dot-dot* to skip past the good bits."

"This is a sexual recovery group," says Joey, "not *Penthouse Forum*."

"Well," Owen says, "we kissed and then, uh, then some other stuff. But when we were, y'know, *expressing our love,* I found I couldn't . . . it was impossible to . . . like, *do* what it is I *do* twenty times a day."

"Are you saying," Joey asks, "you had difficulty reaching orgasm?"

"The guy who loses it in elevators and movie theaters and in *church,* for god's sake, this same guy can't deliver when it counts." Owen shakes his head. "Can you believe the irony?"

"So what?" says Bette. "Did she get off?"

"Think so."

"So what's the big deal?"

"I thought," Owen says, confused, "it was important to a woman that she satisfy her man. Like, a confirmation of her skills or something."

The fluff girl snorts. "Don't care so long as I get mine."

"Ain't that the truth," Bette says.

Owen looks relieved. "So you think it's okay?"

"Did you go down on her ungrudgingly?" I ask.

Owen nods, blushing.

"Then she's yours for life, m'man."

Joey claps his hands and clicks his teeth. "Moving on! We have a new member with us tonight. Please introduce yourself and tell us a little."

The fluff girl speaks. "Hello, everyone. My name is Beatrice. I'm a sex addict."

"Welcome, Beatrice," we say in unison.

"Just moved to town. I grew up out East but lived all over. I've got reflex sympathetic dystrophy syndrome; basically, I'm hypersensitve to touch." As if to prove this, she traces a finger along the tabletop and down the cool steel leg. "Feel everything at a heightened sensory level. When I get with a man I'm not looking for love or even sex . . . I'm after friction. Men are just . . . *vehicles,* is the medical term. Friction delivery systems."

"I see," says Joey. "What do you hope to accomplish here?"

"I'm hoping to get laid."

"I like your moxie!" Baney says.

"Beatrice," Joey says dourly, "that is not at all the *ob-jec-tive.*"

"Wait a minute, now, hear me out." She holds her hands out in the manner of a policewoman halting traffic. "We're all addicts here, aren't we? And the nature of addiction—all addiction—is to hurt. Hurt yourself, hurt others. Am I lying?" Beatrice's fingertips running over the weave of her jeans. "And our addiction's different, isn't it? Alcoholics don't romance the bottle or apologize after drinking it; drug addicts don't worry about knocking their needles up. Our addiction is intensely personal so we need to be responsible. Find that fine line between our needs and the existence of others." Beatrice's fingertips moving along the table's gum-pebbled underside. "It's okay for a viper to lie down with another viper—all vipers know their nature, right? Problem's when the viper lies down with the lamb."

"Is that how you see yourself—a viper?" Joey asks. "And the others here—vipers?"

Beatrice shrugs. "I've been to a lot of these groups. One thing never changes: people don't admit their flaws. Always the rough childhood, the cold wife, stress at the office, the same old piss and moan. Nobody ever stands up and says, Listen: the awful things I do come from a defect in my basic human character, deeply rooted and inseparable from who I am. Never *once* will you hear that. So, yeah, guess I'm a viper. Safe childhood, caring parents, but still. Don't wish to harm anyone but your urges get the better of you sometimes, right? That's why I'm here: searching for someone like me. Only responsible way to go."

ME AND OWEN hunker outside the library doors, smoking. Wind whips through the courtyard, litter scuttling along the cement walls. Two empty vodka bottles wrapped in a white plastic bag perch atop an overflowing garbage can. Beatrice steps out in a leather windjammer.

"Could I bum one of those?" she asks me.

"Don't know—do vipers share cigarettes? I mean, in the wild?"

Standing there in the courtyard's thin yellow light I am again struck by just how beautiful this girl is: Helen of Troy, sack-the-city-torch-the-ramparts kind of beauty, the sort that leaves a wake of helpless shattered men, man-*husks* eaten out and hollow and left to contemplate the paths they'd taken to claim that beauty in those foolish moments when they felt themselves capable.

"You're pretty hot, Beatrice." Hand over my pack. "I'm saying, for a reptile and all."

"Aw, ain't you a peach."

"Just got to town, huh? Where from?"

"Couple different places."

"So, why here?"

"Weary of the same places, the same faces." She hums the opening bars of a song which, though familiar, I cannot place. "Moving on down the line."

"You found a job pretty quick."

"Yeah, well, I worked for a director out West. He made a call."

"You do good work."

Beatrice's long pale fingers caress the cigarette. "Nothing much to it, is there? Not talking rocket science. And how long you been in the biz?"

"Few years. Started after my divorce."

"Like it?"

"What's not to like?" Then: "Anyway, it's safer. Everyone knows the stakes. Everything's laid out in black and white."

She fixes me with a look, the import of which I cannot fully discern. "You think?"

"Yeah I think. Sure I think." A shrug. "Or something. Just my dime-store philosophy."

Baney and Bette return from a coffee shop up the street. We stand in the frosty courtyard, knit shoulder-to-shoulder against the wind. The doors open and shut, mothers and children, college students, old women with satchels of paperback romances passing into and out of the library's welcoming light. I wonder whether any of them pause to consider us huddled here—what might they think? Beatrice's hand moves against Owen's side, a catlike pawing gesture and Owen smiles feebly, looking away. When she laughs the plume of her cinnamoned breath wafts past my face.

Bette shivers. "Got to get out of this cold. Fat chick with thin blood—I'm an enigma."

Baney says, "I could use an enema myself."

The others head inside. Beatrice grinds the butt under her boot heel. "You had a wife?"

"For six years. Swell job, big house."

"Kids?"

"A daughter."

"Love them?"

"Don't know I ever loved my wife. Thought I did for a while. Love my kid to death. Wish there was more room in my heart."

"So, you've hurt people."

"A lot. Haven't you?"

She nods. "Tell them up front who you are and what you're about but still, everyone thinks they're the one's gonna change you. I'm not gonna change. Sure it's miserable sometimes, but it's constant misery trying to be something else. This is . . ."

"The lesser of two evils."

"Yeah." A smile. "Like that."

Down the street two faceless women scream at one another in an unknown dialect until the rumble of a watertruck drowns their voices and through a gap in the courtyard's security fence, a lengthwise slit between decaying housing projects, the moon shivers on the hammered face of the canal.

"What are you thinking?" Beatrice says.

"Don't know." I shrug, suddenly despondent. "Fucking."

"Fucking who?"

"You. Bette. The librarian. Anyone. The 'who' isn't critical—that's the problem."

"Head back inside?"

"I'm easy."

She grasps my jacket sleeve. "Come on."

My name is Sam. I'm a sex addict.

Welcome, Sam.

Do I believe love is possible? Sure. I mean, of course. Certainly as an abstract concept: immaculate love, God's love, whatever.

And you see it every day: a couple passes you on the street and you get this sense that, man, those two really love one another.

The way I feel about Ellie—that's love, isn't it? I don't really know. It's possible, in that *anything* is possible. But I've made a vow to be totally honest about who and what I am; how many rational women would want to involve themselves? Still, I'm an optimist. The understandings and intensities would be different, but there's always that chance. It may not be love by anyone else's definition, but whatever works, right? So, yeah, I think it's possible. Absolutely I do.

STREETS AGLITTER WITH FROST. My eyes follow the yellow dash-dash-dash of the median strip running along dark tarmac. Roads forlorn and devoid of human life. A sickle moon cuts through a bank of threadbare nightclouds to grace shops and offices with a washed-out pall. Beatrice in the passenger's seat fiddling with the radio; every so often she says, "Left here," or "Hang a right at the doughnut shop," leading me through the city grid to an unknown destination. A lamplit billboard towers over the shipyard, the tanned blow-dried visage of some local paragon I should recognize but do not staring down benevolently and I'm left feeling ashamed, the way you feel bumping into a person who knows your name when you cannot recall theirs—ashamed for being unable to remember what it was you'd shared together, however meaningless. Beatrice twists the radio knob and the speakers come to life: a string of garbled syllables devolving into a scream or howl, low and mournful and ongoing, the signal weak, crackling with static and I imagine a ghostly deep-space transmission, some doomed cosmonaut shrieking into an intercom, fishbowl helmet starred with cracks and the steamwhistle screech of pressure hammering his eardrums, a dead man's voice traveling through the empty vacuum of space like a message in a bottle washed ashore on the far reaches of the AM dial.

"Weird," Beatrice says.

"Yeah. Freaky."

"Swing left up at the side street. Almost there."

The building is a deteriorating five-story in the packing district. Faded scorchmarks rise, black tongues against the gouged masonry, scars of some long-ago fire. The intermittent signature of a strobelight flashes across high casement windows. Adjacent parking lot uncommonly packed: BMWs and Mercedes rowed alongside pickups and rusteaten Dodges.

"What is this place? Looks like it should be foreclosed."

"Most likely is," Beatrice says. "This is a one-night-only sort of deal."

Trail her to a green-painted door set between a pair of dumpsters. Her knock is answered by a black man with the rough dimensions of a Morgan Fort gun safe. Beatrice whispers something: apparently the safeword because the man steps aside, allowing just enough room for her to squeeze past. The man is easing his planetary bulk back into position when Beatrice informs him I'm her escort; with a world-weary sigh, he steps aside once more.

"What's the story?" Follow Beatrice up a narrow staircase. Walls graffiti tagged, holes punched through plaster to reveal corroded wires and sodden pink insulation. "Are you leading me into ruin? A snuff film crew? Black-market organ farmers?"

"It's a traveling showcase." She stops, glancing back at me. "Different cities, different participants. I've done it a few times." A wink. "Surprised you don't know about it."

At the top of the stairs a girl with a pierced bellybutton stands beneath a sign reading *Coat Check*. Doff my jacket and hand it over. She taps the sign with a hot-pink fingernail and I notice it in fact reads *Clothes Check*. Beatrice and I strip, turning our shirts and jeans over to the girl. She hands me a claim chit but I've no idea where to stow it. Beatrice slips hers under her tongue. I do the same.

The girl positions herself before a sliding metal door. Spraypainted on the door in pink letters matching her fingernails is the word GOMORRAH.

"Pitter-patter," says Beatrice, hopping lightly from one foot to the other, "let's get at 'er."

The first thing to hit you is heat: this warmth closing around your body. The second is smell: sweet and bitter at once, the scent of bodies in close contact. The way Bette said: like sweat, but deeper. As my eyes adjust I see we're in a warehouse. Steel girders row the vaulted ceiling; small creatures, birds or mice, scuttle across rusted A-beams. Strobelights set on telescopic tripods throw kinetic pinwheels on the walls and floor. A DJ spins trance music on a pair of portable turntables.

"Welcome to the viper's nest." Beatrice's lips next to my ear. "Or is it viper's pit?"

She leads me to the clutch of naked bodies. Thirty or forty people sprawled on swaths of thick velvet. Arms and elbows, calves and knees; occasionally a head will crest, person taking a deep breath as though they've been trapped under water. No one speaks; no voices at all save the sporadic sigh or shuddering exhale. Beatrice is gone, her body twined with a dozen others, amalgamate now, indistinguishable.

Wade in slowly, as a swimmer immerses himself in cold surf. A hand reaches out, grabbing my calf, pulling me down; I'll go willingly enough. Bodies press against mine, limbs hairy and smooth; breasts pushed into my face, a perfumed arm wrapped round my head urging me on; someone's hand, cold and brittle as a talon, clamps onto my leg and delivers a nasty pinch; my lips on thighs and asses, in vaginas and mouths, the crooks of elbows, the undersides of knees; a hard cock crosses the underside of my throat, across lips, gone. A faceless stranger with a dextrous tongue, woman or man I cannot tell, performs fellatio with such wanton bravado I'm left on the verge of weeping. Men and women congregate in well-dressed groups in the warehouse shadows, silent observers. A man stands amidst the teeming surge and emits a high gibbering shriek like some jungle creature and in the plated moonlight falling through the casement windows he appears skinless and I'm thinking about my daughter standing in a green summer field, Ellie's smiling face lit by the July sun. Peace and serenity I'm thinking. Wayne's mangled cock I'm thinking. Pussy tits ass I'm thinking. Admit the existence of a higher power I'm thinking. Flesh I'm thinking. Flesh flesh flesh flesh . . .

At some point I am standing. Beatrice faces me: hands on hips, head cocked to one side, appraising me with a slight smile. She's kicking off this unearthly glow as though her veins rush with phosphorus. Her beauty is crushing and I feel minuscule. Bodies seethe at our feet but in this moment nothing else exists. She brushes at a lock of hair fallen over her eyes and it's ludicrous but I'm envisioning the country cottage and white picket fence, the words SAMUEL + BEATRICE encircled by a heart carved into the wood of an oak tree, all these childish insupportable fantasies. And sure, I've run through this script enough times to know how it turns out but before the guilt and recrimination there exists a state of grace—right . . . *now*—a fleeting span of limitless possibility and hope.

"Think it always has to be this way?"

"The viper bites," Beatrice says. "Can't help itself."

She reaches for me and I pull away. Can't bear to touch her. My body's electric; tongues of blue static lick and pop off the ends of my fingertips. You're gonna exit this world with regrets; it's an absolute given. And okay, I've been burned before—haven't we all? All I'm saying is, there's that chance, right? A longshot, fine, a million to one. Still—it's there.

Maybe. That's as far as I'll go. Just *maybe*.

LIFE IN THE FLESH

TWO MONTHS SHY of my twenty-eighth birthday I beat Johnny "The Kid" Starkley to death in Tupelo, Mississippi. A stiff right to the solar plexus sent him to the ropes, gulping for breath. I clubbed him a pair of overhand rights and a left just below the ear, where the jawbone connects. Brutal punches fired straight from the hip, subtle as a train wreck. The Kid—an apt nickname: sandalwood-smooth skin and clear green eyes, so light on his feet he seemed to float above the canvas—held his left arm out, that arm trembling, red glove bobbing like a buoy on a riotous sea. The Kid's mouthpiece stuck to his teeth, the insides of his lips filmed with white lather, holding his left arm out as if to say, *Please, I've had enough,* but his body too stubborn, too disciplined, to buckle to the will of his mind. I hit him until his eyes glazed over like a dying animal's, until that arm fell away, until the ref signaled for the bell.

Starkley's death hit me hard, but at the time I wouldn't cop to it.

The fight was sanctioned. Marquis of Queensbury rules—I'd done nothing *wrong!*

Started juicing on Ten High bourbon and Schlitz. Went from training five hours a day at Top Rank gym to closing out the Cyclone, the gin joint next door. I shed a sickening amount of weight, skin green and jaundiced, booze destroying the mitochondria in my guts. For a few months I didn't know sobriety: sixpack for breakfast and a flask of mescal on the nightstand, brushing my teeth with apricot brandy. I saw Starkley trapped in the ropes, mouthpiece dangling out, blood filling his eyes. And, in this persistent vision, I knew he was dying, knew I was killing him, but I didn't stop. The worst part was watching Starkley grow younger with each blow—now thirty, now twenty-five, now eighteen, finally my fists slamming into this kid, this skinny-legged, sparrow-chested child hung up between the red and blue ropes.

My manager, Moe Kundler, tried to salvage me. Stumbling back from the Cyclone I'd find AA schedules taped to the door, twelve-step brochures in the mailbox. Then Moe dropped by to find me zonked on the kitchen floor, shards of shattered bottle punched into my palms, pants filled with piss and shit. He filled a pot with water and dumped it on me. I came to sputtering, fists balled and ready to rumble. He slapped me hard and said, "Clean yourself up. I'm making the phone call."

No way could I hack detox or the nuthatch, glimpsing Starkley in those Rorschach inkblots. I gathered up the money I'd ratholed and hightailed it. Thailand was my choice on account of an uninhibited sexual politic and stern non-extradition policy. I arrived in Bangkok twenty-five years ago, and have never left.

Yesterday Moe wired he's sending a hardass. Time and distance have patched our old beefs. The kid arrives on the 9:40 Air Canada out of Vancouver. Late twenties, baggy board-shorts and a garish

Hawaiian shirt, eyes dark behind oversize wraparounds. Workably broad across the shoulders and chest, bull necked, narrow waisted, and small hipped. Underslung jaw and a nose busted eastward. His acute-angled brow would give any cutman the screaming meemies: heavy layers of scar tissue rim the curves beneath each eyebrow, and I know if he tastes the long knuckle the sharp ridges of bone will tear those scars to shit.

"Roberto Curry?"

"Welcome to Bangkok."

He wipes at sweat beading his forehead. "Country this hot all over?"

"Hotter," I say. "Airport's air conditioned."

Don Muang airport sits atop an arrow-headed promontory, the darkened city stretching out below. To the west: the meandering strip of Ko Sanh Road contoured in stark neon. To the southwest: Patpong a bright starfish, lit tendrils spreading from its central hub. Humidity's intense: like breathing through boiled wool.

The taxi traces a route down Thanburi Road, skirting the Chao Phraya river. Oil-slicked waters dotted with coastal trawlers and derelict coalships, floating communes of tin-roofed sampans. Turn onto Ko Sanh Road. Almost every building converted into guest houses, every corner has long distance telephone booths with cooling AC, cafés screen *Rush Hour II* and *Brokedown Palace* on video. Sidewalks strung with stalls trafficking in pewter flasks and teak elephants, knock-off Reeboks, bootleg DVDs. A train of Thai women dressed in garishly colored sarongs walk down the side of the road toting various bundles on their heads: firewood, guavas in large porcelain bowls, sacks of kola nuts, stalks of plantains, volcano fish, deep-fried crickets in beaten tin pans. Their husbands walk in front of them carrying not a damn thing.

The kid pockets his sunglasses stepping from the cab. His eyelids are networked with scar tissue. So he's a bleeder.

Blood ruins some fighters. Since the deaths of Johnny Owen and the Korean Duk Koo-Kim, both of whom were blood-blinded from cut eyelids, paranoid refs and ring docs are kiboshing fights at the first sight of red. Some fighters got tough bodies but weak skin—breathe on them hard, they cut. There's nothing a guy can do about it, any more than a guy with a glass jaw can help being brittle. But if that claret keeps flowing—a bad cut above the eye, say, deep and wide and vein-severed, your fighter's heart pounding merry old hell—forget it, the fight's over even if your boy's not really hurt. But Muay Thai matches are rarely stopped on blood, and trainers are permitted certain measures—double-strength adrenaline chloride, ferric acid—to handle the most vicious cuts. Of course, all the ferric acid in the world isn't going to help with the detached retinas and crushed metacarpals, but that's come what may.

We sit in a curry stall with a dining area open to the street. Green curry for me, red for the kid, plus pints of fresh guava juice. The kid axes the juice in favor of beer.

"So," I say, "what's your record?"

"Twenty-two and three. Two losses on stoppages."

"Blood?"

"Blood."

"Lose the other on a KO?"

"TKO my third fight. Soft count to some unranked tomato can."

"Get cocky?"

"Little, maybe."

"I can see that happening."

The kid digs a chicken claw out of his mouth, grimaces, spits on the sidewalk.

"Ever watch Muay Thai?"

"Sure," he says. "Bunch of skinny guys winging at each other."

Consider telling him about the fight I watched last week, the one where the loser left with hemorrhage-thinned blood pissing from his ears. Consider telling him how Muay Thai fighters strengthen their shins by pounding sand-filled bottles against them, the sound a wooden *huk-huk-huk*, until their skin's tough as boot leather. Instead I say, "How much weight you carrying?"

"Started middleweight, climbed to light heavy."

"Any vision problems, those scars?"

"Peepers are twenty-twenty."

"What kind of condition you in? Don't bother bluffing, I'll find out."

The kid rolls up a shirt sleeve and flexes his biceps muscle, pumping the brachial vein. "And body fat less than ten percent. I'm gripped, stripped, ready to rip."

"You're sweating like a bastard."

"It's the food."

"It's the heat. You'll get used to it. Training camp's outside Chang Rai, two hours south. You'll be doing road work on jungle paths. Sweat off ten pounds the first week—your cardio'll skyrocket."

The kid finishes his beer, signals for another. "Want one, coach?"

"I don't drink."

The kid nods as if he'd anticipated this weakness in me. A local woman stops beside our table. Three-quarters legs, decent tits but hatchet faced, wearing a miniskirt exposing the lower crescents of her can. Red silk skirt and scarf, gold hoop earrings, white frosted lipstick.

"Herro, boys." To the kid: "Wha jo' name?"

"I'm Tony, hon."

She rests a hand on the kid's shoulder. "Oh, ju a stron' boy, hah?" She sits on his lap. "Ju a strong, han'some big boy, hah?"

"Watch yourself with that one."

The woman pouts at me. "Ju be quiet." She wiggles her ass into the kid's crotch. "Ju lie me, Tony?"

"Sure," the kid says. "Me love you long time." His hands knead her thighs. "Thass ni'," the woman says.

I grab the fluttering brocade of the scarf and yank it off. "Adam's apple is a dead giveaway. Now your top-quality ladymen get it surgically shaved down so's you can barely tell. But this one here—well, she's no top quality."

The aggrieved he-she snatches the scarf back. "Ju a horr'ble ma'," she says to me. The kid shoves him-her away, beating his palms on his shorts as if they're coated in flaming oil. Got a look on his face like he ate a handful of rat turds he mistook for Raisinettes.

"Ah, Christ, no!"

"I'd be inclined to blame it on the beer goggles, kid, but you've only had two. Got to watch out for the scarfed ones."

"Why didn't you tell me before I let it bounce on my dick?"

"You didn't seem keen on listening."

"You're a real peach, coach."

An open-top Isuzu drops us off at the training camp shortly after 5 a.m. It is a fine, clean morning, the kind of morning that, as they say, makes you wish you got up early more often. A scarred dirt path leads through the trees alongside a fast-running stream. The path leads into a large dusty clearing fringed by tall palms and dotted with bamboo-and-tin Nissen huts. At the far end is a long-house. The sounds of men in training are audible through its open doors.

"Stow your gear," pointing to one of the huts, "and throw on your road kit."

The kid comes out wearing gray jogging shorts, cross-trainers, a hooded sweatshirt. I retrieve a rusted bicycle leaning against the long-house and say, "Let's go."

The kid starts out in a stiff-legged trot but, warming up, his strides lengthen, smooth out. The path is too narrow for us to navigate side by side so I fall in behind him on the bike. Soon a skunk-tail of perspiration darkens the back of his sweatshirt as we follow the path east into the rising sun.

"Give me that shirt." The kid doffs the sweatshirt and drops it in the bike basket. At the 3K mark his chest is heaving, arms hanging from his shoulders. When the path finally rounds back to the camp he sprawls out in the dirt, sucking wind.

"Piss-poor conditioning, kid, but you got heart. Wind we can work on."

"Fucking country. Can't breathe the air."

"You'll get used to it. Get home, your lungs will feel double-size. Throw on your training kit and meet me in the gym."

"Fucking country."

He comes into the long-house wearing a pair of shorts and his ring shoes, a towel draped around his neck. The tattooed face of a dog, blue and grinning, covers one shoulder. On the other shoulder a crude imp or demon brandishes a pitchfork beneath the words *Li'l Devil*.

The long-house is equipped same as any North American boxing gym. In the ring, Khru Sucharit, the legendary Muay Thai trainer, instructs Bua, a rising fighter. Bua's eighteen and has been fighting since infancy. His body is perfectly shredded, each muscle group distinct and visible beneath rough, dusky skin. He's drilling textbook hook-kicks into punch-mitts snugged over Sucharit's hands, transferring his weight to rock the old trainer back a step with every blow.

"Know what I see?" The kid points at Bua. "Skin and bones and arms and legs."

"Then you're only looking, not seeing."

"Let me know when it's time to snatch the pebble out of your hand, sensei."

Set him off on the speed bag. Hand speed's decent, and the kid's got power: the leather bag snaps hard against its ringed-iron mooring.

He starts mugging, beating a rat-a-tat rhythm on the bag, bringing one knee up and then the other, two pistons in perfect cadence, lisping, "I'm the champeen, the greatest, the king."

"Pop the bag."

The kid stalks over to a tan-colored heavy bag suspended from a crossbeam and tees off. He rips a half-dozen body shots into the two-hundred-pound bag, causing it to buck on its chain. He sways at the hip in bob-and-weave style, shouldering the bag, throwing hooks and short right hands, falling in line with its rhythm before stabbing four left hooks and following with an overhand right.

The kid forces a yawn. "Okay, boss?"

"It'll do."

After a half-hour of rope skipping and shadowboxing I tell him to stop. Brew a pot of oolong tea and pour cups with lemon. We sit on the ring apron and watch Bua run footwork combos in front of a full-length mirror.

"Moe only sends me hardasses," I say. "What's your story?"

The kid wipes his face with the towel. "Moe thinks I'm a hardass?"

"You wouldn't be here otherwise."

"Well," the kid says, "could be he thinks I don't train hard enough."

"Why would he think that?"

"No idea. I win fights."

"People think you win a fight in the ring," I tell him. "But you know where the big fights are won? Right here. In the gym and on the road."

"I know, I know." The kid's heard it all before.

"Moe says you brawl like a Viking. Says you fight with your dick instead of your head."

"He told you all this already, what you asking me for?"

I nod over at Bua. "That kid's won over a hundred fights. Started when he was thirteen, fights twenty times a year. He's not a crowd favorite—he's too smart for that. He doesn't go out to make a show. He goes out to get a job done and absorb the least punishment possible."

Bua's feet flicker across a vulcanized floormat, body circling to the left, feinting, ducking away, back to the right. The squeak of his shoes on the rubber and his breath coming into an even rhythm. The boy's so quick he could fight in a rainstorm and stay bone dry.

"I don't know where Sucharit found him," I say. "Probably on the streets. He doesn't fight for glory. He fights for a paycheck. The boy trains hard and fights for the money because he knows, even at his age, it could all be taken away."

The kids sips tea, wipes his neck. "I don't fight for the money, exactly."

"Then why?"

"I got anger."

"At who?"

"Don't know. Everyone. Not all the time, you know, but sometimes . . . it builds up. This need to hurt, even if it means getting hurt myself. And that's okay, the way I see it, because everybody stepping into the ring knows the stakes. You accept those stakes, you accept the risk— maybe you're going to get fed. No, it's not the money. Fighting, it's like, *therapy*."

Fighters like him are the hardest to train. On one hand, he's managed to inhibit his natural instinct for survival: he understands he will get hurt, bleed, and doesn't run from it. Stifling the survival instinct—to continue fighting after being knocked down, to wipe blood out of your eyes and wade back into the fray—is a trick some fighters never master. On the other hand, his anger is dangerous: it's useless, not to mention foolish, carrying too much fury into the ring. Successful fighters learn to see their opponent as a faceless thing whose weight roughly equals their own, something vertical that must be laid horizontal. But successful fighters respect their opponents: respect their power, their stamina, their will to win. Lack of respect leads to a cocky fighter blinking up into the ring lights as the ref counts him out.

Bua completes his drills and he and Sucharit walk over to the ring. The boy's body is slick with clean, healthy sweat. He smiles. The bottom front teeth have been punched out.

"Your fighter's looking good," I tell Sucharit.

Sucharit frowns: trainers never admit the worth of their fighters, especially in their presence. "He slow," Sucharit says. "Like he eat lead." He slaps the boy's toned stomach. "Hah? You eat lead, hah?"

"I thought he looked slow," says the kid.

"When's his next fight?"

"Two wee'," Sucharit says to me. "Ban'kok."

"Tell him I say he's a weak puncher," the kid says. "Girl arms."

"He understands fine," I say. "Quit making an ass."

"Tell him I got two friends I want him to meet," the kid goes on, grinning. He holds up his right fist: "Bread." He holds up the left: "And Butter."

Sucharit puts his arm around Bua's shoulder and guides him away. "Goo' luck training."

"Why'd you say that?" I say after they've gone. "Something in the air?"

"Air's fine."

THE MOST WIDESPREAD misunderstanding surrounding the death of Johnny "The Kid" Starkley is that I killed him purposefully and maliciously because he questioned my sexuality, called me *faggot* at the weigh-in. But it had nothing to do with vengeance: I'd been trained to fight until my opponent dropped or the bell went or the ref stepped in. The bell didn't ring and Ruby Goldstein didn't step in and Starkley refused to go down so I did as I'd been trained. I didn't want to kill him. My only intent was to defeat Starkley completely, leave him lying there on the canvas. I wanted him dead *to me,* dead as a threat. Nietzsche wrote, *Every man unfolds himself in fighting.* Well, that night in Tupelo, in a ring smelling of sweat and spit and cold adrenaline, I unfolded.

My popularity skyrocketed after the fight. Everyone wanted to ink the "sanctioned murderer" to their card. But by then all the fight had drained out of me. I stared at myself in every passing mirror: nose busted so many times over it couldn't rightly be called a nose any-more, right eyelid hanging half-masted due to nerve damage, cheeks so scarred they looked like carnival taffy. I understood the same thing could've happened to Starkley in a bar or back alley for no payday at all. It's just, that way it wouldn't have been on my conscience. I started juicing hard, haunting the Cyclone with the washups and fight bums, stripping down everything I'd built.

My second week in Bangkok I drifted into the Royal Jubilee Palace arena, drawn by crowd buzz and frantic ocarina music, to see my first Muay Thai match. I was mesmerized by the pre-fight rituals, the lean tan bodies, the thrill of men in close combat. The *pureness* of it all. I knew then I'd never escape. Marvin Hagler spoke for all of us when he said, *If they cut my head open, they would find one big boxing glove. That's all I am. I live it.* You can't outrun this life. Sounds weak, I know, but it's the truth. Whether it was bred into me or whether I'd always harbored the bent has long ceased to matter.

This morning I'm watching the kid shadowbox in a wash of hot, dusty sunlight pouring through slats in the long-house roof. The kid's a bully: in sparring sessions he'll remind you of a vintage Foreman, shoving his partner around before tagging him with jabs, then a hook to the body, finishing with an uppercut flush on the knockout button. Shots so hard the other guy's eyes fog despite the headgear and over-size gloves.

Problem is he can't leave his fight in the ring. Type of alpha male who'll walk into a bar and knock the bouncer's teeth out to prove he's the toughest bastard in the place. He's got serious heart: takes sparring shots so wicked they'd cripple a bear, eats up mile after mile of road like he's starving, punches a dent in the heavy bag. But there's too much of the animal in him.

The kid's sharing the ring with Bua, shadowboxing. Sucharit's in with his boy, pointing up, down, to the side, Bua following Sucharit's pointing finger with a punch, kick, or sweep. The kid's working the opposite corner, wearing ring shoes, red trunks, and wrist wraps, flashing hard combos—double-up jab, feint, hook, hook, straight right, bob back, jab-jab, uppercut—exhaling short puffs with each punch.

"Hey, Boo-boo." He's taken to calling Bua "Boo-boo" or "Boo-hoo." Sometimes he'll creep up behind the boy and holler, *Boo!* "Why don't we go a few rounds?"

"Take a break," I call from the apron. "Don't have to be a prick every day of your life."

The kid dances across the canvas, peppering jabs at Bua's back, coming within inches.

"Come on, Boo-boo, show me what you got."

I say, "Back off. *Now.*"

"What's the matter?" Dancing on the balls of his feet, shuffle-step, pittypat jab-jab-jab. "Is Boo-hoo scared? Boo-hoo a puss?"

Bua doesn't reply, eyes never leaving Sucharit's moving finger. I slide between the ropes and push the kid away. "The hell's your problem?"

He brushes past me and shoves Bua between the shoulder blades. "Let's do this. Let's do it *up*, baby."

I hook my fingers inside his trunks but, as he's a legit light heavyweight and I never fought past welterweight, I can't haul him away. "Keep this up and you're on the next steamer home."

Bua turns to face the kid. Nothing in his eyes speaks to anger—still smiling that gap-toothed smile—but his arms hang loose and ready, thigh muscles fluttering.

Sucharit steps between the fighters. "You wan' fie my boy, hah?" he says to the kid.

"What was your first clue?"

"He fie you, okay, okay. Baa no' here."

"Why not?"

"Who watch? Who *pay?*"

"Over here it isn't about who's swinging the biggest dick," I say. "The boy's not gonna fight, nobody's paying."

"Cool." The kid's throwing jabs that stop inches from Bua's unblinking eyes. "Make a few bucks kicking his ass."

"When were you thinking?" I say to Sucharit.

"Nex' wee. Ban'kok."

"We're gonna get it *on,* 'cause we don't get a–*long!*"

The kid raises his arms and dances in the center of the ring like Ali.

A PRIZEFIGHTER IS A FREAK. He's got maybe ten years in the roughest business in the world, a business ruled by a strict hierarchy: winners and losers. He's not a paperhanger, a lawyer, a beancounter. He doesn't put on his galoshes, grab his briefcase, catch the trolley, the same daily grind for thirty, forty years. He gives it all now, or never.

Moe Kundler told me that. Moe was a fighter himself, cruiserweight, never held a belt or scored a big payday, a crippling right hook but a weak chin led to three consecutive canvas naps and eliminated him as a contender. The ring turns fighters into freaks by aging them prematurely: that twenty-two-square-foot expanse is a time warp.

The Royal Jubilee Palace arena's prep area is located in the building's bowels. Me and the kid in a shoebox-sized room, low ceiling, pipes rattling overhead. Six or seven shattered chicken coops in one corner, floor crusted with plaster flakes and dead roaches. Above, the dim babble of the crowd cheering the semi-main.

I called Moe and asked was it okay the kid fought Bua. I said, "The only way this kid's going to progress is to take a rude beating. Only way he'll learn." Moe was wary when he heard it was a mixed-discipline bout, Muay Thai versus boxing. "Will his record be affected?" I said no, since the fight wasn't sanctioned. Moe said, "So the other guy can kick?" I said yes, and headbutt, and elbow. Moe said, "Could the kid get hurt bad?" I said, "A chance. What he needs." Moe said, "Then go for it."

The kid's perched on the edge of a prep table. I'm taping his hands. Wrap adhesive gauze around his wrists to protect the eight interlocking carpal bones, across the meat of his palms, his thumbs, fingers to the second knuckle. The wrap's got to be tight, but not too tight: a fighter with blue hands is bound to break bones and not even know it.

"Flex your fingers," I say. The kid curls his hands into tight fists. "Okay. Now the gloves."

I help him on with the gloves—ten ouncers instead of WBA-sanctioned sixteens—and tape them to his wrists. The kid hops off the table, high-stepping, rolling his shoulders loose. Then the sweat comes and he's shadowboxing, holding his gloves up, juking his head to the right of them, to the left, cracking hard jabs from the guard.

"Stand back in your stance," I tell him. "Otherwise he'll kick your thighs into ground chuck."

The kid's dressed Tyson chic: black trunks, black ring shoes, no socks or robe, just a black terry-cloth towel with a hole cut in the center to pass his head.

"Remember your elbows," I say. "Legal in Muay Thai. Headbutts, too." Like every pro fighter, the kid's been taught how to fire elbows and butt heads. Only this time he doesn't have to worry about the DQ.

"For the thousands in attendance, and the millions watching around the globe," he intones, slamming his fists together. "Let's get ready to rum–*buuuuul!*"

The kid looks pale under the hot ring lights, skin glowing against his dark trappings. Bua's wearing green trunks fringed with gold, yellow shoes, the traditional Muay Thai headpiece of braided hemp. Although the kid outweighs him by twenty pounds, Bua's arms and legs are long, rangy, his hands huge—*tack hammers,* Moe'd call them. Judging by the stare-down it seems probable one or both will leave the ring on a stretcher.

The Royal Jubilee Palace—nicknamed "The Pail"—is a three-tiered arena: its levels, instead of extending outwards, are stacked one atop another, giving fighters the impression they're fighting at the bottom of a bucket. Ten-foot-high chicken-wire barriers ring each tier to discourage fans from hurling Singha beer bottles and other trash into the ring. The place is rife with chattering voices, like a forest full of monkeys.

I water the kid, grease his cheeks and brows, remove his mouthpiece from the ice bucket and slip it into his mouth. Sucharit is massaging Bua's shoulders and whispering in his ear. The ref, a tiny balding Thai in a sweat-stained zebra get-up, calls the fighters together, makes them touch gloves. The ocarina quartet place their lips to their wide-bellied instruments. The bell rings.

The kid rushes out, gloves held over his mouth, elbows out, head down, looking at Bua out of the tops of his eyes. Bua circles out of his corner to the left, standing high on his toes, hands low, wrists rotating. They meet near the ropes, Bua stabbing two quick jabs.

The kid takes the first one high on the forehead. The second one he slips over his left shoulder and, stepping in with his right foot, brings his left hand up in a tight arc. The uppercut catches Bua on the throat under his chin. His legs jelly a little. Kid goes low, knees flexing, fires another submarine shot. Bua grabs him, pulling their bodies flush. The kid's gloves are high on Bua's chest but he can't push him off. He brings them up into the boy's face, rubbing the laces across the cheeks and eyes. He's looking to the ref for a break.

"No breaks!" I holler over the crowd noise. "Fight out! Fight *out!*"

Bua brings his left knee up into the kid's side beneath the kidney. The kid lets out a grunt. Bua knees him again, putting all his weight into it. The crowd rises to a quick roar. In close, the kid shoves against Bua's face, gets some separation and brings an elbow up into the gap, shearing it across Bua's chin. Bua reels into the ring's center.

The kid comes on, stance switched to southpaw. He jabs once, twice, again, setting up the overhand right. Bua's still groggy, stepping to his left with the left foot and throwing a left hook over the jab. The kid turns under it and, as he takes the punch above the ear, fires his own right return into the short rib, carrying his weight onto the left foot, ripping another hard right into the same spot.

Bua fires a side-kick into the kid's thigh, the sound of meat on meat a bullwhip's crack. The kid staggers but Bua overbalances, too much weight on the back right leg, and the kid recovers to step in low, rising with a powerful right cross.

The boy goes down. He goes down on his butt and the back of his head hits the canvas.

The crowd becomes very still. The ocarina musicians, whose playing had risen to a fever pitch, cease. The boy rises to his knees, gloves pressed to the canvas. Shaking his head violently, shaking the cobwebs off.

". . . t'ree . . . fo' . . ."

He reaches for the rope and pulls himself up. Still shaking his head. The kid's standing in a neutral corner, mugging to the crowd. "It's all over but the crying, coach," he says. But it's not. If he knew anything about anything, he'd know that.

". . . si' . . . seben . . ."

The kid can crack; that cross would've crumbled most fighters in his weight class. But Bua's up by the ref's count of eight. His face is red and glove burned.

The kid charges out of the neutral corner throwing a right-lead haymaker aimed to take the boy's head off. Bua ducks low and brings a sharp left up into the stomach. The kid caves at the waist and grunts in pain. Swiveling to the outside, Bua vises his arms on either side of his opponent's head and, thrusting forward, drives first the left knee, then the right, into his gut.

The kid's tough. But the boy *lives* tough. The kid fights to remind himself he's still breathing. The boy thinks about enduring, surviving. They haven't grown up the same: one has never gone hungry, never watched a man die or fought for his life. All this matters in the ring.

Bua steps back and, as the kid straightens himself, attacks the right leg with three roundhouse kicks. The kid gasps. His knee buckles. Bua feints another roundhouse and, when the kid drops his guard hand, sets both feet and leaps, right arm cocked like a pistol's hammer, fist smashing into the kid's face, opening a deep gash over the eyebrow.

Not knowing what to do, the kid bear hugs Bua, tying his arms up. Blood's pissing out the side of his face and he's spat the mouthpiece. They butt foreheads and, like magic, the other eyebrow opens up. The kid's squirting blood all over the damn place.

They break the clinch. The kid must be seeing black from the blood: he's wiping at both eyes to clear his vision. He's seeing only the outline of Bua, dark arms and legs. He's backing away, staring around at nothing. Now he moves forward, but uncertainly, no strength or conviction in his movements. It happens very quickly.

Planting his left foot on the canvas, Bua pivots forward on his heel. His right arm uncurls like a whip as it comes around, arcing up, a textbook spinning backfist that hits the kid on the left temple and he goes down, eyes closing. He hits the canvas open mouthed—I hear his teeth click shut. The referee kneels, counting, the kid's body lying there, writhing, trying to get up, unwilling to surrender consciousness.

"... ni' ... ten ..."

At one minute and thirty-six seconds of the first round the ref signals for the bell.

The boy walks to his corner and sits on a stool. Sucharit removes the mouthpiece and waters him, smoothing an iced metal swell-stop over the mouse on his forehead. The crowd chants his name but he doesn't acknowledge them. His face shows no emotion. He looks so old.

Helped by two attendants, I get the kid down to the training room. Crack a smelling salt and wave it under his nose. Five seconds later he regains consciousness and sits up on the table. He stares at me with cloudy blue eyes, face sweat-stung and flecked with dried blood. I flush the cuts with hydrogen peroxide, press split meat together and apply butterfly bandages, make him swallow a few vitamin K tablets.

"You came out like a house on fire," I tell him. "Had him dazed but went for too much too soon."

I cut the tape and pull the gloves off. The kid looks at his hands, at his legs, hands again, up at the ceiling. As if he has no idea where he is, as if he cannot quite believe he's here. Quiet in the room, just the kid breathing. His eyes are unfocused and he raises his left hand in front of them, that hand shivering a little.

"You'll rebound from this," I say. "Maybe the best thing for you."

The kid shoots me a look. Feral, that look. *Cold.* He lowers his hand to his lap. His index finger points at the floor. I look where his finger is pointing, thinking I should call the doctor because nothing's on the floor, the floor is bare—

I never see the dummy right uppercut that catches me flush on the knockout button. My legs crumple beneath me and blackness pours in.

I COME TO sometime later. The kid's gone. So is my wallet and training kit. Don't know how long I've been out because my watch is missing. Upper lip split to the septum and jaw not working properly. I don't know what to do. A lot of blood. Pick myself up and walk out to the street.

The city is alien in a way I've never known. Small torn-eared dogs fight over knots of gristle flung behind a curry stall. A figure passes whose sex I cannot determine; he or she smells of cocoa and lemon-grass and something else and carries a small colored parcel. I lean on the wall of the Royal Jubilee Palace beneath a scrawl of graffiti, a battle cry or revolutionary slogan. Blood soaks the front of my shirt and something is broken on the left side of my face. From an open window of a nearby tenement I hear the last notes of "Let It Be," by the Beatles. A shoeless boy stares at the old *farang* shivering in the heat.

The night Starkley died, a writer of no small eminence eulogized: *As he took those eighteen punches something happened to everyone within psychic range of the event. Some part of his death reached out to us. One felt it hover in the air. He was still standing in the ropes, trapped as he had been before, he gave some little half-smile of regret, as if he were saying, "I didn't know I was going to die just yet," and then, his head leaning back but still erect, his death came to breathe around him.* None of this happened, though somehow I wish it had. Nothing reached out. I saw no smile, regretful or otherwise. Starkley's mouth was slack, mouthpiece hanging halfway out, saliva-stuck to his upper teeth on the left side, eyes rolled back in his skull. I didn't feel his death breathe around me. He died twelve hours later at Cedars-Sinai of a ruptured blood vessel in his brain. He'd been clear-headed, chatty I'm told, until, complaining of a little headache, he lay down and never got back up. It was an accident. It happens.

But, those last few punches—I knew something very ugly was happening. I was fully aware. I see it all so clearly now. His left arm held out, trembling, *Please*. My arm swiveling smoothly in its shoulder socket, the pressure of his face against my gloves, the shockwave coursing through the bones of my fingers, wrist, arm—I *feel* it to this day. And it felt good. Christ, it sickens me to say, but there it is. *Good*. Where did it come from, that urge? Starkley never did a thing wrong. He was a fair fighter. A professional. In the training room afterwards, Moe said, "Those uppercuts you landed near the end . . . the Kid couldn't protect himself." I said, "I know." Moe said quietly, "I think you mighta killed him." I said, "I think so." The fact Starkley stayed up gave me all the license I needed. Why wouldn't he just *go down*? It seemed so strange. Why did he give me the chance? I never wanted that chance.

To my left the mouth of a narrow alleyway runs between the arena and the burnt-out building beside it. The brick of the building is charred and words are scratched into the blackness. In the alleyway's dim light men ring an oildrum fire, passing a bottle of Mekong. They are laughing and I wonder at what. One reaches across the flames to touch another's laughing face.

THE APPRENTICE'S GUIDE
TO MODERN MAGIC

Fakery #17: *The Reanimate Fly*. An illusion popular among street-corner mountebanks. Purporting to spot an expired fly on the sidewalk, the "magician" will bet a passerby he can resurrect it from the dead. The cunning fraud sets the fly in his palm and launches into his "act," muttering garbled incantations, rolling his eyeballs about, frantically flailing his limbs, other shameless hocus-pokery. After a minute the fly stirs, then buzzes away. The deceit: the fly is placed in a freezer, whereupon the cold stuns it into a state of suspended animation. The crafty sod then drops it on the sidewalk and waits on a rube. The heat of his palm raises the fly's internal temperature, bringing it miraculously back to life . . . or so it seems.

—*Excerpted from* Hexers, Charlatans,
and Miracle Mongers: An Exposé,
by Herbert T. Mallory, Sr.

[1]

St. Catharines, Ontario. June 5, 1979.

The Knights of Pythias's seventy-third annual Spring Salubritorial was in full swing. Banquet tables littered with congealed puddles of gravy and beer bottles smirched with greasy fingerprints were pushed to the corners of Lodge #57, chairs lined in haphazard rows facing a raised stage. The membership of the fraternal brotherhood milled about in aimless, meandering circles, bumping into one another, shaking hands, exchanging trivialities about children, jobs, the day's unseasonable fogginess.

Norman Greene, newly elected Grand Chancellor of the Judea chapter, stepped hesitantly onstage. Beneath a fall of snowdrop-white hair, a pair of tri-focal glasses sectioned Norman's eyes into dull brown strata resembling ever-darkening layers of soil.

"Welcome, brothers."

No one noticed Norm until Hal Stapleton spied him out of the corner of his eye and said, "Sit down—show's about to start!"

The group seated themselves with giddy expectation. With their faces shadowed by the stage footlights, they resembled choirboys at midnight mass.

"Welcome, brothers," Norman, used to repeating himself, repeated. "Without further ado, may I introduce Herbert T. Mallory—*The Inimitable Cartouche!*"

A man materialized through folds of thick velour draped behind the stage. A tall figure, suave as a toreador, with strong sharp features and eyes of flawless emerald. His hair was sculpted back with mint brilliantine, face clean-shaven save a neatly clipped Mephistophelian Vandyke. Wearing a spotless tuxedo with a frilled olive cummerbund and polished wingtips, he opened an alligator-skin valise to remove a flattened black disk, transforming it into a top hat with a brisk flick of his wrist.

Sid Tuttle, more than slightly tipsy after four Harvey Wallbangers, elbowed Hal's ample gut. "What's this four-eyed fool spent our dues on?"

Two smaller figures stepped through the velour, a boy and a girl. The girl, a few years older than the boy, crossed the stage in lurching, timid steps on account of the high-heeled shoes she wore. Her taffeta dress was held up with thin spaghetti straps, arms clad in evening gloves that sagged off the ends of her fingertips like withered petals. The boy was a miniature version of the magician. Tall for his age and thin, he wore an immaculately tailored tuxedo with matching olive cummerbund; his chin sported a grease pencil Vandyke. The boy strutted about in a manner that might have been seen as arrogant had he been a few years older—instead, it was merely precocious.

"What's all this?" Hal was baffled: last year, when he'd been in charge of the evening's entertainment, he'd lined up an exotic dancer, Countess Carissa, who'd bounded out of a packing crate wearing tasseled pasties and a smile. She got those tassels spinning like the propellers on a Piper Cub, twirling them one way then back the other to upbeat boom-boom music. "Where's the . . . the *real* entertainment?"

"You know what they say, Hal," Norman mumbled. "Variety . . . ah—spice of life."

The truth was slightly less philosophic: Norman's wife—who'd gotten wind of the Countess's performance last year—warned her husband that if she discovered an entertainer of similar ilk had taken the stage this year, well, he'd better buy a warm toque, because it'd be damn cold sleeping in the garage.

"This is a . . . travesty!" Sid Tuttle moaned. Sid's wife, a stern Pythian sister, only let him out of the house once or twice a month—frittering away a precious evening on magic was sacrilege! He shook his bald head, which, being shiny and oddly planed, reflected thin blades of light like the facets of a poorly cut gemstone.

"Come on, Norm!" Hal's fingers compassed his nipples in concentric spirals, a reminder of the Countess's considerable charms. "This is a man's night, not some kid's birthday party!"

"Yeah," a shrill voice piped up. "I want magic, I'll watch *Circus of the Stars!*"

"Oh, my god!" someone else sputtered. "What next—a pinata? *Loot bags?*"

"He'd better be pulling a naked lady out of that hat!"

"Where's my coat? I'm going home."

"Silence!"

The magician's assistants had erected various stage props: two chairs with a wooden board balanced on the backrests, three black cubes stacked one atop the other, a scarred tea chest.

"I find your communal behavior boorish," the magician said. "How would you like it were I to arrive at your places of business and ridicule you?" He glared down upon the grumbling throng. "I am the Inimitable Cartouche. For the next hour I will dazzle you with feats that will cause you to disbelieve your own eyes."

The Pythians settled into a state of muttering acquiescence. A few even looked mildly excited. A voice from the back asked, "What sorta tricks d'you do?"

"I'll perform no *tricks!* You will be privy to acts of mystery and wonderment that will shake the very bedrock of your belief concerning the laws of nature and the spiritual realm."

"Oh, that'll do nicely," the voice chirped.

While the Pythians had been bickering, Cartouche surreptitiously dipped his left hand into his pocket, rubbing palm and fingers with potassium permanganate. Next, he'd slipped his right hand behind his back, where the boy sprayed it with a fine mist of glycerine from a bottle stashed in his cummerbund. When the magician clapped his hands the chemicals reacted, sending twin cones of red fire up from his palms, while smaller tongues leapt off his fingertips.

"That was quite something," Sid Tuttle had to admit.

"Smoke and mirrors," Hal muttered.

Cartouche led the Pythians through a host of standard illusions with the air of a man scattering pearls before swine. First he levitated the boy, passing a Hula Hoop over and above his hovering form—the magician's hand obscured the hoop's missing portion, allowing it to pass around the black iron pipe supporting the board. Next he performed the Zigzag: after locking the girl in an upright rectangular box with sections cut out for her face, hands, and one foot, he thrust wedges of sheet metal through. Dislodging the middle section, he made it appear as though the girl were divided in three. Though bent nearly double to effect the illusion, the girl managed to smile gamely, wriggling her toes and waving the red silk hankies clutched in each hand.

"I received this trunk," Cartouche said, indicating the tea chest, "from an aged swami in the hills of Vindhya." This was a considerable embellishment: he'd traded it for a crystal radio and a ship in a bottle at the Stittsville flea market. "Anyone who enters is transported to a dimension the polar opposite of our own, where black is white and hot is cold, where men toil under the light of the full moon and sleep in daylight, where—"

"Where droning windbags turn into big-breasted strippers," Hal offered.

"*Silence!*" Cartouche knelt before the young boy. "Well, son?" he whispered. "Think you can do this without screwing it up?"

The boy nodded without meeting his father's eyes. Cartouche said, "Alright, then. I hand you the reins."

The girl pried the heavy lid up. Cartouche stepped inside. She clasped the lock as the boy waved his hands over the chest.

"Floobidaa, floobidoo, floobidee . . ." the boy chanted.

Standing off to one side, the girl watched and listened carefully. She did not hear the soft *snik* as the hidden latch disengaged, or the gathering outrush of air as the chest's false back levered down. She'd watched her brother practice this escape for hours in the basement, amidst the mismatched golf clubs and dusty boxes piled to the ceiling beams, and, no matter how many times he'd repeated it, he'd never effected a silent escape: the latch would snap audibly or not open at all, his head would bump the lid or the false back would strike the floor with a clatter. She didn't see the magician scurry from the box, or the drapes part even slightly in the wake of his passage.

The boy tapped the lid three times. "I banish you from this realm!" He nodded to the girl. "My assistant will now open the lid."

She shot her brother a compressed acid look. She lifted the lid. The chest was empty.

"Feast your eyes—banished!"

"Whoop-de-doo," said Hal.

"Now to bring him back," the boy said, brandishing the wand like a fencer's épée, tapping the chest three times. "Return to this realm!"

When the girl opened the lid, the chest was still empty.

Hal said, "Good riddance."

The boy glanced at his sister. Desperation twisted his features. "Jess, what . . . ?"

The girl slipped behind the curtain. The magician was nowhere in sight. She pushed through a swinging door into a narrow kitchen, hating the clumsy sound of her heels on the glossy tiles, turning the knob on another door opening into a narrow alleyway.

"Daddy?" she called softly. "Dad?"

The girl stood in a jaundiced sheet of light cast through the kitchen door, the warm humid night pressed to her temples. Her father's Datsun was still parked at the mouth of the alley, next to four or five garbage cans dragged to the curb for tomorrow's pickup. She smelled, or believed she could, a lingering trace of his cologne, a foreign brand ordered in ten-bottle lots.

He was gone. He'd . . . *vanished.*

A great clamor suddenly arose from the Pythian congregation. She hurried back through the kitchen and slipped through the curtains.

"Oh, no . . ."

Her brother had decided to push on with the show. He'd dipped into his father's valise, where the chemicals and powders for his most stirring illusions were hidden. He'd obviously attempted the Fiery Orb, in which a golden fireball explodes from the magician's chest towards the audience, extinguishing mere feet from their faces. Expertly performed, the trick is thrilling: spectators experience a brief but disconcerting heat as a fireball rocketed at their eyes. But the novice conjurer hadn't anticipated the remarkable combustive properties of powdered camphor.

The front row was in sad shape. The men's faces were flushed red, clear globes of perspiration clinging to their foreheads. Leaning slightly forward in anticipation, Sid Tuttle had gotten the very worst of it: a merry golden flame danced atop the flat peak of his tarboosh.

The boy looked at his sister, at the red-faced Pythians, back at his sister.

Then he started to cry.

Fakery #59: *Mister Sweet Touch.* The practitioner approaches his target in a busy thoroughfare, ideally an open-air café. Before the rube sugars her tea, the swindler snatches the cup, inquiring how many teaspoons she favors. Depending on the answer, he dips his fingers into the cup for up to five seconds (only if very sweet tea is desired). Urged to drink, she will discover that, magically, the tea is sweet. If further demonstration is required, the rascal may touch anything—the table, the parasol, his target's skin—all rendered

cloyingly sweet. The deceit: the magician washes his hands in a
strong solution of saccharine, a compound five hundred times
sweeter than sugar. For hours afterwards, anything he touches
turns sweet. Beware the counterfeit Midas with his sugary touch.
Beware! Beware!

[2]

St. Catharines, Ontario. October 29, 2003.

Jessica Heinz glanced at the red digital numbers on the bedside clock.
Quarter past eleven. Late morning sunlight streamed through the
limbs of the backyard maple, broomstick-thin rays falling across the
sheets. Squirrels dashed along the buttonbush hedge, cheeks fat with
nuts. Her neighbor was burning leaves and the acrid smell wafted
through an open window.

There seemed very little reason to get up. The time one rose was
largely dictated by the amount of work one intended to complete
during a given day. The fewer duties each day presented, the less reason
one had to rise at a reasonable hour. Six months ago Jess would've
risen at six-thirty to watch the line in the sky separating night from
day peel away in ever-lightening shades, a thin band of gold touching
the rooftops and telephone poles. Now she'd become accustomed to
the position of the sun at her present waking hour, its bottom convex
barely visible below the eaves.

On the kitchen table, a note in Ted's pushed-together handwriting
read: *The past is but the beginning of a beginning, and all that is and
has been is but the twilight of the dawn.* Her husband left similar
inspirationals each morning, cut out of magazines or copied out of
books. She often thought he'd missed his calling as a motivational
speaker.

Ted wanted desperately for her to be happy again. After the shooting—*the Incident,* as it was referred to at the precinct—after the TV reports and newspaper articles, after the Ontario Provincial Police placed her on voluntary suspension, she and Ted sat before the fireplace, talking about the places they might go and what they might do. In the darkness Ted spoke of a future she could no longer conceive of, planning the furnishings of their new house in a new city, the Persian rugs they would buy, the brass lamps and calfskin sofa, the exact shades of paint with names like Crab Bisque and Big Sky and Postal Green. Even though these things were unreal and unattainable, he endeavored to make them possible. What he didn't understand was that Jess no longer felt deserving of that happiness. It was as if she could no longer comprehend happiness; its shape and texture, once so familiar, now possessed jagged edges and thorns, impossible to grasp. She sat before the fire listening to Ted's voice, the reassuring and resolute words washing over her, burying her.

Jess sat on the sofa with a glass of orange juice laced with Belvedere vodka, watching the street through a bay window. Two laburnums were shedding their withered flowers in the opposite yard, the once-golden petals now shriveled and brittle. Seeing Sam's Chevy pull into the driveway, she picked up her glass and went to the door.

"Good lord, Jess, just drag yourself out of bed?"

Sam Mallory, all five-foot-four of him, stepped through the door. Sam's most striking feature was his spectacular bristliness, both physically and in manner. A tangled bush of beard covered most of his face, thick and lush, fanning out in all directions and resembling an inverted fright wig. His knuckles, ears, nose, and the V of his open-throated shirt were similarly hirsute. "Son of Sasquatch," her brother called him. In the few places where the skin was bald—the palms, forehead, below his eyes—it was paper thin and drawn tight to the bone, saddleworn leather.

He glanced at Jess's clean-pressed OPP uniform hanging in the hall closet next to the winter coats and old Halloween decorations. "If you're not gonna put it on, why not stuff it in the attic? Damn death shroud hanging there."

"Coming in, Sam?"

"Since you asked." He heeled his boots off and poked his nose into her glass. "Bit early for that, isn't it?"

"Feels about right. Fix you one?"

"Better not. Ole liver's bound to explode like a hand grenade, and I can't afford the transplant."

Sam followed her into the kitchen, where she brewed a cup of tea. Seeing her fetch a fresh teabag, the wrinkles on Sam's forehead bunched up. "Don't have an old bag somewhere around?"

"Nope."

"Awful waste, seeing as I take it weak anyhow. Toss one away lately? I'll take that, so long as it's lying on top yesterday's newspaper."

"I don't serve secondhand teabags." She winked. "Besides, you're worth it."

"Quit it, will ya."

Jess set the cup in front of him, with a plate of digestives.

"You're not looking good," Sam said. "Look . . . worn."

"Last of the honeydrippers, aren't you?"

Sam Mallory was Jess's uncle, her father's brother. As was the case with many siblings, they were polar opposites: Sam was restrained where her father was flamboyant, straightforward where her father was circumspect, solidly rootbound where her father's sail was set to every passing wind. When his brother vanished inside a tea chest twenty-five years ago, Sam assumed wardship of the children—their mother, Jeanne, having passed giving birth to Jess's brother. A solitary and idiosyncratic man, Sam wasn't the ideal surrogate father. But he'd always cared for his niece and nephew in the manner of a man with much love to give and no one to lavish it upon: fiercely and devotedly, yet ever at one step removed.

What Sam knew about raising children could've fit comfortably on the head of a pin, with room left for a dancing angel or two. But, unlike his brother, he was willing to learn. Jess remembered rushing into the kitchen one morning to see him bent over a mixing bowl, whisking its contents into a froth. In a griddle on the stove, a sad misshapen lump sizzled fitfully.

"What's this?" Jess had woken with a dreadful certainty the house was on fire.

Sam shielded the mixing bowl with his body, the way a mother caught wrapping Christmas presents might shield them from a nosy child. Blobs of yellowish batter clung to his wiry mesh of beard. "Can't you see it's breakfast?"

Jess couldn't recall her father ever fixing breakfast.

"It's the most important meal of the day, in case you didn't know." Her uncle spoke with a huffy knowledgeable air, as though this were a fact he'd recently read, quite possibly in a thick book.

Jess sat at the table, upon which Sam brusquely deposited a plate. The pancake was a charred disk; a single mouthful probably contained enough carcinogens to dispatch an iron-lunged coal miner.

"Tuck in," he'd told her. "It's brain food."

Sam's small pink tongue now hunted for digestive crumbs in the bristly forest of mustache. "Been doing some reading."

Jess stared out at the backyard, where a raven and a squirrel quarreled over bread crusts Ted had scattered that morning. "Oh?"

"Read about something called an Act of Erasure, Jess. Happens in the military, when soldiers lose touch with reality and don't care about anything. Fellow puts himself in harm's way when there's no need. Trying to ruin himself, in a roundabout way."

"And that's what you think I'm doing—erasing myself?"

"Maybe I do." Sam stirred a finger through his tea. "Not ruining, but . . . well, shutting yourself off. Take a look, Jess—you're half-cracked at noontime. When's the last time you stepped outside?"

"You're being overdramatic."

Yet Sam wasn't entirely off base. Jess didn't feel herself being erased, but she did feel something growing around her, like a shell. Sometimes she thought of it this way exactly: a shell forming over her body, hard and calcified, enrobing her arms, her legs. As time went by it became more impenetrable, layer gathering upon layer the way nacre forms about a speck of grit to create a pearl. Soon everything developed a gauzy translucent aura, as though she were enclosed by panes of warped, cloudy glass. Lately things had become darker and more indistinct, the outside world—her old job and friends, Sam, her husband, the incident itself—developing a distant, hollowed-out quality, as though these were people and events she'd once dreamed, many years ago.

"What is it about you and Herbie," Sam said. "Both of you hiding away from the world?"

Jess went to the cupboard and pulled down a bottle. That she refused to rise to his challenge, her utter lack of spirit, troubled Sam more than anything.

"Did you come for a reason," she said, "or just to question my mental state?"

"That's not fair, Jess. Not fair at all."

Jess gazed out the kitchen window at the patches of lifeless brown grass crushed by the lawn furniture. It made her think of a little churchyard in some hamlet she'd passed through with her father. She remembered a tidy cemetery and her father guiding them between the gravestones. The knife-edged wind blowing across the flat endless prairie, the corroded flag holders and warmth of her father's hand, tiny pink flowers bright amidst the browned grass.

"There *was* a reason I stopped by."

"Uh-huh. And what's that?"

"Your brother called. Wants to talk to you."

"He's got a phone."

"You know Herbie."

"I know Herbie." As soon as she'd said it, Jess realized the lie. She hadn't spoken to her brother in nearly two years. "What's he want?"

Sam walked his cup to the sink and rinsed it out. He looked up and for a moment she caught something in his eyes. Then he hugged her the way Jess imagined a man trapped in a foxhole rocked by mortar fire might hug the man beside him: with a rough embarrassed ardency. She couldn't remember the last time he'd done it—her wedding, maybe? He wiped his nose and walked to the door.

"Sam? Hey, Sam?"

She caught up with him in the front hall. "Come on. I'm sorry."

"It's a hard time."

"That's no excuse for me acting like a bear."

"It's alright."

"I'm sorry."

"Ah, quit it, will ya?"

Sam shuffled down the driveway and hoisted himself into the pickup. He looked comical behind the wheel: a tame black bear some enterprising soul had taught to drive.

"What did Herb want?"

"Didn't say exactly," Sam called through the open window. "Wanted you to stop by, but . . ."

Fakery #6: *The Fraudulent Flatline.* This tired ruse took root in India, where similar dime-store "miracles" are sufficient cause to bestow sainthood. The robed charlatan—for this fakery, the more aged and desiccate, the better—sits cross-legged on a busy street corner. Once a gallery of gullible rubes has assembled, someone is asked to check the charlatan's pulse. It's normal. Then, palms upturned and mouth closed, eyes staring like a lobotomy victim, his body trembles. Keen showmen emit white foam from the sides of their mouths, accomplished by secreting of a tab of bromo-seltzer between lip and gum. The trickster's pulse slows, slows . . . stops altogether! He has died before their very eyes! Yet, as if on cue, the rogue's eyes open, and his heart beats fiercely once more. The deceit: by squeezing a small smooth stone in the crook of his armpit, applying pressure on the axillary artery to stem the blood flow, the man's pulse "magically" disappears.

[3]

Herbert T. Mallory, Jr.'s house occupied a barren patch of scrubgrass on the banks of the Welland Canal. A towering Gothic monstrosity adorned with carving and scrollwork, parapet flanked by a pair of hideous granite gargoyles, it was truly more castle than house. The yard was fenced in by a crumbling brick wall topped with iron pikes and, at the front, a massive gate closing in the middle to form the letters HTM, the T splitting in half when the gates opened. The tangle of satellite dishes strung around the topmost parapet resembled toad-stools sprouting from a tree stump. It seemed very much the kind of looming, creepy place children would delight in visiting on Halloween, but unfortunately Halloween was among the many holidays Herbert now refused to celebrate.

Jess parked her Jeep TJ on the rough shale outside the gates. Away to her left, the canal lift-locks rattled and groaned. How could Herbert bear that noise?

Thin rosy sunlight washed the stricken brown lawn and reflected off the cardinal-red paint job of Herbert's Jaguar X80—though, to the best of Jess's knowledge, her brother didn't drive. A tentworm-infested elm, shrouded from trunk to highest branch in gray cobweb skin, shadowed the car. The mummified tree brought to mind images of a cocoon on the verge of birthing some enormous prehistoric bug. The infestation had progressed for years, Herbert not lifting a finger in opposition: the concept of a large imperious entity destroyed by a swarm of unrelenting smaller entities suited his socialist leanings.

Jess climbed the worn stone steps. Music through the screen door, a gloomy dirge.

"Who is it?" a voice answered her knock.

"Jess."

After a formidable pause: "Door's open."

She walked down the tight hallway strung with photographs of her brother levitating with Doug Henning and bending spoons with Uri Geller, astraddle one of Siegfried and Roy's white Bengals. Hung amidst the photos were posters advertising Herbert's stunt spectaculars: The Water Torture Cell Escape, The Vanishing CN Tower, and the ill-fated Buried Alive. Music came from everywhere and nowhere at once; judging by the mournful caterwauling, Jess speculated the composer was prone to fits of deep depression.

The kitchen was a high-ceilinged room smelling of Cup-a-Soup and old newspapers. Greasy wallpaper and dull wooden molding transformed any light into gloom, and the tall narrow windows, smudged with lampblack, allowed little sunlight to filter through anyway. The air was dank and smoky, unnaturally so, as though a fog machine were pumping away in secret. A pyramid of television sets tuned to different stations climbed the right-hand wall.

"Good afternoon, sis."

Herbert sat at a table strewn with piles of candy: jujubes and jellybeans, licorice whips, gummy bears. His slender frame was draped in a fur-trimmed robe; a tawny thatch of hair sprouted from the robe's open throat, matching the unruly mop atop his head. A few ropes of hair were plastered wetly to his skull, as if, hearing Jess's knock, he'd hurried to make himself presentable. Silver-rimmed glasses gave his face an antique aspect at odds with his age: thirty-three. He peered at Jess with the doleful expression of a man who'd recently quit drinking and, life robbed of whatever false pleasure it once held, now existed in a state of perpetual sorrow.

Jess sat. "Sam said you wanted to talk."

"Yes," he said. "Yes, I do."

Herbert tented his fingers and pressed them to his lips. His fingers were long and tapered though quite gnarled, recalling the braided roots of a mangrove tree. He reached out and plucked a red jellybean from a pile, turning it over the way a gemologist might inspect a fire opal.

"And . . . ?"

"I'm getting to it."

Jess felt a familiar anger rising.

No creature on earth was more self-absorbed than a magician. Trust-fund beneficiaries, dowager princesses, prima donnas of every stripe—not in the same *league*. It was a lifelong predisposition, a certain stirring in the bosom of an infant boy as he witnessed his nose plucked from his face and wiggled between someone's fingers. Boys who grew up to be magicians learned the power of mystery early on, became brokers in secret knowledge. The problem was, they tended to overindulge this power, which led, in Jess's case, to an endless procession of scenes similar to this one in 1976:

"Pass the pepper, Dad."

"What pepper, Jessica darling?"

"The pepper that was on the table a minute ago."

"Well, it's not there now, is it?"

"You palmed it."

"Palmed it? My dear, palming's a shameless trick practiced by street-corner hustlers."

"Fine. You made it vanish."

"Perhaps so. Say the magic word and I'll make it reappear."

"Please."

"The butcher says *please*, darling. The garbage man says *please*."

"Ugh. *Floobidoo*."

Moments later she'd feel the pepper mill's sudden weight in her pocket. The first time was amusing. The second time, less so. Times three through three thousand were abject misery. Which was why, as her brother milked the moment as her father had, Jess snapped, "Turn this horrible music off."

"You don't like it?"

"Another minute and I'll slit my throat."

Herbert hunted through the jumble of remote controls at his elbow, found the corresponding unit, pushed a button.

"Now," Jess said, "what the hell is going *on?*"

Herbert rooted through a sagging tower of newspapers—copies of the *St. Catharines Standard, New York Post, Calgary Herald,* a dozen more—coming up with a section of the *Sault Ste. Marie Star.* "Look."

The local news headline read: *Magician Dazzles Patients at Institution.* A grainy black-and-white snapshot captured a tuxedo-clad man in mid-flourish, a loose horseshoe of housecoat-clad and wheelchair-bound spectators gathered round. She squinted at the photograph intensely, until the image dissolved into its composite black-and-gray dots.

"So?"

"*So?* It's him! The magician—Dad!"

"I can see that."

"Oh, I see. You don't care, is that it?"

Why *should* she care? He'd forsaken them. It took two years to convince Herbert he hadn't banished him to a horrible parallel universe, two years during which Herbert suffered nightmares of his doomed *pater* reeling and shrieking in a fathomless void. Jess had developed a pragmatic outlook: some fathers skipped out for cigarettes and never came home; her father stepped into a tea chest and vanished. Though carried off with more panache than the average abandonment it remained a crude and everyday act. "Same shit, different dad," she'd told friends.

"You have no desire to contact him? None whatsoever?"

"He's no part of my life. He left us."

"The man had his reasons."

"Don't start on that again."

"He *did*," Herbert persisted. "He was driven into hiding by vengeful magicians upset about the book."

That damn *book*. The only renown Herbert T. Mallory, Sr., ever garnered came with the publication of *Hexers, Charlatans, and Miracle Mongers: An Exposé*. A compendium of "fakeries," the book revealed the science and deception behind illusions practiced by inner-city con men, India's famed god-men, and famous stage magicians. It was purchased by skeptics, hustlers, and the type of people who delighted in peeking through keyholes or leafing through strangers' diaries.

"What are you talking about? What did anyone ever *do?*"

"Well," Herbert picked a fluffball off his robe, "what about the prank phone calls? And the time our house was egged?"

Jess tried to envision the ridiculous scene: a carful of magicians rumbling down the block decked in rhinestone vests and peacock feathers and bright satin turbans with cut-glass gems set in the centers, slewing around a hairpin curve, screeching curses and incantations while hurling eggs at their dilapidated bungalow.

"He abandoned us, Herbert. He's a coward."

"Believe what you want," he said, chin set at a supercilious angle. "You don't want anything to do with him, fine. I do."

"Then hop in your car and drive."

"You know I can't."

She shrugged and went to the fridge. Every rack and tray was stocked with cans of something called Sagiko Chrysanthemum Drink.

"Don't have any beer?"

"It's Korean. Very refreshing."

Jess cracked one and took a sip. "Delightful." She scraped her fingernail over a grimy windowpane, letting in a weak sickle of sunlight. "So, if you're not leaving the house, how . . . ?"

"Well, I thought maybe you'd track him down—"

"Oh, is that what you thought? Herbert's little errand girl?"

"No, not like that—"

"I don't care whether the man lives or dies—"

"Jesus, would you let me—"

"If you want to see him so bad, take off that ridiculous robe and leave this hermitage—"

"You're one to talk!"

"At least I'll set foot outside my door!"

Herbert pushed out of his chair and came at her. Jess flashed back to the days when he'd wrestle her to the ground, straddle her chest, and rap his fingers on her breastbone until she named ten chocolate bars—the dreaded *rooster peck*. Her only defense had been the fearsome *purple nurple*, which she administered with the sadistic glee of a gulag torturer. She wondered if this would end with them rolling about on the floor, pecking and pinching.

But he pulled up short, eyes filled with an uneasy mingling of shame and resentment. He turned his hand over in the weak sickle of light.

Jess looked at his fingers. Long and tapered, nails bitten to the quick. She'd seen those fingers do things no other fingers on earth could do, make cards and coins and tiny Egyptian swallows appear and disappear with the flickering swiftness of stop-motion photography. Yet taken out of their element and set to mundane tasks, those same fingers were inept and clumsy.

After his father's disappearance, Herbert threw himself into magic. He carried a deck of cards everywhere, practicing tricks in the school-yard, on the bus, in the bathtub. He bought a straitjacket from a medical supply company and learned how to dislocate his shoulders; Jess vividly recalled the meaty *tok* of his clavicle popping from its cup of bone. Soon he had cups and saucers, even the pot roast vanishing from the dinner table. Although Sam lauded Herbert's abilities, as he felt was his role, it was with the disconcerting sense one gets watching history repeat itself.

At the age of eighteen Herbert rode the bus to Toronto. He picked an agent's name from the phonebook, walked to the Bay Street address, barged past the secretary into his office and ran off a series of rapid-fire illusions, culminating with a Fiery Orb. The agent, face sweat stung from the lingering heat, inked Herbert to a contract on the spot.

"I'm sorry," Jess said as her brother turned his hand in the soft light coming through the window. "Shouldn't have said that." She sipped her chrysanthemum drink. "Gets better the more you drink."

Herbert's rise was, to use the industry parlance, meteoric. He embarked on a cross-Canada tour. "A latter-day Houdini," the *Toronto Star* raved; "Destined to be the hottest name in magic!" heralded the *Montreal Gazette*. Europe came next, Herbert playing on the great Old World stages where Robert-Houdin once caught bullets between his teeth and made the floorboards seep blood. He rode a gathering groundswell into America, playing to packed houses at Radio City Music Hall, the Emerson Majestic Theater, and the Los Angeles Orpheum.

He flew Jess and Sam in for his New York performance. Jess remembered sitting in a balcony box with her uncle, who looked uncomfortable amidst red velvet and shadowy silhouettes of wealthy men and women.

But mostly she remembered Herbert.

He seemed so small in the footlights' austere glare, a stagehand startled by the curtain's rise. But as he worked into his act, materializing playing cards by the dozens and flicking them with such force they ricocheted off lobby doors and balcony rails, Jess realized she was witnessing a man in his element. Sometimes he responded to the applause with an indulgent smile; other times by scorning his audience altogether. Herbert was forgiven his open disdain. The audience felt privileged to be witnessing a bright new star at the dawn of his career.

There were television specials—*Herbert Mallory's Cabinet of Illusions!*; *Herbert Mallory: Upside Down in the Water Torture Cell!*— and a string of well-publicized relationships, starlets, and supermodels and an adult film star. There were drunken fracases outside Hollywood nightclubs and the inevitable paparazzi scuffles. There were the grand gestures, such as the day Jess found a Mercedes convertible in her driveway. He developed the manner of a prince among commoners. He dispensed favors like gold and expected to be deferred to at any and every moment.

His career ended live on national television, in front of an estimated seventeen million viewers, in a span of less than four minutes.

"I'm not saying I wouldn't try to find him," Jess said. "It's just, I won't go alone. I've got my own problems."

Herbert nodded towards the pyramid of television screens. "I saw the news reports. Wasn't right, what they did. Suspending you."

"I asked to be suspended."

"You did?"

"I don't belong there."

The stunt—or "personal challenge," as Herbert called it—was a re-creation of Houdini's famous Buried Alive, in which the straitjacketed magician was sealed in a casket then lowered into a vault, which was then filled with sand. Escape was relatively simple: after wriggling out of the jacket, Herbert had only to slide open a panel in the casket's base and dig through a foot of sand to a trapdoor.

Jess was at home when it happened, watching on TV. It had all seemed so strange. The sand had been poured in but the vault was still open. Then a deep muted crack, the sound a bone makes fracturing deep underwater. The surface stirred a little; air from the ruptured casket vented in a series of sandy puffs. The cameras pulled back, as though ashamed of their intensity. As she sat in front of the television holding Ted's hand, part of Jess hated Herbert for the manipulation.

One of the producers came onstage, hollering, "Get him out of there—get him *the hell out!*" Workmen rushed out with crowbars and screwdrivers, attacking the vault seams. The cameras zoomed in. An audience member clambered onto the stage, wedging his car key into a seam and prying with what little force he could muster. A technician tore at the vault with his bare hands.

Three minutes and thirty-seven seconds passed before they were able to break the vault apart. The retaining wall gave way, washing a tide of sand into the front row. Jess saw Herbert's arm turning over and over as his body tumbled down the grade of sand, his tuxedo jacket—he must've escaped his straitjacket before the casket fractured—rucked up to his elbow, gold cufflink glinting in the overheads. His body rolled until it hit the footlights.

Paramedics dragged him from the sand and administered mouth-to-mouth. For thirty seconds there was only the artificial rise and fall of his chest, a fragile bellows. One shoe on, the other yanked off. A hole in his sock. Shirt singed from the white-hot foots. He sat up abruptly, arms jerked out, fingers grasping at nothing. His eyes wide, grains of sand adhering to the lashes.

"Are you all right?" the producer asked. "Herbert? Herbert?"

"It's eternity in there," was all he said.

The network cut to a rerun.

Jess sat down. "As far as I'm concerned, our father deserted us. But if you want to track him down, I'll tag along. I don't want to speak to him, or even look at him. But I'll go."

Herbert stared out at the world as he'd known it for nearly two years: vague and filtered, kept at bay by bricks and mortar and filthy window glass. "So you're saying I have to go?"

"Know what Sam calls this place? The Fortress of Solitude." Jess raised the soda can to her lips, mildly surprised to find it empty. "I don't know what happened in that casket. You never told me—I don't know you've told anybody. I imagine it was horrible. And I know you've got money, enough to build this place and pay for that Jag and keep you in foreign soft drinks the rest of your life. But you need to get out."

Herbert gave her a look—a funny, diverted glance, turning away from her as you might from someone who is sick. "You know why I've never talked about it? Nobody's ever really asked. My agent, my publicist, they were always telling me to get over it, forget it, it's the past. Do you really want to know?"

"Do you really want to tell me?"

After a moment, he said, "It was dark. It was dark and I could hear the casket creaking. The sand was imported from Egypt. Powdered bones, mostly, animals who'd died in the desert; supposedly more airy, lighter. I felt the pressure building as they poured it in—my ears popped. I knew it was going to shatter. That was the worst part. It was dark and I knew it was going to shatter. I called out a few times —screamed, I guess. Four tons of sand. That's like, two and a half elephants." He shook his head wonderingly, as if the weight, stated in plain physical terms, shocked him. "It buckled. A shard of wood cut my cheek. That's all I really remember. My life didn't flash before my eyes. All I remember is darkness and pressure. This hard, featureless pressure."

For a long time neither of them spoke. Why would anyone squirrel himself away after something like that, Jess wondered. She'd never want to be cooped up again—sleep in an open field under the stars, no walls, no roof. No pressure.

"A lot of luck in my life, up 'til then." Herbert shrugged. "Streak was bound to end."

For the first time in many years Jess thought of walking home from school with him in the winter twilight, their flesh an oyster-gray color against the snow, Herbert animated beyond all reason, circling her like an excited dog until she'd wrestled him down and given him a snowy face wash, the two of them tumbling over the clean white ground like shirts in a dryer. She couldn't connect the man sitting across from her to the boy she'd known years ago. There wasn't even a vague outline, a silhouette.

"I'll be here tomorrow morning at nine," she said. "You walk out the front door and I'll drive wherever you want."

"Can't you give me a few days?"

"How serious are you about this? The article's dated yesterday."

Herbert followed his sister to the front door. Hazy autumn sunshine streamed through a bank of saw-edged clouds; after the sepulcher that was her brother's house, Jess had to squint. Opening the Jeep door, she cast a brief glance over her shoulder: Herbert stood in the hall, face broken into shadowed squares by the screen door's mesh.

THAT EVENING she sat on the porch with her husband, his hand holding hers under a blanket. Since being promoted off the factory floor his hands had softened, become more careful and defensive, as though, numbed from years on the line, feeling had returned to them.

An early twilight hung suspended over the downtown skyline, patches of pewter burning between the high rises.

"So, you're sure it's your dad in the photo?"

"It's him."

Ted's father was an insurance agent, his mother a nurse. His family history was marked by the characteristic dullness resulting in well-adjusted offspring: no extramarital affairs or crushing debts or manic, right-brain-oriented parents. Having never known people like them, he could conceive of Jess's father and brother only as vague abstractions, over-the-top comic book characters brought discordantly to life.

"Think Herb will leave that house?"

"Depends how important it is to him." Jess touched her top lip to her nose, inhaling. "I think so. Unfinished business."

"And you?"

"With Dad? We're through."

Later, lying in bed, she watched Ted's reflected image brush its teeth in the bathroom mirror. His body was that of a retired athlete gone slightly to seed. A newly acquired paunch overhung the waistband of his boxers, though he carried it well, as some men had the ability to. He brushed with swift, raking strokes, as though scouring a crusty pot. White foam ran down his fingers and wrist.

It really is true, she thought to herself. Men are almost always more attractive when they think nobody's watching.

Fakery #22: *The Bleeding Wall*. Invented by Robert-Houdin, grandfather of modern magic, it is best performed in a public square. The magician draws a pistol, aims at a wall, and fires. Whitewash and plaster chips fly, and where the bullet strikes, blood drips down the masonry. The deceit: earlier that day, the magician drilled into the wall's opposite side, filling it with a solution of ferric chloride. When the bullet—coated in a solution of sodium sulfo-cyanide—punctures the wall, a chemical reaction occurs, causing a thick crimson substance to spill from the hole. Interesting note: Houdin initially used his own blood, but, following a stretch of daily performances that left him wan and depleted, opted for this chemical substitute.

[4]

It was a fine, crisp morning. After last night's rainfall the sun was blanketed by a layer of wrung-out clouds; they streamed down the sky, misty and tattered, a frozen waterfall. Jess unrolled the window to let cool, creosote-infused air rush in. It was the sort of day she wished she could freeze-frame and repeat indefinitely—she'd take this day the rest of her life.

She pulled into Herbert's driveway. Her brother sat on a trunk behind the screen door.

"Coming?"

"I'm debating." Herbert's voice was thin as a communion wafer.

She glanced at her watch: 9:03. "Do I have to hogtie you and drag you out?"

"For god's sake—a minute, Jess, alright?"

Her brother performed a series of rapid in- and exhalations, a powerlifter pumping himself up for a record-breaking clean-and-jerk. He pushed the screen door open with the toe of his loafer and made a timid half-step from darkness into daylight. He wore a six-button double-breasted wool gabardine suit, creases sharp as a soldier's dress uniform. His face bore the squint-eyed, faintly horrified expression of an infant forced prematurely from the womb. He stepped down onto the driveway. To the best of Jess's knowledge, it was the furthest he'd ventured in years.

"Hard part's over now."

"I've been out once or twice," he said defensively.

"Oh?"

"Just last spring, in fact. A hobo took up residence in the gazebo." He tilted his face to meet the sun. "I rousted him with a stick."

The next obstacle Jess faced was her brother's luggage. She'd packed a small knapsack with a change of clothes. Herbert's luggage consisted of a trunk, a footlocker, two suitcases, and a duffle bag of sufficient bulk to smuggle a pair of contortionists.

"We're going on an eight-hour car ride, not around the world in eighty days."

He looked wounded. "I need these."

"Quit being a prima donna. Why?"

"How will he know I've been successful?"

"What, did you pack awards and plaques? I'm sure he reads the paper."

Jess bartered him down to the duffel bag and a suitcase. She hefted the latter, so heavy it may have contained gold bullion, and dragged it to the Jeep.

"I refuse to ride in that bog stomper," Herbert said. "We'll take my car."

Jess's body soaked into the Jag's tanned leather upholstery as water into a dry sponge. The sleek European dials and gauges were ringed by bands of polished teak. The odometer read 7.2 kilometers, which she suspected was the distance separating the dealership from Herbert's hermitage.

She caught the on-ramp at Lake Street and swung onto the QEW. They passed the Henley Regatta, where a solitary sculler plied the calm brown water, and the slopes of St. David's Bench, where vineyard laborers plucked late-harvest Riesling off the vines. At the city limits they passed a flaking sign that read: *Thank You for Visiting St. Catharines, home of Herbert T. Mallory, Jr., The World's Greatest*

Magician!, with an illustration of a disembodied hand yanking a rabbit from a top hat.

Herbert said, "Wish someone would burn that damn thing."

He rummaged through his suitcase, retrieving the pipe Jess had seen jammed in his face during countless media appearances. It was a calabash of a style favored by Sir Arthur Conan Doyle's famous detective.

"Why do you smoke that thing?"

"Because I am a sophisticate." Herbert's tone suggested Jess wouldn't recognize sophistication if it crept up and nibbled her bottom.

"It's a silly affected habit. Not at all you."

"You have your vices," Herbert said, "and I mine."

On the north side of the Hamilton Skyway, Lake Ontario lay flat and emerald against the sun; on the south side, Stelco smokestacks rose in silvery pillars against the blue canvas of sky. Traffic was surprisingly light and they made good time. The Jag whispered along at 110 kph, Jess resting a couple of fingers on the wheel to keep it steady. After navigating through Toronto, Jess unrolled the window an inch or two, breathing the dung-scented air blowing in over the pastures. Herbert's pipe smelled like a pan of scorched cherries jubilee.

She remembered driving this highway with her father and brother, traveling to a birthday party or bar mitzvah or cottage-country fair. The men sat in the front, her father lecturing Herbert on various tricks and illusions, pointing out the deceptions. She sat in the back. Every so often her dad would reach over the seat, squeeze her knee, and say, "Paying attention, dear?" At those times Jess wished her mother was still alive, or that she had a sister, any buffer between her and the men in the front seat. Her father made no allowance for the possibility she might not *want* to dedicate her life to magic; his mania was so all-consuming, and he'd found such a willing acolyte in his son, that he found it inconceivable she *wouldn't* share his obsession. But even at her tender age, Jess knew a dead-end opportunity when she saw one: what role did women play in magic? Sequin-topped diversions. Eye candy. Her father used her no differently: *Just stand off to the side and smile, dear. Let those darling dimples do all the work.* Looking back, Jess realized her major life choices were influenced by a desire to surround herself with individuals and institutions the opposite of everything— whimsy, fickleness, fantasy—that magic, and her family, represented.

The highway wound along the eastern shore of Georgian Bay. Glimpsed through clusters of silver maple and Douglas fir stippling the shoreline, the water stretched like a dark curved mirror, interrupted only by a chain of dimensionless islands.

"So," Jess said, "ever think about getting back into it?"

"What's that?"

"Magic. The life."

"Well, if you mean the sort of tricks I made a living off, no." He opened a window and scattered pipe ashes to the breeze. "I'm interested in real magic."

"Dad's book should've convinced you there's no such thing."

"Not true. Dad believed in true magic. Why do you think he went to such lengths debunking the frauds?"

A sudden trapdoor feeling opened in Jess's stomach. Here was something else her father had kept hidden away from her. She stared out the window, where a flock of migrating geese kept such perfect pace with the car as to appear frozen in place, pinned like moths to the backdrop of sky.

"There *is* real magic," Herbert continued. "A Bedouin mystic sealed in a vault for two years emerges alive and in good health. A Navajo shaman changes into a timber wolf before a gathering of missionaries. A Hindu holy man climbs a rope into the clouds and vanishes. These things happened. Recorded fact. Transformation, telepathy, invisibility—it can be done."

"Get out of here."

"I'm serious. Tell me this: have you ever heard of Swami Vindii Lagahoo?"

"We play croquet together on Wednesdays."

"Aren't you clever. Lagahoo lived many years ago in Persia, where he was a spiritual counselor of sorts to the prince. Lagahoo was known as a great sorcerer—he lived for 127 years, according to the records of the day—and was credited with many miracles: producing sacred ash from his long sleeves, pulling cancerous tumors through the skin of sick men, levitation, transubstantiation. It's written that once, at a palace gathering, he sliced open the gut of a suckling pig that had been roasting on a spit in full view of the guests—a dozen doves flew out of the slit! Astounding!"

Jess emitted a low sarcastic whistle.

"His most impressive feat, the one that I've been practicing, is making oneself invisible to the naked eye."

"Come on, Herbert."

"I'm serious. It's no trick, just a purely mental skill. A basic matter of will. Lagahoo trained for years and was eventually able to maintain invisibility for hours at a stretch. The whole undertaking drove him crazier than a bedbug."

"Did you ever consider he was crazy to begin with?"

Jess listened with mounting disbelief as Herbert described how, for the past six months, he'd passed each day in a room of his house, sitting in a cross-legged yoga position on the bare floorboards, teaching himself to become invisible.

"... first, you must block all outside distractions. The basic human sensations of sight, sound, smell, touch—block them out. One must feel nothing in order to experience everything. Focus the mind. Set aside all material thoughts. Concentrate. See nothing—no, see *white*. Perfect, unending whiteness. Center yourself upon it." He nodded to himself. "Yes, it's possible. I'm living proof." He added, "Totally self-taught!"

"If you're doing this by yourself, how can you tell you've become invisible?"

Herbert sighed the way a teacher might when faced with a particularly dim-witted student. "I just *know*, Jess. I can feel it. A disconnection, I guess you'd call it."

"All I can say is, if some guy walked into the station raving about aged swamis and invisibility, I'd ring up the men with butterfly nets."

"Shut up."

"Off to the loony bin he'd go. For his own good."

"Think I'm nuts, do you? Pull in." Herbert jabbed his finger at an approaching convenience store. "I'll goddamn well show you."

Jess eased off the highway into the lot of Gibson's Groceteria, parking beneath a sign reading: *Utility Turkey—59¢/lb.* Herbert shrugged off his jacket and rolled his shirt sleeves to the elbow. "Shut the engine off and be quiet," he said, unbuttoning the shirt to his navel. "This takes incredible concentration."

Jess made a motion as though zippering her lips shut.

"All right." Herbert rolled his neck and popped his knuckles. "Now, then. *Watch.*"

He closed his eyes. Soon his body was trembling, fingers twitching through a series of paroxysms as though tuning in stations on a finicky radio. His eyelids quivered like a man deep in REM sleep. His lips moved silently, a string of unintelligible syllables. Jess was reminded of a 911 call she'd answered a few years ago, some burnout who'd smuggled a narcotic toad back from Borneo; his girlfriend reported he'd been licking the poor creature's backside all night. Jess found the guy sprawled on the kitchen floor in his boxers. The toad's head poked from under the fridge, appraising its molester with bugged-out eyes. The guy's body shook faintly, as though undergoing mild electroshock therapy. Herbert's body was shaking much the same way.

This went on for five minutes. At no time did he disappear.

"Can you still see me?"

"Afraid so."

"Damn!" His eyes snapped open. "Nothing? Didn't my skin turn opaque?"

"Maybe a little smoky," she lied.

"Hah—I told you!" Watching Herbert smile was like watching a match head burst into flame. "Just needs more practice."

Jess pulled back onto the highway. The highway hooked sharply westward coming through Sudbury. They drove directly into the sun, which, sinking gently into the hills, threw long embers over the landscape. Here or there they passed a motel or trading post or bait shop, but otherwise the land unfolded in great sweeps of pine and maple and poplar. Herbert rummaged through his suitcase and slotted a CD into the player. "Edith Piaf," he said. "The Little Sparrow. One of Dad's favorites." Jess listened to French lyrics sung in a gravelly contralto, trying hard not to hate Piaf just because her father liked her. It was nearly five o'clock by the time they hit Sault Ste. Marie.

The Sleighton mental care facility was situated on the city's western outskirts, surrounded by a dense forest unclaimed by the logging corporations. The grounds were dotted with tall deciduous trees from which all but the most stubborn leaves had fallen. A wrought-iron fence, rusty bars tipped with ornate points, enclosed the buildings. Jess parked in the visitors' lot.

"Cozy," said Herbert.

Jess sat behind the wheel listening to the engine cool. She'd last seen her father as an eleven-year-old girl. Now she was a thirty-six-year-old woman with house and husband and twenty-five years of unshared history. She thought about that night at the Pythian lodge, how her father hadn't held her gaze for even a moment; he'd simply stepped inside the tea chest, tipped his hat, and vanished. She wondered if it had been premeditated, or if he'd found himself on the other side of the curtain when the notion popped abruptly into his head: walk through the kitchen door out into the alley, turn the corner onto the street, keep walking. A snap decision. Two children, a mortgage, all responsibility—*poof*. Gone. Like magic.

"We've got to do this, Jess."

"Says who? Nobody's codified these things, written a guidebook."

"Do I have to hogtie you, drag you in there?"

The facade of the hospital's central building was pitted and water stained, chunks of mortar crumbling from the Catherine-wheel window frames. The receptionist's unsmiling face was framed in a small porthole set in the middle of a pebbled-glass window. The only means of communication was through a perforated metal disk, same as at a theater box office.

"How may I help you?" the receptionist's voice rattled.

Jess leaned close to the metal disk. "There was a magic show here a few days ago. We . . ."

"Ward Eight, fourth floor. Elevators down the hall to your right."

The entrance to Ward Eight: a steel door painted with a faded rainbow; rabbits, chipmunks, and other forest creatures frolicked beneath the colorful arch. The window glass inlaid with chicken-wire.

An orderly sat behind the charge desk reading *Archie's Digest*. The man filled out his white uniform to the last stitch, fabric straining under its hopeless burden. The skin of his face appeared to float upon his features, not quite secure, like the membrane forming on cold soup. His name tag read LEE.

"We're here about the magician," Jess told him.

Without looking up from the comic, he angled his wrist so Jess could see the digital readout on his watch. "Visiting hours end at five."

"We aren't here to visit any—"

"'Tis *past* five, m'dear."

Jess reached for her badge, which she still carried. With her suspended it carried no weight, but the orderly didn't know that. She flipped the top half over his comic and let it hang.

"What do you want with the magician, officer?"

"We have reason to suspect he was involved in a robbery," Herbert said. "The man is a known hoodlum. We have eyewitness reports, and certain . . . corroborating evidences."

"I don't see how that could be," said Lee.

"Look, we just want to ask some questions," Jess said.

"Well, then, guess I'll go rustle up your magic man."

The orderly came around the desk and waddled into the ward, walking with the listing gait of a once-skinny man whose body has ballooned to ungovernable proportions. Herbert shot his sister a distressed look. Was their father a *patient?* Mercurial, recalcitrant, heedless of social responsibility—dear god, he fit the profile! Maybe they'd picked him up years ago, wandering the streets in filthy rags, destitute and mentally unglued. Perhaps he'd been here for decades and every few months the doctors reduced his medication so he could dress up and perform a show for his fellow looners. Herbert couldn't handle the sight of his father in a ratty housecoat and fuzzy slippers, shambling about like a zombie.

"Do my eyes deceive me?"

They turned to see a man coming out of a glassed-in office behind the charge desk. Mocha-skinned and trim, sporting a pencil-thin mustache of a style cultivated by '70s-era adult film performers, sleek body nearly lost within a billowing lab coat. "It *is!*" he exclaimed, skidding to a stop beside Herbert. "Mr. Mallory, can I just say how honored I am—imagine, the great magician in our ward!"

Herbert inched behind his sister, ignoring the man's proffered hand.

"Is there a problem?" The man spoke with a delicate Indian accent. "Have I upset you?"

"He's fine." Jess shook the man's hand. "Just, after the accident . . ."

"Oh my, yes!" A shake of the head. "Terrible accident. Terrible, terrible. I watched on television." He took a step back, embarrassed by his proximity. "Dr. Venky Iyer."

"Jessica Heinz."

"A thousand apologies, doctor." Herbert bowed. "I mistook you for one of the inmates."

"Ha!" Dr. Iyer cackled. "Cannot be too careful. Now, what brings you fine people here?"

"You hosted a magic show a few days ago . . ."

"Very nice, very nice," Dr. Iyer said. "It certainly brightened everyone's day."

Jess glanced around, thinking the ward could use some brightening. The dayroom was covered in olive-green tile, strips of padded foam tacked to the walls at hip level. The light filtering through the leaded glass windows was muted by thick mesh screens.

"So," Dr. Iyer arched his brows, "will Mr. Mallory be performing?"

He seemed to have mistaken Jess for Herbert's agent. "I'm sorry, no." She showed her badge. "We're looking for information on the man who performed . . ."

"Here's your magician."

The orderly gripped a scrawny fellow by the elbow. The man had thick curly red hair and lips so thin they resembled soda crackers stacked one atop the other. A gourdlike head perched atop a spindled neck like an apple balanced on a breadstick. Standing beside him was a shockingly large woman of about sixty. With blotches of mascara smudging her face and a shock of frizzy black hair, she resembled a chimneysweep after a dogged day's work.

"This is the magician . . . ?" Jess managed.

"Who, Oogie?" Dr. Iyer chuckled. "Certainly not."

"Well, he's been practicing tricks all day," said Lee. "I figured . . ."

Dr. Iyer shook his head. "The officer's looking for the man Oogie's been imitating lately."

"I've been off the past week," Lee said defensively.

"I'm the man you're after," the scrawny man piped up in a voice shrill as a piccolo. "I got magic like you never seen!"

"Cool your jets," Lee warned.

Oogie grasped Jess's hand and kissed it grandly. "Yes, milady, your eyes do not deceive you. It is I, Oogie Dellanthorpe." His tone suggested the name passed over people's lips with great frequency. "Or, as my legions of fans know me, the *Mysterious* Oogie."

"Delusional, but quite harmless," said Dr. Iyer. "A fascinating case."

"I've been hiding out with my able-bodied assistant, Rhonda McMurphy." Oogie nodded to his female companion. "The pressures of fame, you know. But don't worry, I'll soon be thrilling audiences again. I can leave anytime I want."

"That's not at all true," Dr. Iyer whispered to Jess.

Oogie's eyes fell upon Herbert. "Is it—could it *be?*"

Herbert performed a polite bow. "Guilty as charged."

"Dr. Iyer, about the other magician . . . ?"

"Of course, officer. I have his address on file."

Dr. Iyer ushered Jess into his office and closed the door, leaving Herbert to fend off Oogie alone. The office was small and cluttered, shelves stacked with outdated medical texts. In the corner, a little heater popped and cracked as its parts grew warmer and expanded.

"An interesting man," Dr. Iyer said, speaking of her father. "Comes in every year around Halloween. Mr. Dellanthorpe was so enthralled he's taken on a whole new persona."

Dr. Iyer handed over a slip of paper with an address in Thessalon, a town two hours east. "I don't even know the fellow's name. He insists on using his stage name—the Inimitable Cartouche."

By the time they exited the office, Oogie's arm was draped chummily over Herbert's shoulder. "You're a fine fellow," he said. "I like the cut of your jib."

Jess pulled at her brother, making for the exit. "Well, thanks for everything."

"No!" Oogie was reluctant to relinquish Herbert's neck. "I'm . . . I'm putting on a magic show. Yes, it's true: the Mysterious Oogie will perform tonight."

"You'd really be helping us," Dr. Iyer whispered. "Otherwise he'll grouch all night."

They agreed to stay. Lee guided Jess and Herbert to a sofa. Their presence prompted a great deal of curiosity; patients wandered out of their rooms, gravitating to the dayroom.

Oogie reappeared with a turquoise bedsheet pinned to the shoulders of his housecoat and a bristol-board top hat on his head at a breezy angle. Rhonda wore a sequined top and hoop skirt.

"Ladies and gentlemen," Oogie said. "Tonight I will dazzle you with illusions guaranteed to leave you questioning your sanity!"

"Ho ho ho, now, now, Mr. Dellanthorpe," Dr. Iyer said in a sing-song voice. "Let us choose our words a *little* . . ." he brought his index finger and thumb together, as though squeezing the juice from an invisible grape, ". . . more prudently, shall we?"

"Use what sense the good Lord gave you," said Lee, ". . . or I'll brain you."

"We do not brain our patients, officer," Dr. Iyer told Jess with a nervous smile. "We have a strict No Braining policy, in fact."

Oogie shuffled a deck of playing cards. He strode over to a shrunken-apple doll of a woman, fanned the deck.

"Now, to remove any taint of duplicity—milady, have we ever met before?"

"I'm Marla," the old woman croaked. "Your room's next door to mine. You keep me up all night with grunts of self-gratification."

"What I mean is, are we in cahoots?"

"I wouldn't be in cahoots with you for all the silks in Siam."

"Wonderful. Please select a card."

Marla reached for a card. Oogie pulled the deck away and angled it differently. Marla reached again. Oogie snatched the cards away, stuffed half into his pocket and offered the remaining deck. Marla reached . . . Oogie pulled away. Rhonda performed a series of pirouettes.

"My formidable mental powers are useless!" Oogie was confused and dismayed. "This lady's resistance is otherworldly. Tell me, aged crone, is there a metal plate in your skull?"

Marla had nodded off.

Herbert had been watching with mounting agitation. "Mind if I have a go?"

"Yes, give it a whirl," Dr. Iyer said.

Oogie took a seat beside Jess, unruffled despite his failure. "I'm learning how to clog dance," he told her. "Ordered special shoes from Scandinavia."

Herbert fanned Oogie's cards and knelt beside Marla, who snuffled into foggy wakefulness. Herbert asked her to take a card and show it to everyone but him. After Marla had done so, Herbert shuffled the remaining cards and directed Marla to slot her card back into the deck.

"When I tap the deck, your card rises to the top." A light tap. "Remove the card, please."

Marla's face lit up. "The four of clubs—will you look at that!"

"Beginner's luck," Oogie huffed.

For the next half-hour Herbert ran through a series of card illusions: the Haunted Deck, Cutting the Ace, the Teleporting Card, the French Drop. Those who'd hung back earlier drew near. Everyone leaned forward, heads tilted slightly upward, bodies inclined towards Herbert like iron filings under a faint yet persistent magnetic pull. Following each trick the room burst with astonished laughter or low *oooohs,* followed by the disbelieving question: "How did he *do* that?" Jess watched her brother's face change. Something peeled away from it, a layer so deeply ingrained she hadn't noticed it until it was gone. The features relaxed, creases smoothing out, softening. She saw a trace of the boy she remembered.

"I must seclude myself in preparation for my final feat," he said. "I ask the lights be dimmed. Everyone must remain completely silent. Any disturbance will ruin my concentration."

"Herbert, are you sure—?"

"Hush, doubting sister."

Herbert entered a room at the end of the ward. Following his departure the dayroom filled with excited whispers, like a cage full of birds. Lee tiptoed over to the dimmer knob and brought the light level down to a mellow dusk.

After a few minutes Herbert cried, "Behold!" and everyone craned to see the fabulous magician striding down the hallway . . .

. . . stark naked.

Herbert believed the only sure way to render oneself invisible required the removal of one's clothes. Though *he* could still see his body—the pasty skin and thatch of curly black chest hair, the teacup-shaped birthmark on his hip—Herbert was utterly certain nobody else could.

"I am in your very midst," he called out triumphantly, "and yet you cannot see me—ho ho *ho!*"

A palpable surge of discomfort passed through the group. Most people looked away, shocked and deeply embarrassed. This only solidified Herbert's conviction.

"Is this normal behavior?" Dr. Iyer asked Jess.

Herbert strutted through the group. He flipped a lock of Rhonda's hair. "What's that—the wind? No, madam, it was I!"

"Fellow's equipped like a fox," Marla said to no one in particular.

Herbert stopped in front of a black man wearing a porkpie hat. "Tell me, friend," he asked. "As I stand before you, what do you see?"

"I see a damn *fool!*"

"Herbert," Jess said gently. "We can see you."

"You're lying."

"Everybody please point at my brother."

Twenty fingers did so.

"I see." Herbert was more bemused than upset. "Well, isn't that . . . odd."

Herbert retreated down the hallway, pale body glowing in the thin nocturnal light. As he walked past the casement windows, burnt orange light of a harvest moon slanting through the glass, Jess noticed something odd: the moonlight did not touch upon the curvature of his arms and shoulders, did not touch his skin at all. It seemed to fall through him.

Fakery #77: *The Possessed Apple.* This ploy was first practiced in medieval days. An opportunistic rogue set an apple on the cobbles of the village square, claiming the ability to move it using only the precipitous powers of his mind. As he bore down with a look of fierce concentration, the apple would indeed begin to tumble over the stones. The ruse: the man cored an apple and placed a large beetle inside, then plugged both holes using potter's glue and the remains of the core. The agitated insect tossed and turned within its mealy cell, causing the apple to move about. Humorous note: a few practitioners, touring this act through superstitious backwoods shanty-towns, were marked as warlocks and burnt at the stake.

[5]

IT WAS NEARLY eight o'clock when they left Sleighton. Dr. Iyer offered directions to the Regal Lodge—actually not a lodge at all, just five or six moss green cottages clustered on a rocky promontory jutting into Whitefish Bay. Their cottage had two cots and a stone fireplace. Stuffed largemouth bass hung on the walls, walleyed and glassy.

Jess sat on the porch beneath a tarpaper awning, looking out over the bay. The moon and stars stood on their exact reflections on the surface of the night-darkened water. A fish jumped in the center of the moon, the image rippling, glazing over, re-forming. She could barely make out the clapboard shacks standing amidst a cluster of pines across the channel.

Herbert joined her on the steps. They sat in silence for a while, listening to the constant lapping of waves against the dock pilings. The air was clean and raw and left the taste of winter at the back of their throats.

"What do you hope to accomplish by all this?"

"All what?"

"Don't be dumb," Jess said. "What do you want to ask? What do you want him to say?"

"I went back to the house, once. Before it sold and the furniture got carted away. Walking around, looking. This was at the time I still thought I'd, you know . . ."

"Banished Dad to an alternate dimension?"

"Right. He was everywhere in that house. He was in the bathroom cabinet, his razors and Burma Shave and that whatever it was, that pomade, to slick his hair. His clothes were lying around, smelling of him, that cologne. He was in the pictures on the walls and food in the fridge, the packet of flower seeds on the table. Hair stuck to a cake of soap. Everywhere."

A bullet-shaped wedge of darkness cut through the moon's reflection, the roar of an outboard motor swelling, dissipating.

"I made him a booklet, once. Cardboard and colored paper, tied together with yarn. I wrote down some of the tricks he'd taught me. Just this thing I'd made. It was childish; it was nothing. But I remember him saying he'd keep it close." Herbert gazed into the sky, the seam where moonlight and darkness swam together. "It was still in his nightstand. There were a few old photos, some yellow slivers of toenail, the booklet. Why didn't he take it with him, if it meant so much?"

They sat in silence. Jess stared out over the bay, starlight bending upon the water's surface. A cold wind came across the water, slightly tainted by the sulfurous smell of the pulp mills. Three or four mallards congregated beneath the boathouse, bobbing bodies illuminated by an outdoor bulb; it took a moment before Jess recognized they were decoys.

"Why did you come?" Herbert asked. "You don't want to see him."

"That's right."

"So, just get out of town for a few days? Away from . . . all that?"

"I guess so."

"It wasn't your fault."

"Herbert, let's not, huh?"

"You should talk about it to somebody. You talked to Ted, I'm sure." He paused, focusing on the billowy white shapes left by his words. "Listen, when I told you about the casket—it helped. I didn't think it would."

She hadn't talked about it—not to Ted, Sam, or the department psychologist. It was a wound too painful to dress, the edges raw and bleeding, and she kept thinking if she treated the pain as something untouchable and beyond her control it might heal itself eventually. But that hadn't happened, and now everywhere, in the trees and the water and the sky, she felt a sadness weighing down on her. And though sometimes the pain receded, washed out on a tide of new possibilities and potential, it always returned, the more unbearable for that brief absence.

"Do you want to hear about it?"

Was it even a question?

"Only if you want."

She told him this:

The call was a routine 412: *Suspicious or overt behavior in a neighboring domicile.* Usually a domestic dispute: shouting, accusations, broken crockery. Jess hated 412s, the women with swollen eyes refusing to press charges, the same depressing minuet played out week after week. The call came from Grapeview Estates, a wealthy development near Port Dalhousie. She pulled into a driveway on Sarah Court shortly after nine o'clock, the night of February 27.

The caller was a man in his mid-fifties cradling a white terrier in his arms. He pointed to a half-constructed house across the street. *Saw people moving around before dark. Arsonists. Lit a fire. Liable to burn the damn block down.*

The house hovered at the lot's back edge in a pool of darkness. Snow-covered roof beams poked at the sky like broken ribs, icicles descending from every unfinished angle. Jess walked beneath the funnel of light cast by a gooseneck streetlamp as new snow fell, flakes alighting on her hair and face. Arson was a summer crime, best when the air was hot and tinder dry; this was likely vagrants seeking shelter.

The flashlight cast a bleached glow on the untreated wood. Electrical cables snaked through holes in the ceiling and wound around exposed beams. The floor was dusted in fresh snow, untracked by footprints.

Officer Heinz, she called. *Police.*

She shone a flashlight down the basement stairwell: smashed cin-derblocks, flattened fast food cartons, gray cement glittering with frost. The ashy, electric scent of a doused fire. Jess's footsteps echoed hollowly as she descended. The radio crackled at her hip, a medley of codes and numbers. She told herself it was a vagrant, some washed-out husk posing no threat. But she'd heard stories of encounters beneath train trestles or shadowy freeway overpasses, men with little hope or sanity lashing out viciously. Her right hand tightened on the butt of a .38 service revolver.

A shape ran past the flashlight's beam. Lit by the stark white cone, the eyes were glassy and feral, the hand clutching something small and silvery.

Jess raised her pistol, the motion almost casual. Her understand-ing that it was a child came a split second too late to stop her muscles flexing under a presumption of danger.

Muzzle-flash lit the boy's face. He twisted away, as though ashamed. The force of impact threw his body back, feet leaving the ground, flying, falling. He hit the ground and skidded.

The flashlight fell from her hands, lighting the left side of the boy's body. He wore a puffy white parka, blue jeans, a Timex wristwatch. His right hand was mittened; the left clutched a silver Zippo. The gunshot had jolted one of his boots off. There was a hole in the heel of his sock. Jess saw all this. His face was white, green eyes dilated, left eyelid fluttering. His mouth was open and there was some blood there, thin and shiny. He drew short, hiccupping breaths. His cheeks were smooth and hairless and freckled, his hair parted to the left. There was a small hole in his parka, frosted black around its edges. The hole was placed somewhere between shoulder and heart. Tiny flecks of blood all over his clean white parka and in the swimming light they looked to move across his chest like aphids.

Another boy stood in the corner. The concrete at his feet scorched black. A pile of sticks, a half-burnt mitten, a soda bottle melted down to a charred lump of plastic. Two boys playing with fire in an abandoned house. The city was growing so quickly, green spaces paved into parking lots—where could boys go to do the sorts of things boys did? Two boys playing with matches, piss-scared they'd be caught. One of them had tried to run.

"Go," she said to the other kid who was already moving up the stairs. "Get help. Get . . . help."

She knelt beside the wounded boy, pressing her hands to his chest. Redness pushed between her fingers, warming them. How old was he? Maybe twelve, maybe younger. She called it in. *Shots fired. Civilian down.* The boy coughed up blood. His fingers were long and shapely; girlish. She pulled him onto her lap and tilted his head, scooping blood from his mouth with her fingers. His nose was slightly upturned—the word *devilish* flitted through her mind. A smear of ash on his chin. His eyes wide open, glazed, looking up into the darkness. Calm, hugely round eyes.

"Please," she said, "please."

In that moment, she saw the boy's funeral. A small group gathered on a grassy hill, bright winter sunlight washing the snow-topped tombstones. She saw the coffin, small and narrow and polished to a high gloss. She saw a blown-up photo leaning on an easel, a picture of the boy as she'd never known, the boy's face wide open and smiling. She saw the boy's father sobbing in the sloppy and frightening way some men have, loud and gasping for air.

"Why did you run?" she whispered. "It wasn't so bad. A little fire. It's okay. Not so bad."

Ambulance, fire, police: standard 911 protocol. Paramedics pulled the boy from her, injected rapid-coagulant into his neck, carried him away. Someone wrapped a blanket around Jess's shoulders. She was led to a cruiser and taken home.

Green luna moths pulsed on the cottage's screen door, bathed briefly in porchlight before drifting into the darkness. Nothing had changed physically—the moon still reflected its quivering image on the bay, water still lapped the pilings—and yet things were unconditionally altered.

"It was an accident," said Herbert. "A terrible accident. But the boy pulled through. He's okay—I read a story about it."

"His name is David Hickey. Eleven years old. The bullet passed within four centimeters of his heart." She held her index finger and thumb an approximate distance apart. "Fractions, you know? Four . . . *centimeters*. Increments."

She wouldn't tell Herbert—or anyone—about the trip to the hospital the next day. How she'd stood outside the ICU, peering through the observatory room window at the boy reclined in a hospital bed. His parents sat beside the bed watching the arrhythmic spike of the EKG monitor. She'd wanted to go to them, to apologize and hold the boy's hand . . . but she was paralyzed with fear: fear of what had happened, and what could have happened. For the first time she could recall, she prayed to God, prayed for the boy to pull through. She prayed for the boy, but also—selfishly, she realized afterwards—for herself. She prayed for the boy's health so she might go on living as she had, the fine job and caring husband and quotidian happiness she'd enjoyed. Her future depended on the boy, so she prayed for him, and for herself.

"I don't think I'll ever escape," she said. "I mean, sometimes it goes away, that feeling, but it comes back. So I'm always wondering, is it possible—escape?"

Herbert didn't reply. Jess felt a blankness rise inside her, flowing through her veins, nasty and slippery like heavy black oil in a drip pan. She stepped off the porch, walking down the gentle slope falling away from the cottage, towards the shore.

"Jess? Hey, Jess?"

She did not run; there was no urgency. She heeled off her shoes on the thin band of soil along the shoreline and went into the bay. The icy water sent a rolling tide of gooseflesh up her body. Cones of mist rose off the water's surface and she felt the mushy bottom between her toes. The water's flat surface was a pane of deeply tinted glass as she passed through it slowly, the chill gone now, water warm, the temperature of blood. She let herself go, not diving but merely sinking. Her mouth filled with the taste of stirred silt and algae; the weight of water forced the air from her lungs. Disconnected images fled through her mind: an improbable barn roof, the gap between each slat exactly four centimeters, sunlight pouring through in neat even bars; a World War II battlefield, mud and blood and shit, she's charging a machinegun nest in a clean-pressed OPP uniform, screaming and laughing at once; a field on a long-ago summer day, the dry earth and smell of hay, tumbling over and over in the tall grass, holding onto someone whose face she cannot make out. Fractions, brinks, increments, hair breadths, verges, moments: she saw all this. Undercurrents buffeted her, pulling her deeper. Strands of hair swept in soft arcs across her face. Her feet lost touch with the bottom and she floated out into the uncertain gravity of the bay.

Hands encircled her waist. Her head broke the surface and she saw the hot white stars aligned in orbit. Her brother's arms were hooked tightly beneath her armpits, feet kicking between her legs. Herbert paddled into the shallows and rolled over on his side.

"Jesus," he gasped, "are you crazy?"

"I don't know." Shivering, she struggled to frame an appropriate response. "I can't see my way clear of it anymore. Like, the things you thought possible aren't truly possible anymore, and they'll never be again. I'm sorry, but, you know, sorry's not enough. It's just . . . not . . . enough."

Herbert peeled his shirt over his head and heaved it onto the grass. His chest was wan and sunken, an arrowhead of dark hair pointing at his chin. Plumes of steam rose off his shoulders and braided from the crown of his skull.

"I don't think escape is something we can hope for," he said. "People have it worse than us; we can't flatter ourselves otherwise. You go on. Put your head down and bull through." He showed her his palms. "What else can you do? Find something that fills that empty space inside you. For me, it's magic. There's something peaceful about it. Calm and steadying. It gives me control. I think that's what it's about: not escaping, just regaining control."

Regain control. It sounded so simple, a matter of mechanical application: turn wheel in the direction of the skid, pump brakes steadily. Go about your business. Jess wasn't sure she could. Her character wasn't weak or resigned, but controlling the terms of her imprisonment possessed no appeal.

"Let's get into some dry clothes," she said. "You'll catch pneumonia. What were you thinking, trying to swim in this cold?"

"Seemed like the thing to do at the time."

THAT NIGHT JESS CALLED home. Ted picked up on the sixth ring.

"It's me."

"It's you." His voice logy, as though his mouth were packed with syrup-soaked wool. "Find your man?"

"No. Tomorrow."

While they'd dated, Ted hadn't known how to dance. Jess loved dancing, the club atmosphere, the way a knowing partner would hold her. Though athletic and comfortable in his own skin, Ted was no dancer. One night she'd made an offhand remark; *I'll have to find me a boy who likes to dance,* the kind of comment a woman might make in the early stages when the threat of other options carried weight.

Unbeknownst to her, Ted started taking lessons. He met with a widowed instructor, Cora, every Tuesday and Thursday. They feather-stepped and reverse-turned across her wide living room, practicing the Paseo con Golpe and El Ocho. On New Year's Eve he'd taken her to the Blue Mermaid, where, at the stroke of midnight, he displayed his skills during a slow waltz. He was still horrible, two left feet, but that'd made no difference.

"I miss you," he said. "I miss your smell."

"My smell?"

"You've got a great smell. It's still here, in the sheets, but—not the same."

"Will it be enough to tide you over?"

"I guess it'll have to. Can't hug and kiss the sheets."

"You *could* . . ."

"But that would be . . . weird."

"A little."

After a beat: "You okay?"

"Yeah," she said. "I just wanted to . . ."

"Hear my beautiful voice. Don't blame you: ladies call at all hours to hear my silky-smooth baritone, baby. So . . . what are you wearing?"

Jess laughed softly. "Ted, your dirty mind."

"Oh, my *god,*" Herbert moaned. "Find a phone booth, why don't you?"

Fakery #44: *Rod into Serpent.* One of magic's oldest tricks, it plays on a snake's nature and instinct. First, chill the snake in an icebox for several hours to render it sluggish. Then, grasping the head between thumb and index finger, apply steady, equal pressure. This stuns the serpent, who believes an enormous beast is attacking. Unable to defend itself, it goes into shock, body rigid as a twig. Finally, set the stunned snake on the floor. Within a few minutes, it will slither away, unharmed.

[6]

The morning sky was dour, the trees to the west a dirty tone of silver. A cover of fog clung to the bay, moving low and fat across the water.

Jess navigated down the gravel track leading to the main road. Fog hung suspended between skeletal oak and maple. Rounding a blind curve, Jess glimpsed the looming shape and slammed her foot on the brake. The car's back end fishtailed over the shale.

"Holy moley," Herbert said in a small, childlike voice.

The bull moose was easily ten feet tall. The front half of its body blocked the road, hindquarters mired in the spillway. Seen in profile, its head was a long dark wedge elegantly downswept, a smooth invert bow connecting its lips to the wet fur of its dewlap, which fanned in finlike ridges. The antlers were mostly shed of their itchy summer hide, though molting tatters hung from the odd point; rising from either side of the skull, tips stained by pine sap, they resembled the wings of an albino butterfly.

"Honk the horn." Herbert recalled stories of cars colliding with such beasts, frames buckling and metal shearing while the animal walked away, stunned but unhurt. "Scare it."

"It's okay," Jess said. "There's room on your side."

She eased the car forward, angling around the moose's projecting bulk. The animal's massive head swiveled, dark eyes focused on the vehicle. The front wheel slipped on the steep grade of the spillway. Branches raked the fender and windows.

"God, Jess. We'll tip over."

Jess's heart fluttered—it felt *wonderful*. "We're okay."

She inched the front bumper ahead, tapping the gas. The moose's head dipped, nose pressed to the driver-side window. Jess's face was separated from the moose's by a thin pane of glass. Beads of moisture ringed its sockets, a thickly sloped nose and teeth the hue of old bone, a corona of horseflies buzzing around its head. She felt a kinship with the animal—an illusive kinship, the kind that sometimes occurs when strangers lock eyes passing in cars headed opposite directions. The creature expelled plumes of steam through nostrils the size of teacups. Flecks of mucus sprayed the window. Its tongue, black and a foot long, licked a diagonal slash across the misted glass, as though it wished to learn of this strange shiny creature by its taste.

Jess edged the car back onto the road. They stared out the rear window as the moose flicked the huge leathery funnels of its ears at the maddening flies.

"That," Herbert said softly, "is its own kind of magic."

They arrived in Thessalon shortly after noon. The main drag conformed to an archaic model, with stores long since wiped from the metropolitan topography—Woolco, Stedman's, Saan—hanging on thanks to stubborn small-town consumers. The streets and trees and shops were bleached out, town suffocating beneath a blanket of low, dark clouds.

Their father's house stood at the end of a block shaded by the knitted branches of maple and walnut trees. The squat one-story was utterly nondescript and bordered on sterile; Jess had known bums to decorate their cardboard hovels with more flair. She thought of the exotic locales her father could've disappeared to: the white sand beaches of Pago Pago, the African veldt, the caldera of a dormant volcano. But no, he'd abandoned them for this shoebox less than five hundred kilometers away.

They climbed the cracked brick steps and Herbert rang the bell. Jess peeked through the slitted drapes: an ancient stereo with dual cassette player and turntable, a swayback sofa, a stack of newspapers propping up an overflowing ashtray. Dust motes hung in the air, turning over and over.

"He's not home," a woman's voice called out through the shutters of the house next door.

"Do you know where he is?"

"Try the bowling alley."

"Are you sure?"

"Sure I'm sure!" The shutters snapped shut.

PARKWAY BOWL-A-DROME was a corrugated-tin building in the shape of an airplane hangar jutting from the back end of the Leonard Hotel, the two structures fused into one grisly unit. Farmland stretched for miles behind the alley.

Stepping through the front doors, Jess was assaulted by an odor peculiar to bowling alleys: an amalgam of cigarette smoke, grease, shoe deodorizer, whatever they used to polish the lanes. Herbert gazed up and down the bustling hardwood floors, the mica-flecked balls spat from return chutes and gaudy red-and-white shoes stacked in cubbyholes, the insectile hum of the ball-buffing machine, thinking his father wouldn't set foot in this place on a dare.

The man behind the counter tried to guess Jess's shoe size. "Size eight wide."

"We're not here to bowl, but yeah." Jess unfolded the sheet of newsprint with their father's photo. "Looking for this guy. Know him?"

"Who's asking?"

Jess showed her badge. The counterman smiled wisely, as though unsurprised to see their father's misdeeds had finally caught up to him. "Lane eighteen, officer."

The man pushed a small white button in the center of the teardrop ball return and rubbed his hands together over the dryer. On the inclined scorer's table sat a rosin stick, a talc pouch, a deck of Players, and a Styrofoam cup of coffee. The man sunk three fingers into a jet black ball, took two strides, launched the ball in a tight spiral; it flirted with the gutter before curving to strike the one pin. He marked it off on his score sheet, pulled a cigarette from the deck, lipped it, and said, "So. You found me."

Herbert and Jess sat at the horseshoe of molded fiberglass seats ringing the lane. Their father wore tan pants and a beige sweater. His dark hair had thinned and grayed; a widow's peak gave his face an elongated equine aspect. Though age and wear had blunted the sharpness of his features, his emerald eyes still shone.

"So," Herbert said after a minute, "you're bowling now."

"Bowling's wonderful. It makes the heart merry." He looked his children up and down. His fingers rose to his face, tracing his lips and cheek as though searching for correspondences. "It was that newspaper article, wasn't it? I told that damn reporter no pictures."

Jess couldn't believe his lack of emotion. Part of her—a very large part, it seemed—hoped he'd cower like a Nazi war criminal brought to justice. But there was no shame, no contrition. It was as though he'd stumbled across a couple of old, not especially close acquaintances, and was struggling to make polite conversation.

"Don't you have anything to say? Don't you feel the least bit guilty?"

"Jess, please . . ."

"I'm too old to feel guilt, and besides, it's a wasteful emotion. If that's why you searched me out, you may as well leave. Excuse me a moment."

He bowled a strike, then turned to his son and palmed the scorekeeper's pencil up his sleeve. "Still got it, don't I?"

Herbert dug a coin out of his pocket and sent it skipping along his knuckles, then palmed it with deft precision. He opened his mouth to show the coin glinting on his tongue.

"I saw you slip it into your mouth," his father said. "Good, but not quite perfect."

Herbert didn't say anything. It didn't matter his father was wrong, as Herbert had slipped the coin into his mouth earlier, anticipating the opportunity; nor did it matter he was infinitely more skilled, his movements clean where his father's were clubbish; the fame and women and wealth—none of it mattered. At that moment he was a child again, the boy forever trying to please but always falling critically short, shamed and confused before his father.

"Why'd you do it?" Jess cast her eyes in a conspicuous arc: scuffed lanes, a glass case full of cobwebbed trophies, everything overhung in a haze of bluish smoke. "Was this worth it? For all this . . . *splendor?*"

"You always had a smart tongue, Jessica. I knew Sam would take you, we talked about it obliquely, and that was a better fit." A strain of subdued pride underlay this pragmatism. Jess got a sense he considered himself somehow herculean, holding on as long as he had. "Your mother wanted children. Never a goal of mine. I sent money when I could—didn't Sam tell you?"

"You abandoned us."

"Didn't throw you to the wolves, darling."

Jess realized that, over the years, her father had been crafting his most brilliant illusion: he'd tricked himself into believing what he'd done was justified. She'd always considered him a confused man who'd made a bad choice—and perhaps, half a lifetime ago, that had been the case. But the man she now faced was completely devoid of remorse. This wasn't an act or a smokescreen; this was self-delusion distilled to its purest essence.

"It was the other magicians, wasn't it?" Herbert said. "Fallout from the book."

"I shouldn't have written that thing. People trusted me with their secrets and I sold them out. Foolish, but I had something to prove."

"Was it magic, then? A search for real magic?"

Jess caught the note of desperation in Herbert's voice. For him, it all hinged on justification: the idea of their father leaving to pursue a higher goal was something he could live with.

"Real magic? No such thing. Please don't tell me any of that foolishness we talked about when you were a child lingered on. It was all ... *bunk.* I was entertaining you; they were pleasant fictions, fairy tales." He squeezed the talc pouch anxiously. "I never told you the tooth fairy didn't exist, but I never felt badly for it. I just supposed the truth would dawn on you sooner or later."

"The truth. Right. Of course."

Herbert's body was trembling. Had he actually believed this would end with hugs and kisses and promises of Sunday dinners? Twenty-five years dismissed and everything reverting to the way it once was, father and son driving to some dustbowl town in the summer twilight, talking of magic?

"He's everything you lacked the courage and ability to be," Jess said. "You see that, don't you?"

Her father's gaze narrowed, then skipped across the surface of the lanes. "Anyone can become successful if their passion becomes an obsession. Set yourself to a single life task, how can you help but become a success?"

"But isn't that what you did, abandoning us to pursue—*this?*" Jess heard the desperation creeping into her voice. "Jesus, was it really so awful?"

"I was miserable."

She would never learn why her father left. The only power he held was the magician's power of secret knowledge, and to relinquish that was to yield whatever slim command he still held over them. She wanted to tell him it didn't matter, he could take his pathetic secrets to the grave ... but she did care, and for a moment saw herself as a young girl in that dirty wash of alley light, squinting into the darkness, wondering what did we do *wrong?*

"You don't believe in magic?" Herbert said. "Come outside, then. I'll show you."

"Herbert, don't do this. Please."

"Stop talking nonsense. I won't watch you make a bloody fool of yourself."

Herbert's hand clutched his father's sweater. "Damn it, I'll *show* you. It's not nonsense!"

"Take your hands off me. You're making a scene."

Jess took Herbert's wrist, trying to pry his fingers loose. Her father beat at his son's arm as he shook the sleeve. Although Jess never shared Herbert's vision of a joyful resolution, she had not imagined a tug of war in a Bowl-a-drome.

"Goddamn you, let *go!*"

"It's real! I can show you—*real!*"

"Knock it off down there!" the counterman hollered.

"Let 'em go at it," a bowler with a limp walrus mustache called back. "About time someone gave it to the old bastard."

Herbert gave a final furious tug, tearing the sweater, tumbling onto the floor with a swath of angora clutched in his fist. Herbert, Sr., fell back, bony backside impacting a fiberglass bowling chair with a thump. His son stood carefully. Softly but with utter conviction, he said, "I know what's real. Whether you believe or not makes no difference anymore."

Herbert walked out of the alley. Their father sprawled in the chair, heaving. His torn sweater sleeve hung between his legs, nearly brushing the floor. The collar was stretched out of shape, baring a pale clavicle.

"I wasn't . . . lying," he panted. "They were just . . . *fantasies.*"

Seeing him like that, a tall frail man with a torn sweater, the harsh light of the scorer's table showing just how deeply his eyes had retreated into their sockets, Jess realized this was a man who'd never really stepped out of that tea chest he'd entered many years ago. Exited physically, yes, tripped the hidden latch and vanished; but the way that body sagged, the defeated slouch of those shoulders, was the same posture she'd seen in men handcuffed in the backseat of her squad car. An imprisoned look.

THE SKY WAS A DARK BOWL quaking and crashing with thunder. Jess scanned the parking lot, then dashed to the car. Rain pelted down in stinging wires. She peered through the window, but he wasn't inside. She called his name and wind snatched the word from her mouth.

Squinting into the driving rain, she saw him standing along the fenceline bordering the fields, fenceposts dark with creosote and the rusty stitchwork of barbed wire. Shirtless, trousers plastered to his legs, hair stuck to his skull. Eyes closed, he swayed slightly.

Jess stood in the lot, one foot mired in a pothole rapidly filling with rainwater. A vein of lightning split the sky, bathing the fields in rippling white light. Rain poured down her cheeks. Herbert swayed side to side. His face was serene. He looked so young, a boy. Jess laughed at the craziness of it all, the beautiful absurdity. "You're nuts!" she shouted, laughing harder. She saw a figure standing in silhouette behind the alley's smoked glass. Herbert swayed, his ears tuned to an unheard harmony, the rhyme of the wind and rain and sky. His hands held out, palms flat to the earth, as though seeking an elusive balance. Lightning creased the sky, whitening his body.

Her breath caught.

For the rest of her life, she will always wonder—did it happen? Perhaps it was a trick of the light, a fleeting disorientation. Later she will think her mind played a trick: she wanted so badly for it to happen that she willed her eyes into momentary belief. She will never speak of it, yet one night many years later will wake from a dream of that faraway afternoon, the wind and rain and the sense of something in the air, a quivering pressure in her eardrums, an odd taste beneath her tongue—not magic; she will never quite bring herself to so blunt an admission. Something feathery and alive that all those years later seems so unreal and yet the vision persists undimmed by time, a vision as bracing as it was during those fleeting heartbeats when it happened, and she will sit bolt upright as a cool night breeze plays through the open window and starlight curves upon the brass buttons of her police uniform hanging in the bedroom closet, and, in a voice so low and tremulous her husband does not stir, she will whisper,

"He disappeared."

The skin of Herbert's chest and arms and head turned opaque as a nearly colorless essence, smoke or mist or fog, rose off his body. For a moment Jess could see the basic structure of his skeleton, the bones of his arms and ribcage, skull gilt with flashing light, then only the arteries and veins pumping blood. When these vanished all that remained were the disembodied trousers standing on their own and the open field beyond. Jess would never forget that Rolex free-floating in the charged air, the dime-sized flash of brilliance as lightning reflected off its face.

Herbert's body suddenly coalesced, the disparate atoms flooding back and uniting. He toppled into the mud. Jess ran to him.

"Did you see it?" His eyes were alive and on fire. "Did you see?"

"I don't know what I saw."

She helped him up, amazed at just how light he felt. A strange smell clung to him, a mixture of singed earth and ozone. She threw his arm over her shoulder and carried him across the lot. By the time she settled him into the front seat, he was fast asleep.

She cast a glance at the bowling alley window. The silhouetted figure was gone.

Recognize that what they peddle as truth is in fact fiction. Look beyond the stagecraft, deception, and sleight-of-hand, and you will always find the truth, which is simply this: there *is* no truth. It is all a lie. Elaborate and brilliantly concealed, but a lie nonetheless. Never trust your eyes. Be forever skeptical. Learn to spot the tricks I have outlined and together we shall expose these "magicians" for what they truly are: frauds, shysters, and villains!

[7]

Herbert slept the entire drive home. At one point he started shivering violently and Jess wrapped him in sweaters and ran the heater until his teeth stopped chattering. The rain let up, leaving in its wake a pristine clarity.

They pulled into Herbert's driveway shortly after nine o'clock. Warm southern air was infused with the plankton smell of the canal. Jess woke Herbert, helped him wrangle his luggage onto the porch. He glanced at the stricken tree on his lawn.

"I really should do something about that poor thing, shouldn't I?"

"Burn it. End its misery."

"Maybe I will. Plant another in its place. Water and trim it. Take good care of it."

He reached into his pants pocket and withdrew a small booklet: soggy green construction paper tied up with fraying blue yarn, clumsy scissoring, words written in a spiky hand. For a moment it seemed as if he would crumple it, but he smoothed it out and returned it to his pocket.

"I don't think he's a bad person. I think he just . . . lost control. It could happen to anybody, don't you think? He's not a bad man."

Jess envied his childlike ability to forgive. Perhaps he would never grow up, be forever a man-child lost in a world of mirrors and brightly colored smoke. This didn't anger her, where before it had. He came forward, an awkward lunge, hugging her. Jess felt his stiff contours, bone and hard angles, a boy's body not yet fleshed into adulthood. She remembered a night when they were young, Herbert waking from a nightmare and crawling under the covers of her bed, his body all elbows and kneecaps. He really hadn't changed over the years: still bony and gangling and clinging to beliefs others had long ago surrendered.

My brother, she thought. Crown prince of Never-Never Land.

"Well."

"Well. Sam cooks dinner for me and Ted on Sundays. You should come."

"But, Jess . . . Sam's a terrible cook."

"Come anyways. Come anytime."

Jess walked to her Jeep. As she pulled out, she saw Herbert standing beside the gossamer-enshrouded elm, laying his hands on the trunk, stroking the black flaking bark.

SHE DROVE THROUGH STREETS wet from a brief night rain, neighborhoods silent in the dark, the clean lawns, the houses low-slung and split-level and modern. Radio tuned to the local station, Chrissie Hynde singing about a picture of you. Moving into the country: the night coolness of low peninsula fields, vineyards and cherry groves, solitary lights of farmhouses and irrigation ditches filled with moonlit water. She thought of the summer she'd picked fruit with a group of itinerant Caribbean workers. They were paid by the basket, and a small Jamaican man with skin so dark it hurt her eyes had shown her how to twist strawberries off the vine so as not to damage the fruit. The Jamaicans shared two old ten-speeds and after the day's picking would bike to the nearest convenience store with a roll of quarters, calling their wives from payphones, talking of the money they'd made and how they'd spend it.

It was almost midnight by the time she pulled into her driveway. Sam's truck was parked at the curb. The living room light burned. She saw figures in silhouette through the drapes: one on the couch, another in a chair.

She sat on the stoop. The sterile scent of late autumn, haloes of misty yellow light making a nimbus around each streetlight. To the west, a few miles distant, a thin column of smoke rose into the sky. It came from her brother's part of town; she wondered if he'd lit that poor tree on fire. She hoped he had, and willed an errant ember to settle on the roof of his house and burn it to the ground, too. There was an inclination in her family to hide away from the world, crawl into dark places and vanish. If they weren't flushed from hiding and forced into daylight, there was a possibility they'd disappear forever.

Leaves skated across the street, pushed by a swirling wind. She stared into the sky, each star a bright pinprick, each realizing a precise clarity. *The past is but the beginning of a beginning, and all that is and has been is but the twilight of the dawn.*

Jess thought of the uniform hanging in the hall closet. Tomorrow she would take it off its hook and make a decision: burn it or put it on. Either way was a beginning. She was ready for a beginning.

Booming laughter from inside. One silhouette threw its head back, the other slapped its knee. Ted and Sam, and, across town, Herbert razing his front yard.

The men in her life.

Jess scuffed her boots on the welcome mat and stepped inside.

Know this: there is such a thing as magic. It *exists*. My intent is not to teach you the art of true magic, but rather to awaken you to its presence in the world and in our lives. Magic is in the water and air and sky; it is all around us, in objects of beauty and ugliness alike. Perhaps this all sounds quite mad; perhaps you think me a fool. All I can say is, I know what is real. My convictions are unshakable.

My only hope is that, even if you never accomplish real magic or see it with your own eyes, you still believe in it, or at the very least its possibility.

I am convinced the world is a much brighter place for those who believe.

—*Excerpted from* The Apprentice's Guide to Modern Magic, *by Herbert T. Mallory, Jr.*

Acknowledgments

MY DEEPEST THANKS to the following people for their input, compassion, care, dedication, and support:

Don and Jill Davidson
David Davidar
Sarah Heller
Starling Lawrence
Francis Geffard
Andrew Kidd
Helen Reeves
Tracy Bordian
Edward O'Connor
Bob Strauss
Brett Savory
Colleen Hymers

Erin Tigchellar
Greg Bechtel
Mark Anthony Jarman
John C. Ball
Alan Burke
Tony Antoniades
Dave Hickey
Sean Johnston
Dave Barnett
Kathy and Randy Blondeau
Shane Ryan Staley

GRATEFUL ACKNOWLEDGMENT is also made to the following journals where some of these stories were first published. My thanks to their fine editors:

"Rust and Bone" first published as "28 Bones" in *The Fiddlehead*.
"Rocket Ride" and "Life in the Flesh" in *Event*.
"On Sleepless Roads" in *Prairie Fire*.